In lighter news, a trio of Florida kids say they've proven that a new breakfast cereal really *CAN* make you smarter!

For more we go to Miami Public Television's Marcos Horchata.

Marcos?

BRAIN FOOD?

REPORTER

It's Science fair season at Breezy Palms Elementary, and fourth graders Amy, Max, and Varga Luna needed a project.

Then Amy saw a commercial for a new cereal: Peanut Butter Clobbers.

Um, I saw the commercial on television? And in the commercial the guy says the cereal will make you smarter.

So I thought...maybe we could make an experiment to see if it really does.

LIVE

AND NOW BACK TO THE NEWSROOM

For two weeks Varga Luna ate nothing but Peanut Butter Clobbers morning, noon, and night. Max ate only a competitor's cereal, and Amy ate as she normally did.

Then we compared our homework scores before and after the experiment.

My scores stayed the same.

Mine, too.

Varga Luna, you singlehandedly ate seven boxes of Peanut Butter Clobbers over two weeks.

Did your scores improve?

LIVE

Your tie is pentagonal. It's covered with an interlocking pattern of tiny lizards. The lizards are based on the work of Dutch artist M. C. Escher. You're either an Escher fan or else a fan of tiny lizards. If I concentrate really hard I can guess what you're going to say before you say it.

LIVE

I'm bothering you. It's because you're a firstborn, aren't you?

Your name can be anagrammed to make ROACH HARM TACO.

What were you asking us?

Nothing. This is Marcos Horcha—

HA, MACHO CARROT.

Marcos Horchata reporting.

ARM TORSO CHA CHA.

UNL
CHA
ADAM

UCKY

RMS

REX

THE
COLD CEREAL
SAGA
BOOK TWO

BALZER + BRAY
An Imprint of HarperCollins Publishers

Also by **ADAM REX**

COLD CEREAL: The Cold Cereal Saga, Book One
THE TRUE MEANING OF SMEKDAY

FOR TEENS
FAT VAMPIRE: A Never Coming of Age Story

Balzer + Bray is an imprint of HarperCollins Publishers.

Library of Congress Cataloging-in-Publication Data
Rex, Adam.
  Unlucky charms / Adam Rex.
    p. cm. — (The cold cereal saga)
  Summary: "Three kids must save the world from the diabolical schemes of an evil
breakfast cereal company, which has been luring magical creatures to our world
through a rift in the time-space continuum"— Provided by publisher.
  ISBN 978-0-06-206005-1 (hardback)
  [1. Cereals, Prepared—Fiction. 2. Magic—Fiction. 3. Adventure and adventurers—
Fiction. 4. Twins—Fiction. 5. Brothers and sisters—Fiction.] I. Title.
PZ7.R32865Unl 2013   2012026714
[Fic]—dc23   CIP
                                                                     AC

13 14 15 16 CG/RRDH 10 9 8 7 6 5 4 3 2 1
❖
First Edition

For Dr. Marie Rex, who is a teacher today

CHAPTER 1

Samantha Doe was going to miss her big red coat. It was by far the warmest thing she'd ever worn, and she'd worn it every day for more than three months, and you couldn't help getting attached to something like that. On the inside it was furry, like a pet. It even had the word DOE on the pocket. Samantha loved her big pet coat. But she was going to have to give it back.

She'd been in Antarctica for fifteen weeks—twice as long as she'd been told. She could swear near the end that Goodco was just grasping at excuses to keep her there. And then there was that business with her laptop.

One of the Goodco people, one of the big men who didn't seem to have any scientific credentials at all, had come to her dorm room and asked why she hadn't been sending any personal emails to her children.

Samantha had, in fact. She'd sent Scott and Polly each

an email every day since the Saturday after Thanksgiving. A hundred letters. But she said, "Well ... since it's *personal* emails I'm not sending, I don't see how it's your—"

The man brushed past her and grabbed her laptop off the bed.

"Hey!" Samantha said. But she stepped back. She was suddenly afraid of this big man. He'd just come in from the cold night, wearing the same sort of coat Samantha wore, that everyone wore. Red on the outside, furry on the inside. On him it looked like an animal he'd turned inside out and was flaunting, like a warning. He scowled at the screen.

"You haven't sent an email to your kids since December first," he said. "And they've never emailed you back?"

Samantha wanted to fold up into herself. Scott and Polly wrote her all the time—what was this guy talking about?

"Here—" the big man, this massive man, told her. "This. Where did you get this software?" He showed her the screen, and a file she'd never seen before. It was called 2003 TAXES, and it was nested inside three folders named for sugar-free candy recipes and a fourth titled PHOTOS OF MY UNATTRACTIVE AUNT. She'd never noticed any of these before, either. Her laptop had a lot of garbage on it.

"Why . . . why does it matter?" Samantha asked the man, who was heaving, who could not possibly be

getting larger, could he?

"It matters . . . it *matters* because it's counteracting the spyware *we* put on your computer. How did it get here?"

Samantha didn't know, though her mind turned back to a drawing Polly had sent, months ago, that took a suspiciously long time to download. Anyway, the big man dropped her laptop carelessly on the bed and thundered out before she could answer, or get indignant, or even ask what he'd meant by *spyware*.

She stood awhile, aware of the shallow tide of her own breath. She wasn't so sure about this Goodco anymore. She didn't care how beloved their cereals were.

Afterward she checked, and it was true: all the old emails to and from her kids had vanished off her computer, as if they'd deleted themselves. All of Scott's curious messages, wanting to know every last thing about the strange phenomenon she was studying. Even Polly's drawing of a cat with a unicorn's horn, gone. She sat on her bed and thought for a long time.

The next day she demanded to leave on the next plane out, and over the following weeks Goodco delivered one feeble excuse after another why she needed to stay. But then finally, when they gave their permission, an unscheduled flight made ready to leave right away—a woman at the Kiwi base had slipped in the shower, and Samantha could hitch a ride on her medical transport. She landed in New

Zealand, and gave back her red coat, and caught a plane to Los Angeles, and then another to Philadelphia. Scott and Polly and their father, John, would be meeting her at the airport—or so they said in an email she could no longer find five minutes after she read it.

She deplaned into the terminal, exited the secure area, and almost didn't see the chauffeur holding a sign with her name on it. She wasn't looking for her name, after all; she was looking for her family. But she approached the uniformed man with a little frown on her face.

"I'm Samantha Doe," she told him. "I wasn't expecting a driver."

The chauffeur tucked the sign under his arm and fished something shiny out of his pocket.

"I've been instructed to give you this," he said, and handed her a small gold octagonal hoop.

She turned it in her hand. "What is it? It . . . heh . . . it looks like a miniature particle collider."

"Put it on."

"What?"

"I've been instructed to tell you to put it on."

"Instructed by whom? My ex-husband?" she said as she slipped the thing onto her wrist. Then, wincing, she asked, "Was it always glowing?"

And then she was gone.

● ○ ★

Thirty feet away, Scott gasped. He couldn't help it. There was no flash of light, no puff of smoke. His mother was just there, and then she wasn't. She wasn't anywhere. She wasn't anywhere in the whole universe.

"GO GO GO GO!" shouted someone in the crowd, and then ten ordinary-looking men converged on the startled chauffeur and seized his arms—Freemen, laying in wait for Scott and his friends to show themselves. Members of the Good and Harmless Freemen of America, a secret society of creeps who did Goodco's bidding. Scott's heart started pounding against his chest like it wanted out—and why not? The last time he'd seen so many Freemen in one place, they'd tried to dissect his friends.

"What the—" sputtered the chauffeur as the Freemen held him fast. "Lemme go! What happened to that lady?"

The surrounding men, in their plain clothes and scarves, looked to an older Freeman in a black cowboy hat and duster, who stood apart and scanned the faces in the crowd. Then he turned to the driver.

"Who hired you?" Scott heard him growl.

"Some old guy," said the chauffeur in a high voice. "Look, what's this about?"

"It's the wizard's work," the man in black told the others. "Must be. Fan out, he might be close."

The man in black was both right and wrong—the wizard was close, but the wizard wasn't a wizard.

Scott started to move, but Merle laid a hand on his shoulder.

"Stay put," the old man said.

Scott's wig felt itchy. His fake glasses felt fake. In his black wig and big black glasses, he felt like Clark Kent. A kind of bizarro universe Clark Kent who removes his glasses and for some reason his hair to reveal that he is actually a perfectly ordinary blond boy with a mild peanut allergy.

Well, not so ordinary, really. He was part fairy, on his father's side. Plus he had a leprechaun in his backpack.

"Is he really Merlin?" another Freeman asked the man in black. "They say he turns people into animals."

"I *wish*," huffed Mick, the leprechaun. Merle could only do a few cool things, and he was already doing most of them.

"*He's* the reason all the magic left our world," another man told his fellow Freemen, glancing around, his voice the reedy voice of the True Believer. "*Merlin*. He's why it's all trapped in another dimension with the elves and fairies."

"Not true," Merle muttered under his breath.

"And now he's trying to ruin the Fay's Grand Plan to bring the worlds together. Him and his friends. He's *powerful*—"

"He's just a very old man who knows some card tricks,"

7

insisted the Freeman in charge. "Nothing more. But . . . assume he could be anyone. Check the women for Adam's apples."

The so-called wizard just to Scott's left in the gift shop was not Scott's father. This man in a Mets sweatshirt and an identical pair of thick black glasses was a time-traveling scientist named Merle Lynn, and the glasses had been his idea. Each pair had a tiny light in the bridge that flashed thousands of times per second, too fast to see, and did something weird to the occipital lobe in the brain of any person looking directly at them. Scott didn't understand the details, but the upshot was that anyone staring you in the face would be transfixed by your glasses and not really notice anything else about you. These glasses were your secret identity. So even though there were evil men in the airport looking for Scott and Merle right this second, they paid no attention to the old man and the boy in the wigs and glasses standing stiffly by the Ben Franklin bottle-cap openers.

The Freemen were splitting up, showing people fake badges and asking them questions. Or maybe real badges—the Good and Harmless Freemen of America had a wide reach.

"They're coming," Scott whispered. "Why are we just standing here?"

"If we let 'em come to us, we'll look like a couple a'

nobodies with interesting glasses. If we move, we'll be a boy and an old man trying to leave. Your call."

Scott exhaled slowly as a Freeman in khakis and a pink shirt walked right through the gift shop and showed them a very authentic-looking police badge. Scott's wig felt like a pile of hay. He tried to maintain eye contact without looking like he was trying to maintain eye contact, which was quite a trick.

"Sorry to bother you two," said the Freeman. "But we're looking for a person of interest. Elderly Caucasian male? Mind if I ask you why you're here?"

"Waiting for my brother," Merle answered. "His flight's late."

"And which flight would that be?" asked the Freeman as he produced a smartphone from his jacket.

Had he really been paying attention, the Freeman might have noticed Scott and Merle tighten up inside their winter coats. Even the backpack flinched. But the fact that he hadn't yet registered that he was already looking at an elderly Caucasian male meant the glasses were doing what they were supposed to.

"From Dallas," said Merle.

The Freeman frowned at his phone. "You're in the wrong terminal. The only flights from Dallas are arriving into D and F. This is C."

"Son of a gun. Well, thanks for the help."

"Sure," the man told them. "You're free to go."

But they didn't. Outside the gift shop an old woman was shouting, "HOW DARE YOU?" to another Freeman who had apparently just asked her to prove she wasn't secretly a man.

"Whoop. That looks like trouble," the pink-shirted Freeman said. And he turned to leave, but here were these two people with glasses, still staring at him like idiots. He turned back.

"Everything all right?" he added. "You don't want to keep your brother waiting."

"Right," said Merle, and he tried to back away without looking away and accidentally knocked a City of Brotherly Love snow globe off a low table. And still he did not look away.

"Oopsie," Scott said weakly.

"Brilliant plan, this," said Mick, knowing he could only be seen and heard by a very few. "A disguise that requires eye contact. Maybe later I'll tell yeh abou' my idea for a bulletproof necktie."

The Freeman backed up. He squinted. He peered at Scott and Merle as if they were one of those posters that look like noise but that reveal a dolphin jumping over a heart if you cross your eyes just right. Then he took a picture with his phone. A picture of Merle and Scott in which their glasses would not flash but would rather perch awkwardly on their suddenly recognizable faces.

"Um," said the Freeman. Then Merle waved a white wand at him and the man fell, snoring, in a heap.

This wasn't magic, either. It was more like a futuristic Taser, Scott recalled as he and Merle plowed through people and Liberty Bell ashtrays and dashed back toward the parking garage.

"There!" shouted the man in the black hat. "Those two!" Nine men peeled away from whomever they'd been interrogating and sprinted after them.

"YOU ARE NOW ENTERING THE MOVING WALKWAY," said an electronic voice as Scott and Merle scampered shakily onto a low-walled conveyor belt for people who didn't appreciate having to walk a tenth of a mile to get to their cars.

"Your fault," yelled Merle. "Just sayin'. No reason we had to get this close."

"I had to see her," Scott answered, probably too low to hear.

"Archimedes," Merle said into his wristwatch. "Bring the van around."

The narrow moving walkway created some confusion for nine men running abreast, so a number of them ran down the center of the carpeted hall instead and fell behind.

"Any o' them wearin' those pink goggles?" asked Mick.

"I don't think so," Scott answered. He didn't want to look. "I think they're trying to blend in."

"Aces," Mick said, and he zipped his cauliflower face out of the backpack. Then he hopped atop the black rubber handrail and ran back toward the Freemen.

"What's he doing?" shouted Merle.

Scott watched Mick curl into a ball and tumble down into the narrow alley of the walkway.

"I think he's bowling."

Freemen tripped and knocked against one another and bounced off the handrails.

"YOU ARE NOW EXITING THE MOVING WALKWAY."

Scott and Merle vaulted onto the carpet again and through the exit, and then they were standing in an alcove, a recessed bay of doors set into the airport building where it met the edge of the four-floor parking garage. They stepped out among the concrete pillars and ramps of the garage, where they were joined by a barn owl and a white van. The former flew to Merle's shoulder as the latter screeched to a halt in front of them.

They had no intention of getting in the van, though. The parking garage only had one narrow exit, and it was sure to be guarded. Mick caught up, and the three of them ran right around the van and hid themselves behind a huge gray column between two SUVs.

Merle spoke to the mechanical owl, Archimedes, and Freemen began pouring through the doors in time to see the white van peel away again.

"Blockade all C garage exits," one Freeman said into a walkie-talkie as the others moved to pursue the van.

"Wait!" said the man in the black hat. "He's tried this trick before. There's no one in that van."

"Great." Scott sighed. "They're getting smarter."

"Listen," said the black-hatted man, and the others listened. "Silence. He's still on this floor."

The Freemen stepped lightly, spreading out, bending to check under cars. When one drew close, Merle put him to sleep with the Slumbro and Mick helped drag him behind the pillar.

"Can you bring the van by again?" whispered Scott. And with his fist and a pair of running finger legs, he acted out a little scenario.

Merle raised his eyebrows and nodded. He gave the Slumbro to Scott and set about trying to explain the plan to his supercomputing robot owl. Scott flicked the wand when a second Freeman rounded the pillar, and they stacked him on top of the first one.

"Gettin' cozy back here," said Mick.

Scott heard an engine rumbling close, closer, but then it was only some lady in a blue hatchback. He whispered, "How long before the van gets back?"

"Maybe a minute."

A minute felt like a long time just now. The Freemen seemed to be everywhere—had more arrived? Maybe some of them were only passengers. A flight attendant pulling a pair of suitcases passed too close, and Scott put her to sleep before he could stop himself.

"Shoot, sorry," he hissed. "Sorry." Mick put her with the others.

Then Scott felt the van's congested engine draw near. Merle was hesitating.

"Can't do it yet," he groused, and nodded at a clutch of passengers entering through the alcove that separated the terminal from the garage. "Regular people in the way." Then they cleared and he added, "Archie, peel out."

Nearby they heard the fuss of the engine, the shriek of tires, the high whine of a belt that probably needed replacing. The van lurched forward, and so did Scott, Merle, and Mick, four bodies running at once toward the same finish line, and Scott really hoped Archimedes had a firm grasp of the geometry of the situation.

"There they are!" shouted someone, and a dozen undercover Freemen in their polos and chinos began to crab walk back through the sea of cars toward the terminal entrance. The fat white van hurtled around the corner, and Scott, Mick, and Merle crossed directly in front of it at top speed, with Archimedes flapping behind.

The van was braking now, filling the garage with a kind of angry whale song.

They threw themselves back into the bay of doors, pitched through those doors and into the terminal, then turned just in time to see the reeling white van parallel park itself neatly inside the alcove.

It was close. The driver's side mirror was nearly touching the door glass. Freemen tried to squeeze through a gap between the van and the wall, but Scott reached through a crack in the terminal doors and put them to sleep.

"Hold back!" the Freeman in the black hat ordered.

On the terminal side, a man with a duffel and a suntan and rubber sandals was just starting to take in the scene.

"Hey," he said. "My car is out there."

The black-hatted Freeman stood out of range of the wand and glared through the gap.

"That was your mom that disappeared, wasn't it, kid?" he asked. "What did you do to her?"

"We sent her into the future!" Scott called back. Exactly a year into the future, to be precise, but they didn't need to know that. "She's *safe* from you people!"

"C'mon," Merle urged. Mick climbed back into the backpack.

"Is this some kind of flash mob or something?" asked the man in the rubber sandals. "Are you going to move that van soon?"

"Sorry," said Scott, and he and Merle proceeded to leave.

"But my car's out there. I need it for driving."

"Sorry!"

They jogged back the way they had come and turned toward a down escalator to baggage claim.

"Stop right there!" someone shouted, and they turned to see the same Freeman who'd interrogated them in the gift shop, running down the moving walkway.

"What's he doing awake already?" said Merle.

Scott squinted at the Slumbro. "You know you have this set on NAP?"

"What? Give it here."

The escalator was crowded, so they fast stepped down some stairs.

"She's . . . she's really safe, right?" asked Scott. "Just in the future?"

"What can I say that'll make you believe me? I double-checked the math. Archie triple-checked it!"

"And Emily checked it too?"

Merle sighed. "Yes, Emily checked it too."

The Freeman was negotiating the escalator behind them and speaking into a walkie-talkie.

"Repeat, subjects are entering C baggage claim. Over."

Baggage claim was a wide tiled hall encircled by doors and big windows, filled with people and luggage and

17

luggage carousels. You could turn in either direction to head outdoors, where the curbsides were packed with shuttles and taxis.

Scott was beginning to understand how to spot the Freemen. They all appeared to be wearing at least a little pink—a scarf, a shirt, maybe a hatband—and a number of them were coming to join him at the base of the stairs. So was a bald and topknotted Hare Krishna in white robes, who'd been slouching over a rattling tambourine and handing out pamphlets near two suitcases in a corner. Everyone else in baggage claim had been doing their best to ignore him, such that most had not even noticed his tall stature or the fact that he'd been chanting "Hairy Christmas" for twenty minutes. But now, standing straight, he towered over Goodco's pawns like the white king on a chessboard.

Scott and Merle stopped on the stairs about a half flight from the bottom, so the Freeman on the escalator just passed them, slowly, with an embarrassed look on his face.

"All right, you two," another Freeman in a pink tie said to Scott and Merle and, to a lesser extent, Mick. "You can't put us all to sleep."

"Can't we?" Scott whispered.

"Prob'ly not."

"Um, sir?" A Freeman addressed the tall figure in

white. "This isn't safe here—please step away."

Just then the Hare Krishna's two suitcases unzipped and released a brown-skinned boy and a pale and dainty little girl. And the tall figure threw off his robe and stick-on topknot to reveal a blockheaded monster of a former librarian. Nearby people gasped, and a family of four burst into applause.

"It's the bigfoot!" cried one of the Freemen, turning from Biggs to Emily. "And the girl!"

"And the boy!" said Erno. "Who's also super scary!" But it wasn't clear that anyone was paying attention.

They had every reason to fear Emily, who actually *had* turned a woman into a donkey a couple of months back. But she couldn't control that sort of thing, so when Merle began wanding people to sleep and Biggs starting lifting Freemen over his head, she and Erno just joined Scott on the fringes and tried to stay out of the way. Ordinary people all around the hall screamed or called for the police. The room was clearing fast. Mick leaned over Scott's shoulder.

"I should get in there," he said. "Start punchin' kneecaps."

"Maybe we should stay together."

"When I thought about all this going down, I imagined us doing something useful," said Erno.

"Can you remember what it was?" asked Scott.

Erno chewed his lip. "It was always kind of hazy."

More and more Freemen. The crew from the parking garage had found their way to ground level and entered baggage claim from the outside. Biggs was surrounded but still fighting. Merle was essentially hiding behind a small pile of Freemen and shaking his Slumbro beside his ear.

"That can't be a good sign," Scott muttered.

"Some of 'em have guns," said Mick. "Why aren't they usin' 'em?"

"Was that Mick talking just now?" Emily asked.

"You could hear him? You're getting better."

"Yeah, but I couldn't understand him. It just sounded like a little mosquito."

"No, that's right," said Erno. "That's what he sounds like."

"Shut it, lad."

"Mick was wondering why they weren't using their guns," said Scott.

"They're going to," Emily said. "Now that all the real people are gone. Watch."

Baggage claim had emptied out. The luggage carousels were choking on unclaimed bags. Freemen glanced about—no witnesses now.

"I better put a scare into them," Emily said.

"What, you?" said Erno. "What can you do?"

"Please. You *know* I've been studying pop culture," said Emily.

"Is that what you call watching a lot of TV?"

Erno and Emily hadn't been allowed television or movies growing up, so lately Emily had been making up for lost time. "I've been catching up on all the horror movies from the last thirty years, and apparently there's nothing scarier than a little girl acting spooky."

"Puppets," suggested Scott.

"Okay, yes. Puppets or a little girl acting spooky. Bonus if she's wearing a pretty party dress. Which I *am*."

"I don't understand," said Erno.

"*What if I talk like thiiiiis,*" she sang.

"Geez. Yeah, do that."

Emily stepped forward, slowly, but jerking now and then as if she herself were a puppet guided by an unsteady hand. Freemen turned and noticed. With a blank face and dead eyes, she raised her arms and slowly sang "Pop Goes the Weasel" in a ghostly voice.

"Oh *no*," a man whispered. Freemen started backing away.

"Look out, something bad's gonna happen! Like in that movie with the puppet."

"She turned someone into an *owl!*" said another.

"That's the wizard's owl. It was always an owl."

Meanwhile, Emily exhausted "Pop Goes the Weasel" and started in on the national anthem.

Merle made his way over to Scott.

"Slumbro's on the fritz. It isn't holding a charge anymore."

"Does it need a new battery?"

"Hope not. They haven't been invented yet. You think this ploy of Emily's is gonna get us out of here?"

"Can't be worse than any other part of our plan."

Two Freemen lost their nerve and ran for the exit.

"You heard them upstairs," Scott told Merle. "They're afraid of you too."

"Good point," said Merle, and he pocketed his wand and waved his arms around, chanting in Latin.

"*Admonitio! Insani magica tempus!*"*

What followed was a lot of tripping, running every which way, and repeated orders from the black-hatted Freeman to "STAND YOUR GROUND." But then the tinted doors of the south baggage claim entrance opened, filling the hall with light, and in glided a lovely, horrible woman. Emily dropped her act and suddenly looked every bit the little girl she was. Biggs roared. Merle muttered something that wasn't Latin but was no less exotic.

"Nimue," whispered Scott. Perhaps she heard, because she fixed her eyes on him and smiled.

"Freemen!" the woman sang. "Behind me!"

The remaining men scurried to her side like children. She looked good, which could only be bad. It meant she'd

---

* "Warning! Crazy magic time!"

22

been feeding on stolen magic and had glamour to burn. Her black hair was pulled up and piled atop her head in glossy ringlets like a tangled telephone cord. Her dress was red as a wound, with a bodice of crow's wings and milky pearls. It was hard to take your eyes off her.

It was so hard, in fact, that no one noticed a girl dash into the hall through the opposite entrance.

Nimue raised her slender arms, looking only at Scott. He could guess why. They'd foiled Nimue last time because she was weak and she didn't know Scott's True Name. He felt certain that she wanted him to know now that she'd figured it out, or was currently so powerful it wouldn't matter either way.

"We should run," said Scott.

"Can't outrun this." Mick sighed.

Then, suddenly, Polly was at his side. Scott turned to his little sister and said, "What are you do—"

"Lift me high!" said a small but confident voice that seemed to come straight from Polly's gut. She raised her hands, and in her palms stood a tiny black-skinned man, no larger than a toy, brandishing a birch-bark shield the size of a postage stamp.

"MACBETH DOE!" shouted Nimue, and a cold flash of roiling light tumbled toward them. "MERLE L—"

Then the light spasmed, rippled, and the woolly haze of it spun down into a single thread that plunged into the

23

center of the birch-bark shield and was gone.

Nimue gagged, wide-eyed, and pitched forward. The Freemen at her sides caught her before she hit the floor face-first.

"Yay, Prince Fi!" shouted Polly. The tiny man shuddered as the shield glowed fitfully like a loose lightbulb. He shook it until it was nothing but dead wood again.

Scott leaned close to Polly. "I thought you were supposed to stay in the car."

"Yeah—like Dad could keep me in the car."

"P-PIXIE?!" spat Nimue. She struggled for composure as the Freemen advanced. "How on this sterile doornail of a planet do you have a freaking pixie?!"

"It's kind of your fault, actually," Erno told her.

"Remind us to tell you about it next time," Merle added, fiddling with his watch. "Kids?"

"YOUR FAULT, MERLIN!" she screamed as they ran for the north doors and the Freemen followed. "EVERYTHING'S BROKEN, AND IT'S YOUR FAULT!"

Biggs burst through first, carrying Emily under one arm, and soon they were all in the sunlit, airy freedom of the outdoors. Two white vans bucked up onto the curb, clumsily—one because it was being controlled remotely by Merle and his wristwatch, the other because it was being driven by Harvey. Harvey was half man, half rabbit, and all jerk. He had just the right mixture of self-regard and disregard for everyone else that you wanted in a getaway driver.

In a moment Biggs had the back of Harvey's van open, and then they were face-to-tiny-smoldering-face with a fluttering, fire-breathing finch. Blue sparks pitched from his beaky nostrils.

"It's us, Finchbriton!" Mick said quickly. "It's us! Snuff it!"

Finchbriton chirruped and flew to Mick's shoulder as everyone piled into the van. Scott and Polly's dad was already there, and when he saw Polly he grabbed her shoulders and pulled her close.

Merle knocked on the roof. "All in! GO!"

The van lurched forward. The second van followed.

John hugged Polly tight—a desperate, crazy hug.

"You are crushing me," announced Prince Fi from somewhere in the middle.

"What did I tell you?" said John. *"What did I tell you?"*

"I thought they might need our help," Polly murmured. "And they did."

"I wished to be of service," said Fi. "The girl should have let me go alone."

The Freemen called for their vehicles and started their pursuit, but then the remote-controlled van opened its cargo doors and released the helium balloons, and the roadway was all fat colorful pandemonium, and by the time they cleared the vans had traded places, and the Freemen followed the wrong one.

"Am I in trouble?" Polly asked her father.

"You're . . . I don't know, grounded or something."

"Am I grounded too?" asked Merle.

"Everyone's grounded."

CHAPTER 2

December and January had been a strange couple of months, and that was saying something—November had been filled with magic animals and dark dealings in secret temples and an exploding cereal factory.

After the cereal factory exploded, Scott and his new sideshow of a family had gone on what his father insisted on calling "the lam." And here was the problem with that.

Scott's party included

- four children;
- an old man;
- an internationally famous showbiz personality;
- an eight-foot-tall librarian who needed to shave his body three times daily or thick, luxurious hair would surge from all but his palms, soles, and a T-shaped patch of face;

- a pixie prince who could hide in your pocket but who rebuffed any attempt to put him in a pocket because it was demeaning;
- a fire-breathing finch who didn't satisfactorily understand which occasions were and were not a good time for fire;
- a cat that tended to rub up against one's legs as if it didn't realize it had a six-inch unicorn horn coming out of its forehead;
- and a duo who were invisible to all but one in ten thousand but who otherwise appeared to be a two-foot-tall leprechaun and a man with a rabbit's head. And the reason they appeared to be a leprechaun and a rabbit-man was because that was what they were.

Scott and Erno and Emily had made a little game of dreaming up ways their group could be even more conspicuous than it already was.

"We could add a clown," said Erno.

"We could wear big sombreros," said Scott.

"I respectfully disagree about the clown," said Emily. "People avoid eye contact with clowns. The clown could actually be a big help." And you could almost see her make a mental note: *Hire Clown.*

"We could all get parrots," Scott said. "Parrots that scream all the time."

"We could get one of those inflatable gorillas they put on car dealerships."

Incidentally, *"Hire Clown"* was actually a pretty good description of their getaway philosophy so far.

"People tend to behave like it's the movies," Emily had lectured to the group. "So the Freemen will be watching all the airports, because that's what you do when you're trying to track people down. But do you know what people on the run never do in movies? They never take hot-air balloons. They never hire a mule train or a paddleboat down the Mississippi. They don't go on luxury cruises. We're going to do all those things."

John raised his hand. "Can we get motorcycles with sidecars? I've always wanted one."

Emily shrugged. "It's your money."

They'd been spending John's money like it was cursed, or on fire. He was their own personal Scrooge McDuck.

And so in this way they'd stayed a step ahead of Goodco and the Freemen while they made their plans. They'd rented an ice cream truck. They'd taken something called the Charleston Choo Choo. After leaving the Philadelphia airport, they abandoned their white van in a Center City garage and hired a guided tour across the Delaware on an amphibious vehicle called the Duck. In New Jersey, thrillingly close to Goodborough, they piled aboard a party bus custom painted to say CONGRATULATIONS ALEX AND STEVE.

"Weird being this close to home and not going there," Emily whispered to Erno. But Scott and Polly had not lived in Goodborough long enough for it to feel like home. Their home had just vanished a year into the future, postponed.

"Three hundred and sixty days until she's back," Scott told Polly.

Each of them staked their claim to a section of the bus. Biggs and Harvey and John traded shifts driving; Erno and Emily selected adjacent bench seats. Scott shifted around based on wherever seemed to be the quietest place to read at any given time—he was on his second book of King Arthur stories, trying to learn all the ins and outs. Polly taped off two whole rows, named the area Fancylvania, and tried to talk Prince Fi into an official state visit. But the little pixie camped instead atop the ceiling-mounted television—the only spot outside the bathroom where he could be certain not to have to watch it. And everybody avoided the bathroom.

The party bus seemed almost specially designed to give you motion sickness, what with its pulsing neon and disco ball and bad transmission. Every time they hit a bump it played Kool and the Gang for three minutes, and they hadn't been able to figure out where it was coming from.

"I don't know this song," Merle told Scott. "Is it from your generation?"

"I think it's more from my mom's," Scott answered. "Or her mom's? People play it at weddings, or . . . parties . . . or—"

"Or whenever they want to 'celebrate good times,' yeah. I sorta picked that up from the lyrics."

Scott smirked. "I can't believe I'm asking this, but . . . have you been born yet?"

"Heh. Later this year, actually. About a month after the fairies take over. If all goes well, I'm thinking of gatecrashing my own baby shower."

"That's weird."

"It is what it is." Merle shrugged. "In five years I enter kindergarten. In sixteen I graduate high school, in eighteen I invent time travel to the future but not the past. In nineteen years I go so far into the future I pop up as Merlin in the next universe, and in about fourteen billion years you and me have this conversation again."

"No." Scott winced. "No, that's not right. You were

trying to invent time travel so you could go back and prevent the invasion, right? If we stop the fairies from invading, you'll never invent time travel, maybe. The next universe'll be different."

"Or maybe I do all of this, every time. Maybe I always fail. Maybe I always say, 'Maybe I always fail.' Every twenty-eight billion years I sit on a bus and say that."

Mick crawled over the back of Merle's bench and thumped down beside him. "If yeh believed that, yeh wouldn't be sharin' this pig's breakfast with us."

"If I *believed* it, I'd know I don't have a choice, and I'd be doing it anyway."

Scott sighed. "This is why I don't like time-travel stories."

At fourteen Merle didn't like time-travel stories either, if only because they never had anything useful to teach him. But he'd read and watched them all.

As a boy he believed that time travel must be possible because it felt possible. Natural, even. When a terrible thing happened, didn't the human mind keep looking for solutions, even after the thing had passed? *If I could just not have been so loud, I could save them. If I could only have been more brave.*

Every new technology seemed to be preparing human

minds for the time travel discovery that could only be right around the corner. Instant replays. Undo buttons. Games that let you save your progress and face the boss monster again and again. After his parents were gone, Merle had a lot of time to himself, and he filled it with physics textbooks and books of folklore and crackpot websites. Friends were a distraction. When the past was repaired, he would have all the time in the world for friends.

At his high school graduation, he was a full four inches shorter than the next shortest boy.

The ceremony was watched over by the usual trolls, the same sort of Redcaps that surveilled any gathering of more than twenty humans these days. But after Merle threw his mortarboard in the air with the rest of his class and pushed back through the crowd to find his aunt, he found her standing stiffly beside a tall and stately elf. A sickeningly familiar elf.

"It was a . . . a *lovely* ceremony," Aunt Meredith said haltingly, as if she were fighting for breath. "Such a . . . *orderly* ceremony. The graduates weren't any problem at all—"

"I am not here as a peacekeeper, lady," the elf said in that way some of them had, where their voices seemed to come at you from everywhere at once. "I want only to congratulate your nephew. Privately, an' it please you."

Aunt Meredith was snuffling. She pulled her fingers

across her eyes. "Allergies," she murmured.

"It's okay, Tante," Merle told her. His heart was going sour in him. "I'll meet you at the el stop."

Other graduates and their families passed, giving them a wide berth, watching out of the corners of their eyes. Aunt Meredith lingered a moment, uncertain, but when Merle nodded again and jerked his head, she bustled off and left him alone with the fairy.

He was one of those regal, Tolkienesque elves that made you feel fat and unlovely. Six-five, lean, sloe-eyed, with short green mossy hair. A soldier's haircut. A strange mix of both human and fairy sensibilities: a silk hoodie, leather shorts, wristlet braided from dandelion greens, Converse One Stars. Off duty, obviously—only the pink dragon insignia on his red cap told you he was a captain of the Trooping Fairies of Oberon.

People his aunt's age and older loved to tell one another how unnatural it all still seemed, even fifteen years on: spotting a centaur waiting to use an ATM, assorted gnomes at Coney Island, the Questing Beast sniffing garbage cans outside the Pick 'N Save. They said it with this tragic air, as if it wasn't a gift to have memories of the world as it was before. Merle would give everything to be surprised by the sight of an elf under his high school bleachers.

"Do you remember me?" asked the elf.

Merle huffed. "Is that a joke?" He felt faint.

The elf pretended to watch other graduates pass.

"My name is Conor, by the by."

"Right. Sure it is."

"I want you to know I took no pleasure from that day. I assayed only to do my duty."

"Then your duty sucks. You have an evil duty."

"If that were so, then my glamour would have failed me, and I would have died, and your mother would have lived. My actions were just."

"Don't give me that bull. Her gun backfired, is all. Don't you . . . don't you *dare* tell me you won because the universe *wanted* you to."

The way Conor was glancing around, Merle wondered if he was waiting for all the other humans to clear out. What happened when there were no more witnesses?

36

Maybe then the elf finished what he'd left undone, six years before. At last they were alone, and Conor frowned at his feet.

"You're being watched, Merle."

Merle felt a chill. "What, right now?"

"Always."

Merle hiccuped, nervously. Whenever he'd imagined this scenario, he'd always carried himself with a little more dignity. He hadn't been wearing a black satin gown, for example.

"They suspect what you're up to," Conor continued. "My superiors. They haven't seen fit to share their suspicions with me, but . . . I remember seeing you before, Merle."

"Yeah. *Six years ago June.* I remember that too."

"No, not six years. Centuries. I observed a dispute over a tower that would not stand, and you were there. And yet you were older, no longer a boy. I think you understand me."

Merle thought maybe he *did* understand. A thrill ran through him.

"And . . . you're telling me this why?"

Conor looked up finally, studied Merle awhile before answering.

"You know, the Fay have always taken human children," he said. "I might've taken *you* that June day.

Raised you as my own. You weren't so old."

Was that some kind of weird threat? Merle hiccuped again, felt empty-headed. Darkness creeped like a stain around the edges of his sight.

"I wonder if I did right, leaving you there with your mother and father. I wonder if I could have taken hold of a wheel then, stopped it spinning. What threads might be lost if I had?"

"You talk a lot," Merle slurred, swaying. "Is it your glamour making me feel like this? You hoping for a mysterious exit? I'm not going to faint, so you'll just have to look me in the eye and leave."

"Take care, Merlin," Conor said. Then Merle drooped, and fade to black.

After a couple of years at university, Merle had a reputation for being obsessive about western European folklore and brilliant at quantum physics, and not much else. It was understood that if you needed an explanation of the Pauli exclusion principle or wanted to know who built Stonehenge, you should get someone to let you into basement lab three, because day or night that's probably where Merle was.

A couple grad students poked their heads in.

"Hey—Merlin."

"Yeah, hey—Merlin."

"What," said Merle. He didn't look up from his soldering.

"Hey . . . how many pookas in a quark?"

"How many . . . ," Merle repeated idly. Then he turned his head to scowl at them. "How many pookas in a quark? That doesn't even make sense."

"What's the problem?"

"Well . . . you presumably have a lot of quarks in a pooka, but pookas in a quark? One's a subatomic particle. The other's one of the shape-shifting Fay. Don't you know the difference between physics and fairies?"

"*I* do." The first grad student scoffed. "I just didn't think *you* did."

The other student laughed.

"That's really funny," Merle told them. "Come closer and I'll show you how a soldering iron works."

"See ya, Merlin."

"Yeah, see ya, Merlin."

Professor Strohmer entered as they left. He stood and watched Merle work for a moment before speaking.

"You're back in the lab already?"

"Not back in it; still in it. Hey, watch the hoses. That's liquid helium you're tripping on."

Strohmer picked the remains of a microwave burrito off an adjacent stool and sat down. "You smell, Merle. And I hope you realize I'm only telling you this because you smell. You need a shower and you need to go to sleep."

"I have classes."

"You do have classes. You have my class, for example. And you know as well as I do that you're going to skip it and hide in here all day with your . . . chimera."

Merle clucked his tongue. "What do you mean, chimera?"

"Well . . . ," the professor began, adjusting his glasses. "It can mean a few things. But I meant 'something hoped for which is nonetheless impossible.'"

"It's not impossible. Just . . . very, very hard."

"I know what you're trying to build, Merle. And why. I heard about your parents."

Merle flinched. "How did you hear that? I never told—"

"I'm sorry. Word gets around. But we're talking about time travel, Merle. Time travel to the *past*, no less. It's science fiction. It's a f . . . it's a—"

"*Fairy tale?*" Merle said, turning. "You were gonna say fairy tale, weren't you."

"Merle—"

"You notice how members of my generation don't use that phrase? I wonder why that is."

"I think I've been giving you too much leeway, Merle."

"Hey—you know what else chimera can mean? It can mean a mythological monster made up of different animal parts. Like a griffin or a sphinx? And I know sphinxes are real, because there's one LIVING ON TOP OF THE LAUNDROMAT NEAR MY HOUSE."

"Okay, calm down—"

"I HAVE TO ANSWER RIDDLES TO USE THE CHANGE MACHINE."

Strohmer got up from the stool. "I'm going to try this again some other time."

"Wait," Merle said, and stepped back. "Sit down. I'm sorry. I'm just a little . . . off. I haven't slept in two days. But I can't leave the lab just yet. I'm waiting for something."

Strohmer had his hands on his hips, watching Merle like he was watching a dog rolling in filth, wondering if he should correct the behavior or just let nature run its course.

"You know I respect your opinion," Merle added quickly. "Your work with fairy metals is the main reason I chose this school."

Everyone knew by now that Fay treasure couldn't be trusted. Maybe some satyr would pay you in gold pieces, more than he should have, even; but if you didn't go and spend them quickly enough, you'd find you had a purse full of buttercups or some such.

Professor Strohmer had been the first to recognize that those buttercups must have been imbued with a kind of energy when they were changed into gold, and that they released this energy again when they changed back. Other scientists took his research and found a way to stabilize the gold somewhat, so that it held its energy like a battery and only let go a little at a time. Suddenly any mundane thing could be powered by fairy gold, with unpredictable results. Even old guys like Strohmer had to admit that what they were doing might not strictly be science anymore.

Merle had a robot owl that he'd hacked and tinkered with, and this owl had a fairy battery that would keep it running for centuries.

"Those fairy metals have given us a lot of things," Strohmer reminded him. "We're going to beat global warming because of fairy metals."

"Uh-huh."

"I'm just saying . . . maybe this whole crusade of yours is a little misguided? The resistance movement your parents were a part of has all but died out. I know we've lost some things, some freedoms, but . . . have you read the new paper in *Nature*? The average human lifespan has increased by almost five years just since the Fay came! Some believe that a baby born this year may live to two hundred!"

"Yeah, a lot of animals live longer in captivity," Merle muttered.

The professor exhaled, then slapped his legs and rose

from the stool again, looking for his exit strategy.

"Hey, speaking of kids, whatever happened to your toy owl? I remember when you started here, that thing never left your shoulder."

"He's helping me with an experiment," said Merle.

"Well . . . when he gets back, tell him I said you should both power down for a while."

"If I did my math right, you can tell him yourself in . . ." Merle consulted his watch. "Six minutes."

Merle must have had a look on his face. Strohmer eyed him suspiciously.

"What happens in six minutes?"

And then, suddenly, Archimedes was there. He appeared, flapping, just above their heads. He clasped a golden octagonal ring in his talons.

Strohmer started and tripped over the helium hose in earnest. Merle was short of breath. "Okay. Wow. It worked." He checked his watch again. "I guess I got the math wrong, though."

"What just—" Strohmer sputtered. "Where was he?"

The owl landed and held the ring out to Merle.

"Nowhere. He was nowhere. I sent him into the future, one year ago."

"Why is it always a year?" Scott asked now, on the bus. "Couldn't you just have sent Archie five minutes into the future?"

"Could," Merle admitted. "But then I'd never have seen him again. Remember, the earth's always looping around the sun. In five minutes, the planet and everything on it would have moved five thousand miles to the right, and Archie would've popped up in empty space somewhere. Same with your mom. In a year the earth'll get back around to exactly where it was when she left, and she'll materialize in the same airport terminal."

Scott pictured it: his mom appearing suddenly, a little woozy maybe, wearing a bracelet made of fairy gold and wondering where her chauffeur had disappeared to.

Their tire grazed a pothole, and the music started playing again. Tiny spotlights fractured off the mirror ball and swam in schools around the inside of the bus. The unicat chased these around while Finchbriton pecked at the mirrors.

"Here's what I don't get," Scott told Mick. "You say most Fay aren't spellcasters. Your magic is like really good luck. So how do you turn worthless things into gold?"

"We don't," said Mick. "I mean, not deliberately. It's like . . . yeh know when you're walkin', an' yeh think yeh see somethin' valuable on the ground maybe? Silver, or a diamond, or even just a quarter. But then yeh look closer, an' it's only a candy wrapper, or a piece o' glass."

"Sure."

"Well, when one o' the Fay thinks he sees a treasure, he's almost always right."

"Hey," said Erno, and he glanced over at where Harvey was sleeping, then back at Scott. "Hey, your dad's still driving the bus, right? Because the TV says he's at a French disco."

John (or rather Reggie Dwight, or rather two goblins masquerading as Reggie Dwight) was shown exiting a cab and entering the club above the caption "'Knight' Out on the Town." Then they flashed a few clips of Reggie from his movies and music videos, and then they showed the cab-to-club footage again in slow motion.

"What was that?" John called back from the driver's seat. "You say I'm on the telly?"

"I would never say telly, but yeah."

45

"Who's got the remote?" asked Emily.

"Hey, Fi," said Scott. "Can you reach the volume?"

"I see no volumes," Fi answered.

"I got it," said Polly, and the bus speakers blared with the voice of the entertainment reporter, which had all the artless tenor of a toddler announcing to a crowded room that she has to go tinkle.

"... cameras inside, but sources say he danced the night away with nearly everyone in the club. Vive la différence! Including this American college student studying abroad."

A redheaded girl tried to keep from grinning before the cameras outside the club. She wore a tiny T-shirt that showed that she was from Colorado, or Wyoming, or just a fan of rectangles. "I asked if I could take his picture with my phone?" she said. "So he took my phone and he put it in his mouth."

"In his mouth?"

"It was a really small phone. Then he swallowed it? Then he said I could get my pictures back in twenty-four hours. Do you think that means we have a date? I gave him my number, but he didn't write it down."

"Did he punch anyone?"

"He punched three people."

"Tell us about the punching."

"He punched one guy who asked to be punched 'cause

46

his girlfriend's a fan? Then he punched a girl I think by accident 'cause of his dancing. Then later he punched a guy who wouldn't let him cut in the bathroom line."

"ARE YOU KIDDING ME?" John bellowed from the front of the bus. "Oh my lord."

Goodco had only targeted John in the first place because they were rubbing out knights—it was nothing personal. But now it was like the goblin impostors were going out of their way to behave badly.

"All the better to make John look like a lunatic if he tries to tell the world what Goodco's up to," Emily suggested.

"My career is *over!*"

"Shh!" Erno shushed back.

"Those goblins are ruining my life!"

"*Shhh!*"

The cameras had gone back to Entertainment News Central or whatever they called it. The show's logo rotated on three big screens, and the anchorwoman stood rigidly in front of them like a pedestal with a smile on it.

"Reggie Dwight's bad-boy behavior began when he punched Queen Elizabeth II at a horse racing track last November. Fans of Reggie Dwight and royal watchers the world over want to know when the singer-actor and the Queen of England will sit down together and bury the hatchet. Sources close to the queen say that Her Majesty is still upset over Sir Reggie's unprovoked attack, but officially she's keeping 'mum.' It could be that rambunctious Reggie won't rest until his queen says 'good knight.' Now in celebrity baby news—"

"TURN IT OFF TURN IT OFF TURN IT OFF," said Prince Fi from atop the TV, where he crouched in a ball with his arms wrapped around his head. Polly did as he asked. Fi sighed and uncurled. "Like the foul wind of a thousand harpies," he explained, straightening. "Every television is surely swarming with demons too coarse for Pandora's box."

"Yeah, it's a pretty bad show," Erno agreed.

Despite having no good times to celebrate, they hit another bump.

CHAPTER 3

In Halifax, Polly wrapped John's head in bandages, save for a bare strip around his eyes that she covered with sunglasses and a thin slit over his mouth. If anyone asked, they were going to say he'd burned himself horribly somehow.

"We could tell people you were looking down the barrel of a flamethrower," Polly suggested.

"And why would I have done that," John sighed.

"To see why it wasn't working. Like in a cartoon."

"We could say you took a hot omelet to the face," said Merle.

"Couldn't it be something a little more . . . heroic?"

"Are you okay?" Scott asked Emily. She was rubbing her temples. She didn't look like she'd slept.

"Just a headache," she answered with a feeble wave. But you couldn't help but get Scott's sympathies with the word *headache*. He used to have migraines all the time. Every time he saw magical things, actually, but he'd finally gotten used to them, and his headaches had mostly gone away.

"Weird dreams," Emily added absently.

They abandoned the party bus and walked down to the water toward a massive white cruise ship that rose like a cathedral from the dock. Harvey carried the unicat, which he was calling Grimalkin in defiance of every other name that had been suggested so far (Pointy, Stabs, Cat Stabbins, Lance, Pierce, Al Gore), in the hope that he'd be able to sneak quietly on board without getting either of them noticed. Mick and Prince Fi played gin rummy in Scott's backpack.

"Welcome to the *Canadian Diamond Queen!*" said a polo-shirted young woman when they reached the end of the queue. Then she put the brakes on her smile a little bit. Her attention swerved to avoid the giant and the man in bandages and finally parked itself on Merle. Here was someone familiar: a senior citizen, just like the last fifteen passengers she'd admitted. You could see her struggling to find the common thread that bound him to everyone else. Carnies? Circus people?

"Carnies," Merle told her.

"Uh-huh. Well! Welcome aboard! Make sure to have your picture taken with one of our cast at the top of the gangway!"

"Cast?" asked John. "You don't mean crew?"

The woman jumped when he spoke. "We . . . call them cast."

"Everyone wants to be in show business," John muttered as he passed. "Did you see how she flinched?" he added when they were out of earshot. "What, just because I burned my face I'm not allowed to speak?"

"You didn't really burn your face," Scott reminded him.

"Maybe she expected you to be mute," said Merle.

Erno said, "Maybe she expected you to cackle about how you're going to show all those fools, those fools who thought you were mad."

They entered the ship and plowed past the photographers. "We wrapped my face so I could be anonymous," John groused. "This isn't anonymous, this is just a worse kind of famous."

The inside of the ship looked like a floating Cheesecake Factory. It looked like a huge fancy gift shop. It looked like the tomb of King Hallmark III.

It also looked like Biggs was going to be doing a lot of slouching. The guest areas, with their hallways and cabins, were all narrow and low ceilinged. The rooms themselves were barely larger than the beds, with closets the size of bathrooms and bathrooms the size of closets. But each had a dozen free movies on the TV and chocolates on the pillows and a balcony that overlooked the ocean. Finchbriton met them on one of these balconies.

"There yeh are," Mick said to him. "Wanna join me under the bed? 'S roomy."

Mick and Harvey, who both preferred the undersides of beds, were sharing a room with Scott and Erno. Polly was rooming with Emily and Grimalkin. John was with Merle, Biggs was by himself.

"Come to our room, Prince Fi," said Polly. "I'll make you a little apartment out of a dresser drawer."

Fi sighed. "Thank you . . . no. That would be unseemly. I shall share quarters with the boys."

Polly hugged her shoulders. "Yeah, you're . . . you're right. Unseemly."

After a safety drill the ship got under way. And Harvey got immediately seasick.

"Why didn't you tell us you had trouble with seasickness?" Scott asked through the balcony door during a brief spell in which Harvey had either just finished or was about to commence vomiting onto the balcony below.

"HOW WOULD I KNOW?" Harvey sputtered, shivering. "I'm a pooka! I uthed to live underground. I went through a hole in the univerthe to get to thith turd of a planet. I've never thailed an ocean before."

"Yeah." Scott tried to sympathize. "Mick told me all about how he just turned up in this world suddenly, in a baby carriage. I guess it must have been a weird surprise for you too. When you made the Crossing, I mean."

That's what the Freemen had called it in their secret papers: the Crossing. The Walk Between Worlds—when a person or animal from the shrinking magical land of Pretannica traded places with some other person or animal here.

"Yeah, big thurprize," Harvey answered. "Didn't thee it coming."

"So . . . how did it happen with you?" Scott asked the pooka. "How did you make the Crossing?"

"I would love to have thith convertbation with you? But I'm thuper busy. Thith boat ithn't going to throw up on itthelf!"

Polly stepped out onto the balcony and plunked down into a plastic lounge chair. Harvey watched her out of the corner of his eye, as if she might weave him a friendship bracelet if he wasn't vigilant. She watched him back, appraisingly.

"I like your ears," she said.

"I wish I could thay the thame," he replied, wobbling.

"I think you must have been a really important fairy back in Pretannica," she continued, undeterred. "Girls are experts on this kind of thing. Like you must have been a prince or a jack or something."

Scott stared at his sister. Harvey did, too. "Showth what you know. I wath a *king*. Harvey the First of the

Lepusian Kingdom."

Polly nodded. "In my homeland I was known as Princess Babyfat Von Pumpkinbread. Before I was adopted by *commoners*," she added, indicating Scott. Harvey gave Scott a sneer.

Scott frowned. "Hey, I was just—"

"Leave uth! Leave uth before I—" shouted Harvey; but he didn't finish his sentence, unless the remainder was "vomit," in which case he finished it spectacularly.

Scott pulled his head back in.

"So wait . . . ," said Erno to Mick. "A five is higher than a king?"

"If it's a trump, yeah."

"This game is stupid."

"Harvey's pretty sick," Scott mentioned.

"The mongrel has brought it upon himself," said Prince Fi, who struggled to hold playing cards that were nearly as tall as he was. Like at any moment they might seize him and bring him before the Queen of Hearts, and then off with his head. "Hares are meant to eat vegetable matter, are they not?"

"I think he might have gotten some relish accidentally on his last hot dog," Scott offered.

"Harvey's got a little glamour left," said Mick. "It'll sort him out."

Scott watched them a moment, then shrugged. "All

right, whatever. I'm going to go play video games."

The thing about a moving cruise ship was that you couldn't get *too* lost. There was never any need for the parental admonishment, "Don't go too far." Unfamiliar adults, who in any other situation might have reported an unattended child or even tried to corral him like he was an unleashed dog, tended to ignore Scott even more than usual. Over the next few days he ate a sundae for breakfast, saw three movies while floating in a heated pool, failed to watch any whales during a whale watch, and accidentally took a Zumba class.

The fourth night was a formal night, which meant that everybody was expected to dress up extra nice for dinner. John had taken them to a tailor, so all the men and boys had tuxedos. Even Mick, who could wear the clothes off a ventriloquist's dummy if he took them in a bit. Even Biggs, who'd been greeted as if he were the natural disaster the tailor had been preparing for all his life.

Only Harvey couldn't come to dinner. His stomach had settled, but his rabbit head was still a rabbit head. If anyone saw Mick, his size could be explained by dwarfism or Made-Up Disease Syndrome or whatever. But Harvey? Harvey was stuck, and getting cabin fever. He claimed he could handle it after decades of confinement at Goodco headquarters, but in truth he'd been sneaking out while the rest were at dinner and idly stealing things from both passengers and crew—bath towels, cell phones, cocktail shakers, sunglasses and shoes left poolside while their owners swam. He didn't keep any of it; he threw it overboard—he wasn't a *thief*. It was only to pass the time.

On this night, servers flitted about in feathery masks, offering the adults free champagne. Violinists circled like mosquitoes. There were grand staircases that served mostly as backdrops for having one's picture taken, since every other passenger exclusively rode the elevators, of which there were twelve. But the staircases were nonetheless wide and made from great slabs of polished marble with gleaming gold banisters. Only if this gold could have been peeled back to reveal chocolate might the cruise have gotten any more stupidly self-indulgent.

John had a personal rule against using elevators if stairs were available, so they were always shooing photographers out of the way as they descended to Triton's Promenade Deck for meals. Passengers who had never considered using the stairs nonphotographically turned now to watch Scott's group make its entrance: first John, with his bandaged face and sunglasses; then massive, monstrous Biggs; and then . . . Polly and Merle. You could see their disappointment—just one wolfman or a Dracula away from a solid theme.

All food was included in the price of the cruise, so when their waiter came to the table Erno indulged his new habit of ordering the first three things on the menu and deciding later what he actually wanted to eat. Scott ordered two things himself, but the second was for Mick. Mick sat in an empty chair and tried not to grumble when the server always took his utensils away.

Their food came. Scott thought he knew what salmon looked like, so he was surprised to find a spiral of green foam topped by a puff pastry covered in yams.

"I think they brought me the wrong thing," he said. "I don't see any fish."

"We need to discuss our plans," said Emily.

"Oh, wait—I found it."

"We're going to want to move fast once we reach England," Emily added.

They had two good reasons for going to the British Isles. Papers in the Freemen filing cabinet Emily had memorized said that the real queen was being held captive in Avalon, in the west of England. And they also had indicated that Prince Fi's pixie brothers were prisoners of the Goodco U.K. headquarters in Slough, a town west of London.

"Perhaps I should reach out to . . . some other knights while we're near London," John suggested.

The table swooned with silence for a moment. Merle said, "Yeah. Yeah, maybe that's a good idea."

"Just as a sort of plan B, you understand."

"Right."

Eventually they all expected to run afoul of a colossal pink dragon, and only knights could beat dragons. But Goodco had been quietly getting rid of knights, so the only one who was preparing for this was John.

Scott had noticed his father's confidence slipping. One day John would behave as if he was destined to slay the largest dragon in two worlds; the next you could tell he was thinking that a proper knight should be known for something more valiant than performing his own stunts in a stage production of *The House at Pooh Corner*.

Scott swallowed a yam. "You can do it." He shrugged. "Slay Saxbriton, I mean."

John's head lifted; even through the bandages he looked like someone had just given him a tiara and a dozen roses. "Do you think so?" he asked, with such a rainbow of a smile on his face that Scott found he couldn't look at him.

"Sure. Maybe. I don't know. Maybe we should get some other knights anyway."

"Hmm," Emily mused. "Not to be indelicate, John, but who do you know who isn't already dead?"

Merle coughed. Everyone picked at their food. Scott excavated a piece of salmon from inside its pastry shell.

"A few people. I know Richard Starkey."

"Who's he?" said Erno.

John nearly choked on his Roasted Winter Vegetable

Tower with Bacon Lardons. "Richard Starkey? Drummer for the Quarrymen? Only the most important rock-and-roll band of the twentieth century?"

"Oh."

"We should warn him," said Emily. "Where does he live?"

"In the Holland Park district of London, in a house formerly owned by the painter Frederic Leighton," Scott answered, his cheeks still full. Then he frowned at his own mouth, if one can do such a thing.

"Ha," said Erno. "That might be the first time anyone's known anything Emily didn't."

Mick was glancing back and forth between Scott and his plate. "Wait a minute," he said, pointing at the fish. "Is that . . . ?"

Scott nodded furiously, his eyes wide.

"The Salmon of Knowledge!" gasped Mick.

"The . . . what?" said Emily.

"The Salmon o' Knowledge!" Mick whooped. "First caught by the great Irish hero Finn McCool! One taste an' yeh gain ultimate wisdom. Yeh know everythin'! But I thought Finn killed it centuries ago."

Scott shook his head. He pushed the bite of fish around with his tongue. "Dere's ahways a Salmon ub Knowwige. Iffit dies, one ub iss shildren eecomes da new Salmon ub Knowwige."

"How do you know all that?" asked Erno.

Scott pointed at his mouth.

"Oh, right."

"Iss too mush," he added, wincing. "Too mush knowwige. Can't concendrate."

"Finn got all the wisdom o' the world from just a wee bit o' salmon fat that got on his thumb," Mick explained. "For the rest o' his life he could suck that thumb an' answer any question."

"Scott's the new Emily," said Erno. Emily scowled and crossed her arms.

Scott was shaking his head again. "Finn ried."

"Ried?"

"He . . . didm't tell da troof. He rost . . . *lost* all da knowwige as soon as he swawwowed! Juss rike I'm going to! Finn juss *bretended* to know ebrything."

Emily huffed. "Typical. Boys."

"'Tis a wonder the Salmon ever came to be in this world in th' first place," said Mick.

"Rifts open petween da worlds in oceans, too," said Scott as he pushed his fists against his eyes.

"It's hurting him," said John. "Scott, you should swallow."

"No!" said Merle. "Wait. We could learn a lot."

"Everyone ask him questions," said Mick. "Help him focus."

"Maybe he could guess what word I'm thinking of right now," Emily muttered.

Scott stared at Emily in shock.

"*Useful* questions," suggested Mick.

"Okay, um . . . ," said Erno. "We spoiled all that Milk-7 back at the Goodborough factory. Did we stop Goodco from putting out a cereal with Milk-7 in it?"

"No. But dey onwy haf enough to sell it in big cities at first. Dey're trying to get more dragon milg agross so dey gan sell it ebrywhere."

"Shoot."

"That doppelgänger of mine . . . ," said John. "The goblin Reggie Dwight. What's *he* up to?"

"Da goplins are in London, regording your negst album."

"Good lord. Can they sing?"

"But lissen," Scott spat. "Goblin Reshie Dwight is gonna meet wif goblin Queen Erizabef. Live, on gamera. Dey're gonna bretend to make up, wike eberyone wants dem to."

The table fell silent.

"This is big," said Merle.

"If we get close enough to goblin Reggie, I can take his place," said John. "I could expose the goblin queen as a fake."

"How many goblins does Nimue have, anyway?" asked Erno.

"Seben."

"We should split up," Emily said quietly. "One group helps Scott's dad, the other rescues the real queen."

"It's going to be dangerous," said John.

"Too bad we can't all take some of that chemical that makes everyone huge and strong," said Erno. "Like it did for Biggs."

"Didn't make everyone bigger," Biggs mumbled. "Just the boys."

"Is Emily right about the queen being held in Avalon?" Erno asked Scott.

"I . . . dunno? Yeah, I dink so. Ish . . . hazy."

"That's weird," said Merle to Mick. "Shouldn't he know?"

Mick shrugged. "Maybe they've got the location protected by a spell?"

"I guess it's a good thing I memorized *an entire filing cabinet*, then," said Emily bitterly. "I mean, it's no *magic fish*, but—"

"Wait," said Scott. "Yes. Afalon. In Somerset. Deffinidly."

"You can see her?"

"Yeb. She loogs . . . weird? Dere's someding weird about her."

"What a super-useful piece of information," said Emily.

"You're being mean begause you habben't been

sweeping," Scott told her, and their eyes locked.

"Sweeping?" said Erno.

"Sleeping," Emily corrected. "It's no big deal."

"And also you're sgared. Sgared you'll get dumb now dat you're nod daking the Milk."

Emily curled up in her chair. "Why'd you say that?"

"Id's drue."

"That doesn't mean you had to say it."

For a moment nobody could think of anything to add. Biggs cleared his sinuses.

Scott grimaced. "It'sh breaking up in my mouf! Too delicate. Hafta shwallow soon."

"I'm not surprised," said John. "The chef here is quite good."

"He shtudied at Le Cordon Bleu!"

"I had the salmon last night," said Erno. "It was really flaky."

"The shecret ish a citrus marinade!"

"Maybe we should stick to business?" said Emily.

Polly made a noise, and everyone flinched.

She'd been uncharacteristically quiet that evening. Normally she could keep two or three conversations going all by herself. Now she simply asked, "Will my . . . will Prince Fi ever forgive me?"

Scott just breathed a moment. "Can't tell the fujure, Pully. Onwy the present."

64

"Maybe I made him mad when I said he could sleep in our dresser drawer?" Polly said as she tore a piece of bread into little pills. "Like maybe it reminded him how I used to make him live in a shoe box? Back when I thought he was a toy?"

"He'll forgive you," Scott answered. He had no idea if it was true.

But just then he knew Fi's story. He knew everything there was to know.

CHAPTER 4

The prince himself had remained in Scott and Erno's cabin, and from atop the television he was watching an oblivious old woman with headphones clean the floor with a stick vac. He was only four inches tall, but his proud eyes and regal bearing made him appear five, easily. His indigo tabard brought out the faint blue of his dark face.

"I expect you cannot hear me through your ear cradles," Fi said. "Can you? No. Still and all, I will honor you with my speech. For though you are lowborn and gruesomely ugly, you will be audience to the story of Prince Fi, last son of Dun Dinas."

The maid didn't answer. Nor did she look up, which gave Fi a certain freedom of movement, and he paced the television like he was treading some high stage above an imaginary crowd of pixies assembled on the bedspread.

Pixies were not naturally invisible to humans, like the Fay; but after ten months as an inanimate toy, Fi was possessed by a powerful need to fidget, not to mention the kind of recklessness that comes of having very rich parents.

"King Denzil XXXIII and Queen Rosevear had four sons: Fee, Fi, Fo, and Denzil. And we were all happy on our islands, away from the savage humans and inhospitable Fay. Beautiful Lady Morenwyn often stayed at court, and my brothers and I undertook contests of courage and skill to win her hand. And the sun never set on the pixie empire. Nor anywhere else, I'm given to understand.

"But darkness fell nonetheless. Morenwyn was

kidnapped by her mother, the witch Fray, and stolen away to a secret island. My brother Denzil was oldest, so the honor of rescuing Morenwyn fell first to him. He took up our grandfather's peerless sword, Wasp-Mare, and sailed east in an enchanted boat. And was not heard from again.

"Next was Fo. And Fo chose the girdle Giantkiller, which gives a pixie the strength of a man, and the Hammer of the Jötnar, cold forged from ice that neither breaks nor melts. And he sailed south in an enchanted boat and was not heard from again.

"The honor of saving Morenwyn should have next fallen to me. But while I made my preparations, impulsive Fee slipped into my chambers and took Armaplantae, the Living Armor, and the bow and quiver of the great pixie hero Cornwallace, whose arrows always flew straight and true. And he sailed west in an enchanted boat. And was not heard from again.

"Here I asked around to see if anyone knew of a fourth enchanted boat, but no one did."

In the cruise ship cabin, Fi paused while the maid went to her cart for fresh towels. He cleared his throat as she returned. Her headphones buzzed with the waspish sounds of tinny Europop.

"The pixies have a great talent with birds," said Fi.

"We speak to them in their own language and may even persuade them to serve as mounts, though we do this but seldom—a bird who has let a pixie ride on its back will never be accepted into polite society again. In happier times the witch Fray had sometimes flown to the castle on the back of a red-billed chough. They were monstrous black birds, some as many as seventeen inches long, but I hunted the sea crows across coastal cliffs with the best weapons left to me. I wielded the marginally enchanted sword known as Carpet Nail, and for protection a thin scrap of birch bark that I have named Hoarskin."

It wasn't a dry throat now that made Fi cough. He could call his shield anything he wanted, but he knew he couldn't make it special—it was merely one of the sort carried by every member of the pixie infantry. Hardened by resin, these shields were really only useful against fairy magics. *All* pixie magic, rare though it was, tended to cancel out fairy glamour, and vice versa. It would surely offend Fi's pixie pride to admit this, but their oil-and-water magics were the only reason the Fay had not taken the pixies' islands generations ago.

"On the third day of my hunt I found a mangy old crow that stood apart from the rest of the flock. Indeed, if he dared come near, the others would peck at his head and

neck and beat him back with their wings. A pariah. But I let him close. I speared him plump grubs and earned his trust. And when I was near enough to whisper, I told him, 'Take me to your mistress.'"

The maid arranged and straightened the bedclothes and struggled with the contents of one of her pockets. Her beige uniform was really too tight for her, Fi noted, and it gathered in the pits and folds of her plump body. She was like a polyester walnut.

"I soared north, over the Irish Sea, stiff fingered and shivering as I held tight to the bird's scruff. And when we neared the Isle of Man, I . . . oh, dear." Fi trailed off and watched what was shaping up to be an epic clash of forces, suitable for song or myth. The maid had gotten her hand stuck in her own pocket and couldn't get it out again. She looked like she was playing tug-of-war with a dog.

"You'll have to let it go," Fi advised, though of course the maid couldn't hear him. "You can't hold on to whatever's in there and pull your hand out at the same time, woman; give it up!"

But with a spirited pull and a rip, the maid proved Fi wrong and produced a small white envelope from the ruined pocket. She stood still a moment, panting, then leaned over the bed and placed the envelope on one of its pillows. The pixies had their own written language, but Fi was reasonably certain that the name of the boy, Erno, was written on the front.

"Every other evening a little dark maid has left a chocolate on that pillow," Fi told her as she fixed her smock and made to leave. "Tonight, a secret message. What game is this?"

In the end, Scott had not so much swallowed as sensed the salmon dissolve, like some helpful spirit evanescing back into the unknown. The séance was over.

"It's all gone." Scott sighed. "My head feels like an empty circus tent."

"I was *going* to get the salmon," muttered Emily. "It was my second choice."

"I knew that," said Scott, holding his head and pointing.

"I totally kinda remember knowing that."

Everyone stared at their plates for a moment.

"This dinner was fun," said Erno. "What's for dessert, the Cheesecake of Courage?"

CHAPTER 5

The next morning John found Scott and Polly out on deck. He'd been jogging a circuit around the ship—sneakers and socks, shorts, hoodie, and bandages—and he stopped and rounded back after he passed their lounge chairs.

"Isn't it kind of awful, running with your head all wrapped up?" asked Scott as John sat at Polly's feet, breathing hugely and evenly.

"The worst part is changing the bandages at night," John answered, "and finding all these tiny bugs trapped in the gauze. I mean, do they really like gauze, or is this just the regular number of face bugs?"

Polly didn't say anything. The silence was conspicuous. Her face was cycling through expressions like a traffic light—hopeful to cautious to halting, then back to hopeful again.

John put a hand on her shoe. "Fi will come around. Just

give him time. Getting treated like a little plaything . . . it was a big hit to his ego."

Polly sniffed.

"Maybe you can give her some tips," Scott told John. "You actors have huge egos, right?"

John laughed. Or huffed, or something—it was hard to tell through the bandages. "Just the opposite, really. The best actors have no ego at all. No ego makes it easy to play a part, become somebody else. But it can also make you want to be loved by everyone. And when you need love that badly . . . you never stop being afraid of rejection."

"I don't think Fi's like that," Polly said.

"No," John agreed. "I think Fi *does* have an ego, and it's been bruised by all that toy business. He just wants to forget, and you're not letting him."

"I'm being nice!" Polly protested. "I've been extra nice ever since I found out."

"Yes—you're so *very* nice that it's like a box of chocolates every time you speak. He wishes he could move on, but you keep giving him big Mylar balloons that read SORRY FOR YOUR HUMILIATING EXPERIENCE."

Polly winced and chewed it over.

"My two bits, anyway," said John as he rose to resume his run. "See you in three and a half minutes." Then he charged off like a fit mummy.

After a pause Scott felt compelled to admit, "That

might have actually been good advice Dad gave you just now. I mean . . . assuming it really *was* Dad. Could have been anyone under those bandages."

"It was Dad. He's smart."

"Maybe when you cover up his face he gets smarter."

One very early morning the *Canadian Diamond Queen* docked at Dover. They had an official disembarkation time, which they ignored, and instead sneaked out through the luggage bays.

"Hey," said a man in a jumpsuit as they passed. "You're not supposed to be here."

"That's so true." John sighed through his bandages. "I should be sleeping in my big feathery bed after a night on the stage, dazzling my adoring fans," he added, and patted the man on the arm. "Thank you for saying so." Then he joined the others down the loading platform.

Erno sidled up to Emily. "So you haven't been sleeping?"

Emily shrugged. "Nightmares. I keep dreaming of Mom. I mean . . . *my* mom."

Erno nodded. They'd been raised as brother and sister, and Erno had to remind himself sometimes that it wasn't true, too. "How do you know it's her?"

"In my dreams I know what she looks like. When I wake up I can't remember. She's always looking for me, calling my name. But she can't find me. I try to call out to her, to tell her where I am, but my voice won't work." When she saw Erno's concerned look, she added, "It's nothing. Maybe bad dreams are a side effect of not taking the Milk-7 anymore." She glanced over at the envelope Erno was holding, the envelope he'd found on his pillow the previous night.

Erno had examined every inch of the envelope and its contents. He'd inspected it for fingerprints, knowing full well that he hadn't any other fingerprints to compare it to. When he thought no one was looking, he'd sniffed it.

"It couldn't have been Mr. Wilson," Emily told Erno. "How could he have known we'd be boarding that cruise ship? Why would he sneak on board dressed as a maid and . . . not even say hello?"

They passed quickly through the loading dock and bribed their way around customs. Erno read the enclosed riddle again, aloud. He was trusting Emily to handle this bolt out of the blue from Mr. Wilson, even though she'd been a bit high voiced and fidgety ever since learning about it.

> *The new year has a week to wait till waking.*
> *The water's almost frozen in the well.*
> *The hours of the day*
> *pass swiftly by, then drift away,*
> *and yet there's nothing, less than nothing left to tell.*

"He sounds depressed," said Emily. Erno continued:

> *Soon the final days are numbered, then forgotten,*
> *and the new year's hardly worth the time it's taken.*
> *By degrees the hourglass reckons*
> *all the minutes, all the seconds,*
> *and the next year still has weeks to wait to waken.*

"And that's it," said Erno.

"I don't get it yet," Emily groused, rubbing her temples again. "But . . . I will, don't worry."

"I'm hungry," said Polly.

"There's a grocer's," said John. "You lot stock up while I give Sir Richard Starkey a call."

Harvey sighed and thumped down on the concrete by the store entrance with Finchbriton and Grimalkin. Merle and Biggs veered off into the produce section for fruits or vegetables or some nonsense. The rest of them paced up and down aisles, grabbing bread and cheese and odd British snacks they would later regret. No one said as much, but all of them—Erno and Emily, Scott and Polly, Mick and Fi—were dreading the inevitable cereal section, as if it were lying in wait like the killer in a slasher film. Then, there it was: cheery boxes, cartoon animals, photo after photo of tumbling cereal pieces splashing up goopy crowns of whole milk. Nearly half the cereals were Goodco brand.

"Weird," said Erno. "In England, Koko Lumps is called Soy Capitán."

Scott paused in front of one box in particular. "There it is," he whispered. "Peanut Butter Clobbers. 'Now with Intellijuice.'"

"It's already out?" said Erno. "When did it come out?"

Mick leaned out of Scott's backpack to look. He groaned and said, "The queen on the Clobbers box— that's just me in a wig, innit?"

"It's not *just* you in a wig. You're also wearing a dress."

Prince Fi, for his part, couldn't take his eyes off the Puftees. Or the three blue-skinned Puftees Pixies on the box front. There wasn't much of a family resemblance, but apparently it was enough to get him thinking about his missing brothers.

"We should be talking about rescuing Fee, Fo, and Denzil," Fi said, clenching his little blueberry fist against his chest. "There is a correct order to things: we find my brothers, and my brothers help us rescue this human queen."

"Fi's right!" said Polly. "I mean, probably."

For a moment no one spoke. Scott waited for Emily's rebuttal, but she was off in her own little world.

"I . . . I don't know," said Scott. "This meeting between the fake queen and the fake Reggie Dwight is a really big opportunity, and it's happening so soon. We can't miss it. The whole world will listen to us about Goodco if we show them the queen's just a big puppet."

Fi was silent. Everyone was, and Scott felt like a jerk. Eventually Polly asked if Fi would like to be picked up.

"You may place me astride your hair tail," he told her.

"Ponytail."

"Yes," said Fi. "That." He still wouldn't go in a pocket. Polly lifted Fi atop her head, and he straddled her hair tie like it was a saddle. Scott suspected that he preferred to think of Polly as just a weird horse.

They should get out of the cereal aisle, Scott thought. They should keep moving. But he wanted to tear all these poisonous boxes off the shelves. He wanted to kick them around the store. Emily, he thought, had other ideas. She touched at the corner of one of the Clobbers boxes lightly, like she was worried she'd scare it away.

Intellijuice (or ThinkDrink, or Milk-7) was a chemical additive Goodco had developed after testing it out on Emily for ten years. Actually, *chemical* was a polite way of saying "mostly dragon barf and saltwater," but it made people smarter. It opened doors in their minds. One day soon Nimue would throw those doors wide and storm into those minds, and a million kids would become her private army of sugar zombies.

Maybe Emily was worrying about this. But Scott thought she looked more hungry than worried.

79

Erno noticed this, too. "C'mon," he said. "Let's go."

"Wait," said Emily. "Look."

She'd pulled a box of Clobbers out a bit, and now they could see Scott's last school picture printed above a recipe for Clobber Bars.

"Oh boy," said Scott.

Erno pulled other boxes out at random, and they found pictures of Emily, Merle, Polly, Erno, Biggs. HAVE YOU SEEN ME? was printed beneath each, with a phone number and a web address. They were all too stunned for a moment to move. Then Scott quickly straightened the boxes. "Leave the groceries," he said, and they walked quickly, but not too quickly, out of the store.

John met them out front in a truck with a squarish cab and a boxy cargo area.

"I got us a lorry!" he called from the driver-side window. "Just bought it off the driver around back! Paid way too much." The sign on the side said it had been carrying Poppadum Crisps in Minted Lamb, Bubble 'n' Squeak, Baked Bean, and Prawn 'n' Pickle flavors. The kids reread the sign a few times, but it kept saying that. They piled into the back.

Biggs drove and shared the cab with Erno and Emily. The rest sat around an electric lantern on the cold steel cargo floor, feeling it rattle against their butts as the lorry rumbled toward London. John undid his bandages and scratched his face.

"We could play a car game," Polly whispered to Fi, in the corner.

"What is a car game?" asked Fi. Polly considered how to answer, but she couldn't think of any games that didn't need at least one window to look out of.

The unicat (who'd apparently forgotten what had happened last time) stalked Finchbriton. It crept close, its body low and discreet but its tall tail twitching like it was advertising the Grand Opening of a tire store. Then it crept too close, and Finchbriton whistled a puff of blue fire that lit the tips of its whiskers. They burned down like fuses and ignited a little explosion of activity as the cat leaped up, and back, and ran around and around the truck interior, full tilt and sticking its claws in everyone. Then it went to sleep.

"You could tell me about how you got here," Polly suggested, kind of softly, kind of not wanting the others to hear her asking. Fi didn't respond right away, and she was on the verge of repeating herself when finally his voice descended like a deflating balloon.

"The lady Morenwyn had been kidnapped," he began. "Taken by her witch of a mother, the lady Fray."

CHAPTER 6

"Why was she a witch?" asked Polly.

"She was a sorceress," Fi answered. "The only one born in a generation. Pixie magic is rare, but powerful. We aren't all possessed of little glimmers like the Fay."

"But why not call her a sorceress or . . . enchantress or something? Seems like a witch is just a sorceress who doesn't get asked to parties."

"Do you want to hear this story?"

"Sorry."

"One by one my brothers quested to rescue Morenwyn, and one by one they disappeared. Only I was left, so I hunted for a sea crow that Fray might once have used as a steed, and when I found such a creature I asked it to take me home to its mistress."

"You can talk to birds?" asked Polly.

"Forsooth."

"Can you teach *me* to talk to birds?"

"No," said Prince Fi. "So: I flew north over the Irish Sea on the chough's back, shivering from cold, shivering with the thrill that soon I would see my brothers again, and sable-haired Morenwyn. In my reverie I'd scarcely noticed that the bird was plunging down toward

something jagged and dark rising out of the ocean, like a colossal bit of backbone. Then I saw this was a castle, larger and stranger than any I'd seen. It was squat and bowlegged, jutting up from a forsaken strip of rock and strutted with buttresses and staircases too monumental for any pixie. Blunt stone towers jutted out at impossible angles like new antlers. A web of windowpanes comprised the whole of one end of the fortress, as delicate as a snowflake but tall as a tree. The chough sailed toward it and might have taken me directly into Fray's sitting room if I hadn't the presence to leap off its back and onto the parapet."

"Parapet?"

"Yes, parapet. The . . . toothy bits on the tops of castles."

"Oh, right."

"How I wished for the ancient times of story and song when the great Spirit had cloven the hours 'tween night and day. I might then have waited for cover of darkness before acting. Instead I steadied myself against the salty wind and vaulted over the parapet. I slid slowly down the sloping castle wall and caught hold of the first window ledge I encountered. And now I pried open the wide windows with my sword and tumbled into the warm scarlet bedchamber of the most alluring pixie woman on a thousand shores.

"Morenwyn leaped to her feet and dropped her sewing. She had been mending some white sail or tent that lay curdled all about on the floor. Now she stood, tall and proud, brandishing her sewing needle. Her hair like a storm cloud, her face as rare as a night sky. The lost stars, remembered in her eyes."

Here Fi seemed suddenly to compose himself, and shift uncomfortably atop Polly's ponytail.

"So she was pretty?" asked Polly.

"No, not *pretty*. Not merely *pretty*. She was the dream

of the world. She looked down on me, kneeling in the folds of that white tent, or sail, and sighed.

"'And finally Fi,' she said. 'Goody.'

"'Lady.' I bowed.

"'That's the last of the princes, now. Who's next after you lot, the dukes? Are the dukes going to rescue me next? Just tell me how long I've got before it's butlers and washerwomen.'

"'Lady,' I said. 'I am here for my brothers, and for you, if you need a champion. Do you need a champion?'

"Morenwyn covered her plum mouth then, with her fingers. 'You're asking?'

"'I am asking if you require rescuing.'

"I didn't get my answer," Fi told Polly, "not then. For the window beside me shattered, and the white hand

85

of a giant yanked me out by my cloak. I was whipped through the air, half choking, and understood that Morenwyn was mending neither sail nor tent as a shirtless monster of a man dangled me in front of his thick, bovine face.

"He was on the tallest landing of a staircase outside her bedroom. It sickened me that he'd been watching us there.

"'Gentle!' Morenwyn called from the window. 'Don't hurt him!'

"'Won't.' The giant grinned. 'Much.'

"'I like to think,' I rasped, 'that she was talking to me.' And then I reached as high as I could and drove my sword beneath the giant's black fingernail.

"He howled and I dropped, holding my shield like a canopy above me to slow my fall. I caught hold of his leg on the way down and slid into the rolled cuff of his pants, where I huddled and waited. It was nauseating, being lurched this way and that as the giant turned about on the slick bricks, searching for me. He peered over the edge of the landing to the rocks below.

"'Where he go?' the monster bellowed. 'You see?'

"I heard Morenwyn say, 'Sorry, Nim, lost track.'

"The monster rushed off and wist not that he had a passenger. He took me to the mouth of a dry sea cave and down beneath that cathedral of rock, to a fire pit where sat four other giants in queer and mismatching dress.

"'Pixie man!' my giant, Nim, told them. 'Help me find!'

"Three of the giants jumped to attention and made ready to follow. A fourth giant, wearing only his undergarment, hesitated. Nim took a serious tone.

"'You come also, Rudesby. New ones must come when Nim say.'

"When this Rudesby spoke, his language was strange, the accent unfamiliar.

"'Pleez.' He seemed to plead. 'Aye juhst haave too tahlk too thaat tynee wumman. Aye dohnt beelahng heer!'

"Nim grappled with Rudesby and pulled him along by the ear, and that's when I jumped free of his pant leg, dashed across the sand, and tucked myself into the shadows until they were gone.

"'Pleez!' Rudesby struggled as Nim led him aboveground, his voice getting washed out by the sea air. 'Aye juhst wahna goh *hohwm!*'

"I ventured deeper into the cave, this cave that must form a hollow under Fray's castle, then scrambled up a set of steep and rough-hewn steps until I noticed another staircase of pixie proportions running parallel to the first. I climbed for an age, toward faint light. Finally I came to find a kind of metal grate, albeit one so large I could just squeeze up through its openings, and found above it the largest room I have ever seen.

87

"I think you'd call it vast even by human measure. Vast enough to hold hundreds of humans, or even to play a match of that sport of yours, with the basket and the ball?"

"Basketball," said Polly.

"Yes. Basket and ball. What is the sport called?"

"It's called basketball. That's what we call it."

"Ah, of course. You are the poets of the new world. So: I could see that the castle was immense on my approach to the island, but never could I have guessed that below Morenwyn's bedchamber it housed little more than one cavernous void, lit on its end by the tall leaded window I'd seen outside. Here was a room like the belly of a whale, with stone ribs buttressing the margins, each curving to the floor and pointing toward a golden monument in the center. The monument was almost ten pixies high, broader than it was wide, taller than it was broad. It was inlaid with silver, symbols, jewels, and it looked like a flaming sword against the ruby sky, framed in that vast and faceted window.

"The air in here was teeming with motes of dust.

"An animal voice screeched in the darkness, high above. I crept around the edge of the chamber. I had no wish to see the golden monument any closer—there was something distinctly Fay about it—and my duty was to my brothers. And to Morenwyn, I thought, if she would have me.

"But then the dust in the air shone like fire, the room lit with ten thousand tiny lights.

"'Aha,' said a voice like a growling house cat. 'Fi, is it? You princes are positively interchangeable.'

"A pixie woman stood far off, on the dais near the base of the monument. I don't like to say that she looked like her daughter, but of course she did. She resembled her daughter like the charcoal resembles the tree. She was dressed in the rags and ribbons of a hermit.

"'Well met, Lady Fray,' I said, and touched at the pommel of my sword. 'You keep a lovely home. Airy.'

"'Yes, I do think the airiness is its best feature.'

"'Anyone else would have cluttered up the place with furniture, things. But you know all a person really needs is one good gold monolith.'

"'That,' Fray agreed, 'and I find nothing really complements a monolith like a stupendously large tapestry.' Fray gestured to the wall opposite the giant window, and now I saw something that before had been shrouded in darkness: a woven tapestry depicting two overlapping spheres, stabbed through their hearts by some sharp stake, and all the heavens torn asunder by fierce light. And beneath that: a multitude of people great and small, all weeping. 'I wove it in a day and a night,' Fray added, though this could only be a lie. 'I don't remember a moment of it. But I emerged from my trance

with cracked and bleeding hands and looked at what I'd created—a vision of the end of all things.'

"I didn't know what to say. It was a bit modern for my tastes.

"'So,' said Fray, stepping forward. 'Here for Morenwyn, I suppose?'

"'That is her decision to make. I'm here for my brothers.'

"Fray lifted her brow and nodded, as if in approval.

'At last, a worshipful son of Denzil. What a shame. Be a sport, will you? Make a pretty speech about freeing my poor daughter and leading the armies of pixiedom to my doorstep. It makes this next bit so much easier.'

"Fray whistled, and the floor grate lifted. Five giants, the same five I'd seen underground, climbed up into the chamber and formed a half circle around the monolith. The one called Rudesby was still being manhandled by the others. Fray gestured and muttered, and hurled a dart of light from her fingertips that struck the stone floor where I'd been standing only a moment before. I didn't think my pixie shield would protect me from this witchcraft. But I maneuvered to keep the golden tower between us, thankful at last for its Fay magic. Fray cast another spell, but the monument blew it like a wind, swept it off course.

"'Nim?' said Fray.

"'Rudesby!' barked Nim. 'You first! New ones always first!'

"He prodded Rudesby in the back, and the half-naked giant stumbled forward. 'Aye'm saahry!' he told me, advancing. 'Pleez dohn't hurt mee! Aye haffa wyfe in Sanfransisgoh!'

"He lurched at me, bent at the waist, fumbling with outstretched arm. I ran up the length of that arm, stabbed him in the ear, then leaped off his shoulders. Grabbing hold of his underpants, I arrested my fall, then dropped again to the floor behind his left heel and sliced his tendon. He dropped, clutching his head.

"'Tapping owt!' Rudesby said, slapping the floor. 'Aye'm tapping owt!'

"'Worthless,' grumbled Nim. 'Clara! Tom-Tom! Marty! Go!'

"Fray came around the golden tower, calling forth some new spell from the ether, but now her own giants blocked her sight. The three of them surrounded me, but like the pixie heroes of old, I confounded them. Three giants hunting the same pixie could only get in each other's way. They struck heads, crossed arms. I sliced one in the toe, and he was compelled to tackle another, while the third searched for me among their flailing limbs. But then I made my great error and saw nothing protecting me from Fray's mischief. She spoke, and I was blinded by light, and a moment later I could see but could not move.

"Again, some piercing voice called out from above.

"'There,' said Fray. 'By the Spirit, you're a clever mouse. I see why she likes you.'

"Fray stepped aboard Nim's hand and disembarked again after he'd brought her only inches from my face. To say that I strained with every muscle against Fray's enchantment would be a lie. I could not do even that. Only my mind raged against its cage.

"'Wonderful thing, this magic,' said Fray. 'I wish you

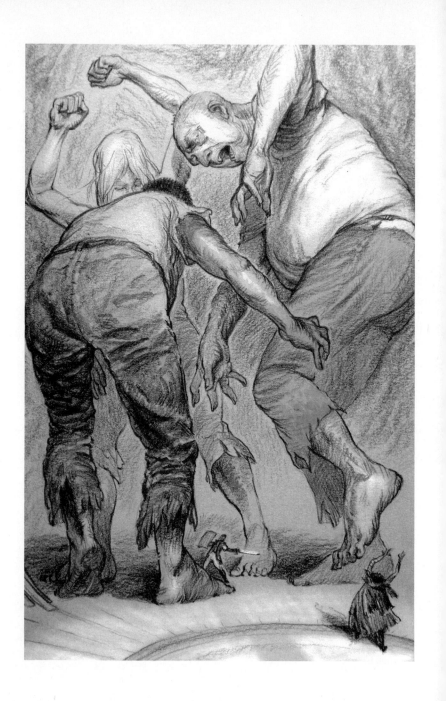

could see yourself. It's like the thinnest coat of glass. You needn't eat, or drink, or even breathe. You'll never die. But you'll never move again either, so here's hoping you end up someplace with a view.'

"She circled around me and was joined again by her giants.

"'This world is truly dying,' she whispered in my ear. 'I know I've said that before. And when I said it before, all the kingdom turned against me. Suddenly all my useful little spells, the magic arts that enchanted *your own sword and shield*, branded me a witch. Well, now—here's good news: I'm going to send you to a place without magic. A tedious groan of a place. You were so good with my giants, so I will send you to a world of giants.'

"'Mother,' said Morenwyn behind her.

"'Daughter.' Fray turned and answered. 'You've been attracting flies again. Look at this dirty little thing I've caught.'

"'Mother, I think he's different.'

"'Oh, they're *all* different. Our differences make us special, darling—I think I saw an embroidered pillow once to that effect.'

"'I'll deal with Fi,' said Morenwyn. 'Please. Leave me with him.'

"'We can't let him go, Morenwyn. If he told the elves—'

"'Why would he tell the elves?'

"'Morenwyn,' the witch said flatly. 'You know what's at stake.'

"I thought they both might have looked across to the tapestry then. It was hard to say. Morenwyn sighed.

"'I will do what needs to be done,' she said. 'But *I* will do it.'

"'Fine. Good. I'll leave Nim to help you.'

"And Fray and the other giants did leave us then. Morenwyn stood before me. I would have bowed if I could.

"'You always stood out, Fi,' she said. 'Even at your father's court, even when you were all stumbling over one another to impress me with your contests. I could tell you let Fee win sometimes.'

"I could neither confirm nor deny this at the time, though in the interest of accuracy I'll admit it's true.

"'Of course you know that Fee was here just before you. He didn't ask me if I wanted a champion. He had me three-quarters rescued before he even asked me how I was doing.'

"I smiled then, in my mind.

"'I was never kidnapped. I liked neither the warp nor weft of the future they were weaving me at court, so I sent for my mother. I *tried* to tell Fee this. Then Mother caught Fee, and she brought him here.' Morenwyn strode briskly toward one wall, and Nim lifted me up and followed. Where she stopped there was a low stone stall, a pixie-sized stall, jutting out from the wall, and an octagon traced in chalk. She seemed to be taking some care not to get too close. 'All of your brothers were brought here. Did Mother tell you about the doors?'

"*No*, I whispered back in my thoughts.

"'Mother learned from her travels that the world is shrinking, dying. She meditated on this for a long time. And then she had the vision of the tapestry! And she learned more. There are doors all across the world, and they can't be seen. Most, most by far, only open and close for a moment, and rarely in the same place twice. They lead to another world. A world, as my mother told you, without magic. A world without pixies or elves or any magical creature, she thinks. She's explored but a little of it.

"'But some of these doors, certain special doors, are open for weeks at a time. Rarer still are the doors that are always open. The Fay are desperate to find such doors. And we have four of them.'

"She gestured at the chalk octagon.

"'This one goes to a kind of twin England. We know it to be filled with humans. Now look up there.'

"She raised her arm straight in the air, pointed at

97

something too high and too dark to see. But then she tightened her fingers, and the motes of light far above us burned brighter. A crooked tower tunneled up from the castle ceiling. Across the base of it was strung a strong net. Near the top of it perched a dozen eagles.

"'There's a door up there, too. It opens onto a cliff face high above a desert. From time to time a human on the other side falls through and trades places with one of our eagles. We catch him in our net, and he joins our . . . happy family. I'm told Nim's grandfather came here this way.'

"'Yes'm,' said Nim.

"'The one they're calling Rudesby joined us only weeks ago.'

"She paused and looked at the tapestry.

"'There's a door there, too.'

"After a moment she motioned to Nim, and he carried us both past the golden monolith and to another corner. There was a larger stall here, a gaping octagon.

"She stepped down lightly onto the floor. 'The Fay want to find doors so they can escape this world, invade another, but Mother says they've turned wicked. She's foreseen that the fairies will tear both worlds apart with their folly, and she fears that you'll reveal her secret, tell them about these doors. She'd have me send you through that first door, to the human town. Like she did your brothers. I think . . . I think Mother's too careless in sending good pixies there. I won't send you through the second door either, which I understand leads to certain death. And the third's a frozen desert. But this one,' she said, nodding at the octagon, 'nothing ever goes in or out of here.'

"Nim set me down inside the stall, right in front of the octagon. He set me down facing the wall.

"'Mother says we'll have to go through to the other world one day, too. She says our world is drying up. I think she's saving this door for us. I'll send you through, and you'll be awaiting us when we come! Surely by then mother could be convinced to undo her spell.'

"'Good-bye, Fi,' she added. 'May the Spirit keep you.'

"I did not know what I was waiting for, then," Fi told Polly. "I did not know how the rifts worked, that a body had to change places with something of similar size on the other side to make the Crossing. So I stood rigidly in silence for a while, listening to Morenwyn breathe behind me."

Fi was quiet. The road rumbled along beneath them. "Then what happened?" asked Polly.

Then Fi had felt a sensation as if something was moving through him, and a second later he wasn't in the witch's castle anymore.

"Oh," Morenwyn said to the wriggling fish that had taken his place. "Oh, dear."

CHAPTER 7

Fi had barely registered that he was underwater before he was swallowed by a different fish. A fish that had been fixing to eat the one Fi had just traded places with. The inside of a fish is generally less diverting than the outside, so Fi was left alone with his thoughts. He thought of the great pixie hero Cornwallace, whom the

legends said had also once been swallowed by a fish, and had cut his way to freedom with his enchanted dagger. But Fi could not lift his arms, so he contented himself by merely wishing the fish misfortune, and would have been pleased to learn that it was eaten by an albatross a few moments later.

Still and all, getting swallowed by an albatross was nothing if not a step backward. And one relatively unimproved by the fact that the albatross was shot by a tuna fisherman that same afternoon.

The fishermen of the *Albacore Four* had been watching a World Cup match, and South Africa had just won, and Jerry had taken his gun up on deck to celebrate by shooting at the sky for a bit. The sky, disgruntled, threw something back: a great white bird, plummeting, pinwheeling from the hole Jerry had just made in its right wing. An albatross, looking as preposterous as a biplane on the deck of the *Albacore Four*.

People claim that so many things are bad luck. Black cats and broken mirrors and sidewalk cracks. What you probably don't know is that it's also bad luck to kill an albatross. And why would you? You are presumably not a sailor, and you've likely never seen an albatross, and even if you have, you probably hadn't anything against it personally and so you managed not to kill it. Unless it was an accident. But in general terms it is terrifically easy not to kill an albatross—you're probably not killing one right now.

The point is that you may not have known it's bad luck to kill an albatross, but Jerry the sailor knew. He knew this very well.

The usual custom in this sort of situation is to wear the albatross around your neck for a while, but instead Jerry scooped it up and, glancing about, rushed it belowdecks to one of the freezer holds, where he hid it inside a first aid cooler. Then he rejoined his crewmates and remarked loudly what a nice, birdless day it was outside.

When the *Albacore Four* was destroyed by lightning, Jerry found the first aid cooler useful to hold on to as he kicked for shore. On land, he found a buyer for his well-preserved and mostly intact albatross carcass, and bought

a fresh suit of clothes, and landed a new job, and was killed a week later in an unrelated pumpkin-catapulting incident.

The albatross was freeze-dried and resold to the New Jersey Museum of Natural History, where it was displayed with a plaque that failed to mention that it contained any pixies. A week later it was stolen by mistake.

"How will I know which one is the eagle?" the thief asked, fidgeting outside the museum.

"Aw," Haskoll answered. "And to think people say there's no such thing as a stupid question. Good for you!"

"Sorry, but not everybody's a . . . a bird doctor or whatever."

"You sure you're up for this, big guy? I bet I can find another hobo at the bus station who's willing."

"If you got the two hundred dollars, I'll get your bird. Just don't want to grab the wrong one . . ."

Haskoll smiled. "It's easy. You bring me the biggest bird they have, okay?"

"'Kay," the thief breathed. Then he headed across the quiet street to the rear of the museum.

When Haskoll saw him again at the meeting place in the parking garage, he was carrying an albatross and a pelican.

The albatross had been freeze-dried with its wings extended, and it caught the air like a kite as the thief ran.

"There wasn't any eagle, boss!" the thief said. "I swear!

There was a little sign that *said* eagle, but it was in front of another sign? And that one said 'exhibit removed for cleaning.'"

"And so you just grabbed every other bird you could carry," Haskoll replied. "What a go-getter you've turned out to be. You gonna make me an eagle out of spare parts now?"

The thief waggled the albatross in front of him, and it was one of the singular experiences of Haskoll's life. There's really nothing like having a dead albatross waved in your face.

"The sign said this bird has the biggest wings!" said the thief. "Bigger than the eagle, maybe? I thought it might be just as good."

"So why the pelican?" said Haskoll.

The thief was giving Haskoll a look now, a look that said, *Man, why NOT the pelican?*

Haskoll sighed and glanced down, and that's when he noticed that the small chunk of iron on the tether around his neck was glowing. Faintly, sure, but there was definitely a glow. The little nugget was a coldstone, a lump of meteoric iron that gave off pink and purple sparks when it was near magic. Only now it was glowing black. *No, that's not right*, thought Haskoll. *Nothing can glow black.* Still, it was making a color he'd possibly never seen before.

Haskoll was part changeling, and like all changelings

he had a natural talent for seeing elves and magical creatures. He worked for a hunter named Papa who liked to shoot such creatures. But Papa was not a changeling and had to take Haskoll's word for it that his trophy room was filled with the heads of fairy-tale beasts, and not just empty wooden plaques.

Recently Haskoll had been contacted by a private collector who wanted to pay him good money to steal Papa's griffin head and replace it with just such an empty plaque. Haskoll had planned to give this collector an ordinary eagle head instead, and keep both the griffin and the money. Now he needed a new plan.

"I can give you a hundred for the both of them," he told the thief. "Minus fifty to pay the pelican disposal fee. So that's fifty, total."

The thief sighed and nodded. Haskoll paid him and waited until he was out of sight, then left the pelican on top of a Subaru.

He had to wait a week before he met his secret buyer, a week he'd originally intended to spend gussying up the eagle head. He'd only spoken to the collector on the phone, so the man's appearance was a bit of a shock.

"Mister . . . Mister Smith?" Haskoll said when the tall, thin man arrived.

"Mister Haskoll," the man replied. "Is there something wrong?"

"Sorry, it's just . . . you look *exactly* like Prince Charles. Of England?"

"I get that a lot." The man smiled. And of course he couldn't be Prince Charles. He didn't even have an English accent. "Do you have something for me?"

Haskoll exhaled. "I . . . didn't get the griffin head. I thought about it, and I just couldn't steal from Papa, you know? But I have something else that might interest you."

He produced the albatross from the tarp he'd wrapped it in, and set it on the table between them.

"A seagull," said Mr. Smith. "I don't think this is quite the prize you think it is."

"It's an albatross," said Haskoll. "But look at this." He pulled the coldstone over his head and held it at arm's length. Except now it was glowing quite pink. Pink *and* black, actually, as if the colors were fighting each other. "That isn't what it—" Haskoll began to add. Then he narrowed his eyes at Mr. Smith. "What *are* you?"

Mr. Smith stood, smiled, and then his skin split and fell away like laundry. Underneath were two goblins, one standing atop the other's shoulders. They were wearing little suits.

"Misters Pigg and Poke," said the goblin on top as he hopped to the floor.

"Conductin' a test of your loyalty," said the other.

Haskoll stood. "A test? For who? Did Papa set all this up?" It didn't seem possible—he just didn't give the old man that much credit.

"For our current employer," said the first goblin. "A very important lady from a good family. She prizes loyalty, you see."

"And yet she's able to make an exception and work with goblins," Haskoll said. "I think that kind of flexibility is really great."

"Oh, but Our Lady is righteous, don't you know."

Haskoll understood. You could always fool the righteous.

"You've shown loyalty to this Papa," said the second goblin with a conspicuous wink. "And yet also a willingness to work with other . . . interested parties. Our Lady would like to hire you, on retainer."

"Hire me to do what?"

"Maybe nothing. Maybe she'll never call on you at all. But for fifty thousand dollars, you will be at her beck and call. Much like we are."

Haskoll thought. "It's gotta be fifty thousand in *real money*. American money, capiche? No fairy gold, no enchanted bills. I don't wanna open my safe one day and find it full of bark or whatever."

The first goblin stood atop the other's shoulders again, and they grew a new Prince Charles skin. They shook Haskoll's hand.

"We'll take the albatross," they said with one voice. "And in return, a little gift."

They reached into their suit coat and removed a gun. Haskoll tensed, but then they turned the pistol and offered it to him, handle first. Haskoll took it.

"An enchanted weapon," said the goblins. "It never runs out of bullets."

"Sweet."

"And here's something for free," said the goblins. "A foretelling."

Haskoll looked up from the gun and frowned. "You mean, like . . . my fortune?"

"All the Fay get little glimpses of the future, though we never know quite when to expect them. But we had a peek just now when we shook your hand."

Haskoll shifted from foot to foot. "Good stuff, I'm sure?"

The goblin Prince Charles smiled. There was possibly something not quite perfect about the disguise—the smile was wider than it should have been.

"Something big is coming your way," said Charles in one of the goblin's voices.

"Soon," he added, in the other's. "Something *very* big. It's going to drop right in your lap."

Haskoll grinned and peppered them with questions about this big something, but they insisted that it should be a surprise. So he thanked them, and they left with the albatross.

It was the middle of the night. Pigg and Poke liked this world, with its nights and days. The other Fay could talk all they wanted about the perfection of twilight, but a goblin's rightful place was in the dark.

The Goodco factory was staffed at night by a skeleton crew, so it was easy for the goblins to find a quiet spot where they could tear the albatross apart.

"How now?" they addressed the pixie at the heart of the mess.

Prince Fi, still immobile, stared up at this poor counterfeit of a human face, searching for any trace of compassion.

"You know, I do believe it's the last of King Denzil's

boys," said the man in a goblin's voice.

"Right as usual, Mister Pigg," he answered himself in another.

Fi screamed in his mind.

"You know, I do think Our Lady Nimue would be pleased to meet you."

"She'd certainly thank us for making introductions, Mister Pigg."

"She would at that, Mister Poke. She would."

"We *could* set up a meet and greet."

"We *could*."

The goblins paused.

"Or we could just throw His Tininess into a cereal box and let the gods sort him out."

So that's what they did.

A Puftees box, of course. He was found by one giant girl and sold to another, who took him home and introduced him to a trunk full of princesses.

CHAPTER 8

"—Oh, Princess Barbie, I love you. Please honor me with a kiss."

"—But what will my father say?"

"—He won't mind at all 'cause I slayed the Dorkmonster, and now he must give me your hand. Kiss me, I love you so."

But I don't love her, thought Prince Fi as the tall blonde pressed close. *I don't even know her. Not that Barbie doesn't possess many . . . agreeable qualities, but—*

The giant knocked Fi's face against Barbie's and made kissy noises.

—Mwah mwah mwah.

The poor woman, he thought as he looked into Barbie's rapidly advancing and retreating eyes. *To be disgraced in this way. Were both our curses lifted, I might make an honest woman of her—if only she weren't three times my height.*

"—We shall be married in the springtime, in the Castle Fun playset."

It had been impossible to tell how long he'd spent in the darkness inside the fish, inside the bird, inside the museum. But now Fi could see that he'd traveled to a world with a sun that still rose and set, and he hit upon the idea of counting the days by composing a sentence. A sentence in his mind, one word each night.

At the end of the first day he chose the word *I* to remind himself that he was a man and not a toy. But by the end of the second and third days he'd written

   I, Prince Fi,

and now you must realize that he had truly begun to despair. In three days he might have written "I will escape," or even "I am sad," and still you would have understood that the prince was hopeful, because these were complete sentences. And to complete a sentence would have meant that he felt the witch's magic wearing thin. But instead he wrote

I, Prince Fi,

and those commas were the commas of the hopeless. Each was a dark teardrop from a single *i*.

The giant girl, who he'd gathered was named Polly, carried him everywhere. Her accent was strange, but he soon came to understand her when she held her face close and whispered to him every asinine thought.

"I think I saw a little man in our house yesterday," she told him once. "Dressed in red. Well, not so little, I guess. Bigger than you." She lowered her voice even further. "I see lots of weird things. Even more now that we've moved here to Goodborough. When I was little I told Mom about them, but she always said they were my imagination, so I stopped telling her."

On the morning that Polly told him they were going to a commercial shoot with her father, he'd written

I, Prince Fi, decree that the Giant Girl is enemy to all pixies, and I hate her, and

And, and, and. It felt pointless to continue.

Fi was in the inside pocket of Polly's coat when she and her father were seized by the camera crew at the Goodco factory. He didn't see Polly's dad struggle free and punch a gaffer. He didn't see the Lady of the Lake step out from the shadows, and speak their names, and immobilize them with a spell. But he felt the spell wash over him. Frozen by pixie magic, he was now unfrozen by Fay. He felt his joints creak and come to life. With the mildly enchanted sword Carpet Nail, he ruined the lining of Polly's coat and slid free of her pocket.

It was nearly as dark in this room as it had been in Polly's coat. He gave his eyes a moment to warm up with the rest of his body, and adjust. They were alone in here—Fi, Polly, and her father. Fi climbed down Polly's leg and onto the floor. The humans were still frozen, and tied up to boot. That seemed unsporting. He could just leave them now, make his escape, find his brothers . . . or he could cut through the ropes and give them a fighting chance if the spell wore off.

"You know the rest," Fi told Polly in the back of the truck. "I severed your bonds, and you regained your mobility while I searched for a way out of the room. I didn't do it for you. I did it because you had been frozen by Fay magic, so you could only be an enemy of the Fay. And my people have ever struggled against the Fay."

Polly was faintly snuffling. "I've said I'm sorry," she whispered. "I've said it a million times."

"Some transgressions are beyond apology."

"We're stopping," said John. "I think we're here."

They were let out of the back by Biggs. The truck was in the middle of a vast parking lot in front of a shopping center. They'd arranged to meet John's friend here.

"Now to find Sir Richard," he said, hopping down to the asphalt in a hat and sunglasses.

"How are we supposed to find one knight in all this?" said Scott, scanning the parking lot.

"He'll be the only one on a horse," Erno suggested.

"I shall stay in the lorry," Fi announced, and slid down from Polly's head. Polly shuffled off to the edge of the cargo bay with everyone else. Then she turned.

"You think you're Prince Charming," she told Fi. "You think you're so good. But good people forgive mistakes. You're not even *trying* to forgive me," she said, wiping her eyes. When they were clear, she added, "You can sit on someone else's head from now on." Then she jumped to the ground, and Biggs pulled the steel door down between them.

CHAPTER 9

Harvey stood with his hands in his pockets while Mick scoured the field of clover at the edge of the parking lot on his hands and knees. Finchbriton hopped about looking for food, and the clearly amnesiac unicat stalked Finchbriton.

Mick glanced up at Harvey. "Little help?"

"Help?" said Harvey. "As if the courtly leprechaun Ferguth Ór needth my help finding a four-leaf clover. I wouldn't inthult you."

Finchbriton found a bug and cooked it a little bit before eating it. The brief reappearance of blue flame jogged the cat's memory, and it slunk off in another direction.

Mick tried to see what the rabbit-man was looking at, and his gaze paused on the big black town car parked in an empty part of the lot. Biggs stood stiffly beside it. Inside the car, John, Merle, and the kids were trying to convince Sir Richard Starkey that the world was in danger.

"Sooo . . . ," said Sir Richard. "All these invisible fairies are going to take over the world?"

The others wished he wouldn't keep putting it like that. Scott glanced at Emily. Emily shared a look with John. Scott and Erno and Emily and Merle were all a little cramped in this limousine seat, sitting backward, facing John and Polly and Sir Richard. They'd hired the limo to collect the famous drummer at his home in London and bring him here, and it was the biggest car they could get without renting another party bus.

Sir Richard was bearded, bald, wearing tinted glasses that made it hard to read his face. His hands were burled with thick gold rings, and he clacked these together.

"They'll only be invisible if they want to be," John explained. "Which they probably won't. It's like a . . . pride thing. Or something."

"But those fairy friends you mentioned . . . they were both invisible?" said Sir Richard.

Scott felt the conversation slipping away. "Mick—" he said. "That's the leprechaun—Mick is out of glamour."

"Out of glamour."

"Out of . . . magic. So he can't turn visible. And the rabbit-man is just a jerk," Scott added under his breath.

"Why can't Sir Richard see them anyway?" Erno

whispered to Merle. "He's a knight."

"Yeah, but he's not a changeling like Scott and Polly and John. Or an invasion baby like me."

"So he's magic enough to slay a dragon but not magic enough to see fairies?"

Merle shrugged.

"You couldn't see Mick and Harvey," John explained to Richard. "So they left to look for four-leaf clovers."

"Four-leaf clovers," repeated Sir Richard. Scott thought he could tell how badly things were going based entirely on how often Sir Richard repeated things.

John nodded. "Apparently we need them for a . . . thingy."

"Potion," said Erno.

"Potion," said Sir Richard.

"Come to think of it," said John, "we should have asked the finch to stay. Everyone sees the finch, for some reason."

"I saw that," Sir Richard agreed, brightening. "I saw it earlier."

"It breathes fire," Erno told him. This was followed by kind of a longish silence.

"Maybe one of us should fetch Fi," said Scott.

"No," Polly flatly answered.

"And so the cereal company . . . ," said Richard.

"Which is run by a fairy queen," John interjected.

". . . is rubbing out Knights Bachelor because we can kill dragons?"

Emily leaned forward and handed Sir Richard a piece of paper. He flinched as if expecting it to fold itself into something dangerous.

"This is a list of Knights Bachelor who have died in the last five years," Emily lectured, "categorized according to cause of death. Note the high number of accidents and sudden declines in health. Knights Bachelor have been seven times more likely to die during this period than an average Englishman of similar age."

Sir Richard studied the list, and his eyebrows lifted.

"I know it's a lot to swallow, Richard," John added.

Sir Richard frowned. "Your behavior has been so . . . uncharacteristic lately. I've seen the news."

"That isn't me. That Reggie Dwight is an impostor. These people will all corroborate that I've only just returned to England this morning."

Everyone nodded.

Sir Richard frowned and sucked on one of his rings.

"You don't have to believe all of it, Sir Richard," said Scott. "But . . . you're not safe. You need to believe that."

Richard thought for a moment. "Well. I guess it can't hurt to go away for a while."

"There you are." John smiled.

"What are you lot going to do?"

"John's going to trade places with the fake Reggie so he can meet with the queen and expose her," said Erno. "She's a fake, too."

Scott sucked air through his teeth. He wouldn't personally have volunteered this information.

"I see," said Sir Richard. The car was fidgety for a moment.

"The whole world will know what's going on," stressed John. "Soon. I swear. I just need you to trust me, Richard."

"I do." Sir Richard smiled and slapped his knees. "God help me, I do. But if it turns out you're wrong, I'm going to tell everyone I haven't seen you since the Grammys."

John laughed, and a pall lifted. "If I'm wrong, you can claim we've never even met."

Everyone smiled. Even Emily smiled. "So," Erno said. "You're a famous drummer."

Sir Richard beamed. "I was with the Quarrymen, a lifetime ago. You've heard our music?"

"No," Erno admitted.

Mick watched the car doors open, and everyone get out. He couldn't tell if Harvey had been looking at the car. He didn't know what the pooka was looking at.

Mick squinted back across the field of clover for a minute, then sighed.

"Why don't yeh go ahead an' insult me, Harv," he said.

Harvey slapped his hand over his eyes, bent over, and plucked a sprig at random. "Here ya go," he said.

Mick stared at the four-leafed clover for a moment, then put it in his pocket.

CHAPTER 10

A makeup girl cried on the London set of *Salamander Hamilton and the Three Ghosts of Christmas*. A production assistant cleaned what appeared to be vomit off what appeared to be Winston Churchill. Reggie Dwight loudly explained how neither thing was directly his fault. The assistant director sighed to the second assistant director. "Forty-three takes and his scene *still* isn't in the can," she said. "*And* he's supposed to record something for the soundtrack this afternoon."

The goblins dressed as Reggie Dwight faked a tantrum and locked themselves in his trailer for two hours, just so they could shed their Reggie skin and breathe awhile. One goblin napped while the other insulted people on the internet. When time came to return to the studio, they hid away their old skin with the others and grew a new one—you couldn't reuse them. If anyone decided to look inside the trailer's back closet they were going to wish they hadn't.

The goblins dressed as Reggie Dwight ate three sandwiches from the catering table, more quickly than Reggie was really able, so when they choked they did it in an entertaining way. Because they were entertainers. Afterward they got into a shoving match with an assistant who tried to give them what they later learned was the Heimlich maneuver. The goblins dressed as Reggie Dwight asked the assistant's forgiveness with a hug that went on just long enough to be uncomfortable. Then they went into the recording booth with pickle on their chin to see how long it would take someone to tell them.

At the piano, the goblins dressed as Reggie Dwight announced that they would not be performing "The Little Drummer Boy," as previously discussed, but would instead sing a new song they had themselves composed only that morning during toilet time. The assembled assistants and sound engineers all looked at one another and shrugged. It actually made a sound, so many people shrugging. Goblin Reggie played a chord and sang,

"*I didn't mean . . .*"

He closed his eyes and leaned into the next chord.

"I didn't mean to punch the queen."

The assistants and sound engineers looked at one another a little more pointedly.

"I didn't plan to greet Her Grace 'n'
Sit for lunch 'n' punch her face in.
Such a scene.
I didn't mean to punch the queen."

Goblin Reggie sighed wistfully.

"I didn't mean to spook the duke.
Oh, whoah whoah WHOAH . . .
I didn't mean to spook the duke.
I guess I should have thought of that
before I swung the cricket bat.
It was a fluke.
I didn't mean to spook the duke."

Between that verse and the next, there was a ninety-second whistling solo. Then,

"Oooooh,
I didn't mean to grope the pope—"

"Uh, Reggie?" coughed some human in the sound booth. "Reggie? Hi. I think maybe that's enough for today."

The goblins thanked everyone for their good work and stepped into their private car. "Won't be back tomorrow, though!" they called. "Have a secret meeting! An ecret-say eeting-may with the Queen of England-way! Okay, bye-bye."

"Home, sir?" asked the driver.

"Yes, Jeeves," they told the driver, whose name was Michaels. "I'm going to fill a big bath and soak in it until my skin puckers and falls off."

"Sir," Michaels answered. He drove them to Reggie's home in St. John's Wood in the north of London. The gate opened onto a three-story stone house surrounded by trees, and Michaels edged the car up the drive.

"You should join me, Jeeves," said goblin Reggie. "It's a big bathtub."

"Thank you, sir, no."

The goblins dismissed Michaels and let themselves into the dark, empty house. They pulled the door shut behind them and paused. Centuries of being the things that creep in darkness had given them some insight into unlit houses. The darkness here was most certainly alive.

They could sense it without knowing just exactly what it was, and for a moment it made them afraid. They smiled.

"So *that's* what that feels like," they said, just before they were jumped from all sides.

CHAPTER 11

"JACKIE IS A PUNK! JUDY IS A RUNT! THEY BOTH WENT DOWN TO BERLIN, JOINED THE ICE CAPADES! AND OH I DON'T KNOW WHY! OH I DON'T KNOW WHY! PERHAPS THEY'LL DIIIIIEE, OH YEAH! PERHAPS THEY'LL DIE!" sang the goblin Reggie Dwight, tied to a banister. "THIRD VERSE! DIFFERENT FROM THE FIRST! JACKIE IS A PUNK! JUDY IS A RUNT—"

"Can't we gag them?" asked John, his fingers in his ears.

"They're two goblins inna suit," said Mick. "The singin' isn't even technic'ly comin' from their mouth."

"Well, then can we at least make them stop looking like me while they do it?"

"That we can," Mick answered, and trotted off toward the kitchen.

Polly came to a stop near her father. "This is a nice

house," she said. She'd spent the last ten minutes running all over it with Erno. "He has this big cabinet full of gold records and awards and things in the bathroom," she told Scott.

"VERSE EIGHT! I AM REALLY GREAT! JACKIE IS A PUNK—"

"In the bathroom?"

John smiled sheepishly. "So I can display them while pretending I don't care if they're displayed or not."

"Uh-huh," Scott said, turning to wince at his father's duplicate. The goblins were bound to the iron staircase with iron chains festooned with horseshoes. Biggs kept them under close watch. Prince Fi menaced them with his sword, for all the good it did. Scott didn't know the song the goblins were singing, but he doubted it had as many verses as they were currently claiming.

"VERSE TWELVE! WORD THAT RHYMES WITH TWELVE! REGGIE IS A—"

Mick returned from the kitchen with a pot of tea. "Helped myself," he told John. "Hope yeh don't mind."

"Of course not. Why . . . ?"

"Yeh'll see." Mick lifted the lid of the pot and dropped a four-leaf clover and a little yellow primrose into the steaming tea and swished it around. "Hey, fellas," he said to the goblin Reggie. "Yis want a cuppa?"

"NONE FOR ME, THANKS."

"Biggsie?"

Biggs took the teapot from Mick and opened the goblin Reggie's jaw like a change purse. The goblins gargled and growled. Then Biggs poured a stream of scalding tea down the passable replica they'd made of Reggie's throat.

They sputtered. They cursed in dead languages. Then they shuddered and rattled and their Reggie skin peeled like a banana.

"Yeesh," said Merle.

"That's what we're going to do to the queen?" said Scott.

"She's not the queen," said Emily from her corner of the sofa. "And if she is, it'll just be tea with some yard clippings in it."

The goblins, now laid bare, tried to wriggle out of their chains. Biggs pulled them tighter. One goblin sat atop the other's shoulders. They were wearing familiar little suits.

"This isn't Pigg and Poke, is it?" said Scott.

"The same." Pigg grinned.

"Cretinous hobgoblins!"

"Yis two really get around," said Mick. "Who's 'mpersonatin' the queen, then?"

"Misters Katt and Bagg," said Poke. "Took over for us after we got demoted to permanent Reggie duty."

"And where're yis supposed t' meet wi' them? Where

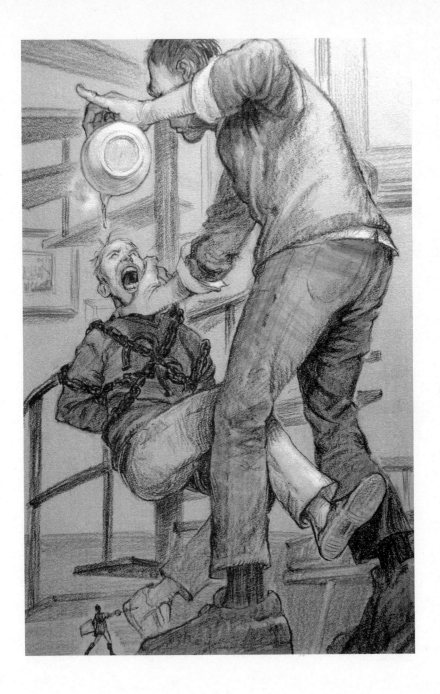

was fake Reggie gonna meet wi' the fake queen?"

"Ah, you know about that, eh?" said Pigg.

"They're clever, Mister Pigg," said Poke. "There's no gettin' around it."

"The royals're sending a car tomorrow mornin'," said Pigg. "Location TBD, though I unnerstand it'll probably be the British Museum."

"They're being awfully helpful all the sudden," said Emily.

"Maybe it's the horseshoes and clovers and such," said Poke. "*Makin'* us help."

"Or maybe we're secretly wonderful people," said Pigg.

"Everyone except Biggs, upstairs," Emily ordered. She started up the spiral staircase past the goblins, and the others dutifully followed. Finally the goblins were left alone with Biggs. They jiggled their chains.

"Left behind." Poke smiled sadly at Biggs. "They don't trust you."

"Trust me to do muh job," Biggs replied, staring over their heads.

"What's your job, big feller?" sighed Pigg.

"Peel your skins again if yuh try to 'scape."

And now the goblins were still.

"Our group should leave right away for Somerset," Scott whispered as soon as they were upstairs. "It'll take a couple hours just to get there, and we're not even sure what we're looking for exactly. Apart from the Queen of England."

"The Freemen files definitely didn't say anything specific except that she's being held in Avalon?" Merle asked Emily. She closed her eyes.

"I . . . I don't think so."

"You don't think so?"

Emily scrunched up her face. "I don't remember! Why are you asking me? Ask the owl! I told him everything I learned."

Archimedes turned his head and whistled, and Merle looked at his watch.

"'In a secure location in Avalon,'" he read. "I guess that's all the Freemen knew."

They reviewed their plans for the next day, such as they were, and separated. Scott, Merle, and Mick left for Somerset in the poppadum truck. Erno scooched up to Emily with Mr. Wilson's poem.

"Wanna work on this?"

"I just want to go to bed," she replied, and no wonder—she looked tired. "You know that kind of headache where it feels like someone's rummaging through your brain?"

". . . Nnnnno."

"Good night, Erno."

She left him alone in an odd little room that didn't look

like it got much use. It was snugly fitted with furniture that was better to look at than sit in, and shelves lined with matching spines of the sort of classics of Western literature that you could buy by the yard. He reread the poem:

> *The new year has a week to wait till waking.*
> *The water's almost frozen in the well.*
> *The hours of the day*
> *pass swiftly by, then drift away,*
> *and yet there's nothing, less than nothing left to tell.*
>
> *Soon the final days are numbered, then forgotten,*
> *and the new year's hardly worth the time it's taken.*
> *By degrees the hourglass reckons*
> *all the minutes, all the seconds,*
> *and the next year still has weeks to wait to waken.*

The unicat brushed up against his shins, stabbing him lightly in the leg.

"The new year has a week to wait," he told it. "Christmas Eve is a week before the end of the year. I wonder if that's important." In the margins he wrote *Christmas, Xmas, eve, 12/24.* "I guess it's about winter? Or time? Half the words are about either time or temperature."

He puzzled over the poem as the house slept around him.

CHAPTER 12

"Tired," said Merle, hunched over the wheel of the poppadum truck.

"I'd drive if I could," said Mick.

"You could teach me," Scott offered. He felt wired. "It's left brake, right accelerator, right?"

"Maybe you should just concentrate on keeping me awake."

"Tell us more about the good ol' days," said Mick. "The good ol' days that haven't happened yet, in your case. If yeh stop talkin' we'll give yeh a shove."

"Well . . . ," Merle began, hesitant, feeling his way back into the story. "I kept working on the time-travel question. I knew I could send things like Archimedes to the future, maybe even people to the future, but travel to the past seemed really impossible."

"You weren't sure you could send people to the

future?" asked Scott.

"I hadn't tried it yet."

Scott huffed. "I would have tried it right away."

"Would you?" Merle asked, turning. "Are you sure? You'd really be in a hurry to be the first human in all creation to try that, to have all your atoms taken apart and put back together again?"

Scott saw his point.

"Besides, I wasn't prepared to explain to everyone why I'd disappeared for a whole year. But word must have gotten out about my little trick with Archie, and soon the Fay showed up to ruin everything, like they always do. No offense, Mick."

"None taken, ugly."

"I'd just gone outside for some fresh air," Merle began, "when I got the feeling I was being watched."

He'd just gone outside for a smoke break, actually—arguably the exact opposite of fresh air—but like all former smokers he was ashamed to admit this in the presence of children. He was pacing the strip of sidewalk between the physics building and the tennis courts when a chill raised the hairs on the back of his neck.

Maybe it was because he was an invasion baby—a human born in the year the elves came, when magic swept like hurricanes over the earth—that he could sense something was wrong. Maybe, he'd think later, it was because one of the Fay *wanted* him to know. Whatever. He tossed his cigarette under his heel and walked swiftly back into the building.

Merle worked in a secure wing—the college had put locks on all the doors after some laptops and a bike had been stolen, years ago—but he cursed these locks now, even as he heard them click behind him. Put a keyed lock on a door, and one of the Fay might still get through it if you're careless, if you neglect to *make certain* you've shut it tight behind you. But these doors had combination locks. And a fairy's guesses were nothing if not lucky. Merle still had his hand on the knob when the door's small window filled with the face of Captain Conor of the Trooping Fairies of Oberon. There were more elves behind him, and Conor looked at Merle, then at the keypad below.

Merle turned, stumbled, raced down the hall shouting, "Archimedes! Octagon!" The mechanical owl met him at the door of his lab with the golden octagon, the time machine, in its claws. They turned the corner toward the wing's only other entrance and saw that here too was a group of elves, just on the other side of the door, patiently punching lucky guesses into the keypad. They'd get it right, and soon.

"Archie," Merle gasped, turning to the owl flapping in place beside him. "Calculate a time jump for both of us.

For both me and you." The owl whistled back, and Merle checked his watch. It said DURATION?

Distantly, from around the corner, Merle heard the click of a door.

"One year," he said. "No! Wait! They might think of that, come wait for me. A hundred years! No, that's nothing to an elf."

Archimedes whistled again. The sound of light footfalls tapped down to them from the far door. The nearest door clicked, and the elves pushed through.

"Five hundred years," he whispered to Archie. "Execute as soon as you've done the math," he added, and grasped the underside of the octagon so that he and the owl were holding it together.

Three elves stopped close on his left; another three turned the corner on his right. Conor was at the front of these.

"Put the device down, Merle," said Conor in that creepy voice he had. "Oberon himself requests an audience."

"*That's* kinda desperate, isn't it?" said Merle. "Collecting an audience at sword point? Must be a pretty bad show."

Five elves cocked their slings, aimed sharp flint missiles at Merle's head.

"Is Queen Titania gonna let him be the ventriloquist this time, or is he still the—"

Merle and Archimedes winked out of existence.

"—dummy," Merle finished, five hundred years in the future. Then he commenced falling.

The math of a five-hundred-year jump was, it turned out, tricky. He hadn't reappeared in his lab or even on solid ground. He found himself, instead, crashing downward through a canopy of leaves, then another, then grasping hold of a lean branch that bowed, snapped, and deposited him roughly on the forest floor. Archimedes fluttered down to meet him.

Mick punched Merle in the arm.

"Ow! Why?"

"Yeh hadn't said anythin' for a bit," said Mick. "Thought yeh needed perkin' up."

"I was thinking!"

"So where did you end up?" asked Scott.

"Near as I can tell, Costa Rica somewhere. I don't know for sure because I discover at this point that there don't seem to be any satellites for Archie to sync up with. But that's fine, I think. Five hundred years have passed, technology is probably so different now that Archie can't recognize it, and vice versa. So I nearly kill myself hiking out of the forest, living off fruit and rainwater, dreaming about my new plan, which is this: I find some future person here who's invented time travel to the past, and I use it to go back and save my parents and the whole world. I dream about this plan, even though I know there's something fundamentally wrong with it."

"What?"

"That if time travel to the past were ever really possible, then the past would be lousy with time travelers. But it wasn't. Nobody from my time had ever met a time traveler from the future, so what does that say?"

"Maybe . . . ," said Scott, not yet ready to give up on the possibility. "Maybe all the time travelers were really secret about it," he said, though he had to admit that didn't seem very likely.

"Well, whatever, it's a moot point. Because I spend the next six months traveling the earth, and I never meet another person."

"Not one?" said Mick. "Not even a fairy?"

"Not even a mouse. Not a creature was stirring. I find canned food, I find a bicycle, but everywhere it's empty towns, overgrown cities. I've jumped too far, and something terrible's happened."

"Jeez," said Scott. Immediately he wished he'd said something a little more profound.

"Yeah. Well. Eventually I can't take the loneliness anymore, so I ask Archie to jump us again—so far into the future that the earth itself will be dead and gone. Just to be on the safe side I settle on twice the age of the whole universe—twenty-eight billion years—and tell Archie to flip the switch. And he does, and we reappear in a cage in medieval England."

● ○ ★

Again the peasant rattled the wooden cage, which shook the wagon, which prompted the soldier who wasn't driving to turn and glare.

"Ignore him," said the driver.

"Please please *please* let me go," pleaded the peasant.

"We're under oath to bring you to King Vortigern," said the soldier.

The peasant pressed against the wooden slats. "When I said I never had a father, I didn't mean I *never* had a father. I meant I never *knew* my father. He died before I was born."

"Listen," said the soldier. "In good sooth? I believe thee. Of course I believe thee. But we're going to sacrifice thee anyway. We have to look busy."

"Look, what's this all about?"

The soldier turned entirely around and addressed the peasant. "King Vortigern has a tower that keeps falling down. His wise men tell him he needs the blood of a boy born without a father, to mix with the mortar. Thou wantest my opinion? I think the wise men just sayeth things like this when they don't know the answer."

"Verily," said the driver.

"Perchance they tellest the king he needs ice in August or a serpent hatched from a cockerel's egg or some similarly impossible nonsense. And the king tells us to go chase after phantoms. So fine—we get some fresh air and no one can ever check up on the so-called wise men."

The wagon creaked along the Roman road, in the north of Wales, toward Dinas Emrys, the Castle Ambrosius. Or what would be the Castle Ambrosius, if it didn't keep falling over.

"So . . . so let me go," urged the prisoner, "if it won't make any difference. You could change your mind and give me my liberty."

The soldier frowned, clearly confused. "So . . . thou proposest we take one who hast drawn the lot of sacrificial lamb and . . . just raise him above his station? Like a promotion?"

"I wasn't a sacrificial lamb this morning," argued the prisoner. "I was a peasant."

"Thou wert always a lamb," said the soldier as he shook his head and turned his eyes back to the road. "Thou just didst not know it. If Fortuna or . . . society or what have thee marks thee for death, then thou art a dead man. It's not our place to argue."

"Wait now," said the driver. "Are you saying there's no upward mobility? None at all? Does not the babe become a boy? Is not the boy promoted to a man? The squire to a knight? A knight to a . . . a . . ."

"Aha!" said the soldier. "You see, you've stepped in your own snare. Does the knight become a king? No. The

143

greatest knight will stay a knight, and the king will pass his crown to his own son, worthless though he may be. And is not the babe just a young boy? Is not the boy a young man? There's no upward mobility here, my friend. Each only comes of age and assumes the role he was born to."

The prisoner listened, and scratched his bottom. Then there was a kind of popping behind him, and he turned to see another man in the cage, holding an owl.

"Marry!" shouted the peasant. "Look here! Fortuna has sent you another lamb, to bleed in my place! A man with an owl! And is the owl not Fortuna's favorite?"

The soldiers turned to look. "Thou'rt thinking of Minerva," one said, but they both seemed pretty impressed with the new mystery prisoner.

The man with the owl staggered, looked around him with wild eyes. "Where am I?" he muttered. "When . . . when am I? How did I get here?"

"You see?" said the peasant, hurling himself against the front of the cage. "How he questioneth, like unto a child! How he gazeth with the eyes of a newborn babe!"

"This is impossible," Merle murmured. "Twenty-eight billion years into the future, and I'm standing in a donkey cart."

"What rubbish he gibbers! Surely he was born just now from the ether, a man without a father! Conjured from nothing to meet King Vortigern's swift justice!"

"Quiet," said Merle, remembering his Slumbro Mini. He flicked it at the peasant, who fell snoring in a heap in the straw. "Wait. Did that guy just say King Vortigern?"

The soldier in the front of the wagon was still a little dumbfounded, but he nodded. "That's where we're taking thee. To Dinas Emrys. We'll probably sacrifice both of ye, just to be safe."

"Dinas Emrys," repeated Merle, taking a seat. "King Vortigern. I know this story. All right, I got nothing else to do. I'll meet your king."

CHAPTER 13

They drove the wagon, and Merle with it, off the Roman road and over a rough path cut through the trees. Then straight through a narrow river and up an embankment that had been cleared of anything growing. Gray stones lay in ragged piles around the barest hints of castle walls.

"Ho there!" called a mason to the soldiers. "You've strange chickens in that coop!"

"Not chickens," answered the driver. "Lambs."

The mason frowned, then seemed to understand. He dropped his head as they passed. "Lord Vortigern is in the west pavilion," he said soberly.

Beneath a large peaked tent was Vortigern, a big man with a big red beard, dressed in furs and with an unfussy gold circlet atop his head. He strode out to meet the wagon and looked delighted by its contents.

"Two!" bellowed the king. "I' faith, that's good work, lads!"

One of the soldiers bowed and immediately set about managing expectations. "My liege. The sleeping one claims now that he hath a father, but that he didst know him not."

"Fine, fine, we'll kill him anyway. And the other?"

"I am Merle Lynn!" announced Merle, standing up in the cage, trying both to look and sound imposing. "And I wish to speak with these wise men who would have my blood!"

"God's teeth! I doubt they'll like *that*. If thou wert the wise men, wouldst thou want to meet the lambs? I wouldn't."

"This one just appeared in the cage," the soldier explained. "We didn't even have to catch him."

Vortigern grinned expansively, shot the grin around the hillock for a bit. "Well, that sounds promising! You have to admit! The wise men might have hit the bull's-eye on this one. And he has a bird! Cute."

"Lord Vortigern," Merle said, undeterred. "I know what you must do to make your tower stand."

"I bet thou dost. I bet thou dost. And I bet—I'm just guessing, now—but I bet thou thinkest it *doesn't* require bleeding thou dry and mixing thy blood in the mortar? I'm right, aren't I. String them up!"

Merle tensed and gripped his Slumbro tight as the cage was set upon by soldiers and laborers. The peasant beside him finally woke.

"Mwuh?" said the peasant as he raised his head.

"Still in the cage," Merle told him. "Still going to die."

"AAAH! No!"

"Stay behind me," said Merle, but the peasant didn't obey, and when the cage was opened he was grabbed roughly by a half-dozen hands. Merle waved his wand, and the peasant and two soldiers fell asleep.

"That keeps happening," said the driver.

Vortigern eyed the wand. "He must be a sorcerer."

"Yes!" said Merle. "A powerful sorcerer! So you'd better—"

"Aha! That's why his blood's so good for making

buildings out of!" Vortigern concluded. "Magic blood!"

The soldiers and laborers all nodded at one another, saying, "Oh yeah, magic blood."

"Nuts," said Merle. He backed away from the door of the cage and was surprised when a pair of arms grabbed him through the bars from behind. Startled, he dropped his Slumbro, and the strong arms of the laborers held him fast.

"Many thanks for putting our lamb to sleep, great sorcerer," said Vortigern. "So much less thrashing and dolorous lamentation if he sleepeth. Now: we only built the one truss for the sacrificial bleeding, so I'm afraid thou wilt have to wait."

They were dragging the sleeping peasant toward a wooden frame built over a cauldron. Soon they'd hoist him up on it and cut his throat, Merle supposed, and then his own turn would come.

He promised himself he'd think about it some more when he was no longer under threat of imminent death, but for now Merle figured one of three things had happened: that he'd strained the forces of time and space so considerably during his last jump that he'd gone backward instead of forward somehow; that he'd maybe (and this seemed too fantastic) jumped past the end of the universe and into a virtually identical new one; or that he'd really jumped into oblivion, as expected, and was dying and this was all some crazy dream he was having as his brain ran out of oxygen.

Still—if it was a crazy dream, it was one he'd read about a hundred times.

"Our blood won't do anything!" he shouted, struggling against the clutches of the king's men. "Your wise men can't even tell you why your tower falls! How can they know the solution if they don't understand the problem?"

"Quit your bleating, lamb," said one of the men.

"And I suppose thou knowest why my tower falls, sorcerer?" asked the king.

"I do. I do. Set that man free and I'll tell you, and if I'm wrong you can still sacrifice me."

They'd tied the peasant's ankles and were just beginning to hoist him up on the frame. King Vortigern chewed his lip.

"My . . . blood's probably really magical right now," Merle added. "I've been eating a lot of unicorn and stuff."

The king thought this over, then shrugged theatrically and ordered the peasant be released. They cut him free, and he continued to snore beside the cauldron. Then all eyes were on Merle, and the men let him go. He snatched up his Slumbro and crammed it into his jeans pocket before speaking.

"Beneath this hill lies a hidden pool. And in that pool two dragons fight—one dragon's red, the other's white." He hadn't meant to rhyme just then, but he figured it was all to the good. He stepped down from the cage to lead them to the secret tunnel beneath the hill, then realized he hadn't a clue where it was.

"Archie," he whispered. "Assume this hill is Dinas Emrys in Wales, United Kingdom. Do any geological records mention a cave entrance?"

Archie sent a map to Merle's watch face, and he led the king and his men to a gap in the rocks, shrouded by moss. The others lit torches; Merle lit the flashlight on his key chain.

"What rare light that burns without heat!" Vortigern said of the flashlight.

"Thanks," said Merle. "I got it free for opening a checking account."

They descended into the hillside, through a narrow passage, each hunched and a little fearful beneath the suffocating patience of the earth. There was a breeze against their faces, rising from below, and here and there thin roots breached the rock walls like hairs, like they were plunging into the cavernous nostril of some sleeping giant. The nostril rumbled, as if snoring.

"There," said Merle, worried he'd lose his audience.

"See? The dragons fight, and their fighting shakes the earth. The red dragon represents—"

Merle stopped short, realizing he'd just stepped into a large open chamber. It should have been dark, but the space was lit dimly by some source he couldn't identify. It was a huge, damp vault, enclosing a dark pool. And that pool was turbid and foaming with the struggle of two magnificent dragons.

Merle had known what to expect, and still he could only stare, stupid and gaping, at the creatures. Dragons. One white, one red. Each the size of an elephant, slick as a fish, tightly built with coiled, ropy muscles and a whiplashing neck, like lightning made flesh. He'd never seen a dragon. He'd heard of the colossal pink one that had terrorized the world before he was born, of course, but it spent most of its time in Ireland or someplace.

The dragons, mercifully, couldn't seem to care less about Merle and King Vortigern and his men. The men had all fallen silent, watching. The white dragon was dominant, trying to bite the red on its nape and hold it down. They crashed together into the deep of the pool, and again the earth rumbled.

"Um . . . so. The red dragon represents the Britons," said Merle to whoever might be listening. "The white one represents the Saxons. The Saxons have the upper hand

now, but one day soon, the red dragon will rise up and prevail."

"Why'd you tell them that?" asked Scott. "It's kind of a weird thing to say."

Merle shrugged. "I have no idea. But the books said that's what I said, so that's what I said."

"But . . . wait. If the books say you said it, but you only said it *because* the books say you said it, then—"

"I'm either too tired or not tired enough to have that kind of conversation right now," Merle told him. They were winding through a cramped little maze of a town, and Merle added, "We should be close now."

"We won't know we're *really* close until we see water," said Mick. "Avalon is an island."

"Yeah," Scott agreed. "When I saw it with my . . . salmon sight, on the cruise ship, it was definitely wet. Swampy."

Merle checked the map again, but let it be. "Anyway, there's one more thing to tell. Eventually Vortigern and his men leave, and while I'm standing there watching the dragons, an elf steps out of the shadows. A real *familiar* elf."

He was one of those regal, Tolkienesque elves that made you feel fat and unlovely. Six-five, lean, sloe eyed, with short green mossy hair.

"You're name's Conor," Merle said.

The elf frowned almost imperceptibly. "My name is Mossblossom."

"Yick. I can see why you changed that."

"King Vortigern called you Merlin," said the elf.

"That's what he called me, yeah."

"You know much, Merlin. My Lady of the Lake will be curious about you."

Merle didn't know what to say to that. He winced at the dragons—the white had finally succeeded in subduing the red, and now the waters calmed. "They're . . . they're not actually fighting, are they?"

"Not fighting, no."

Merle coughed. "I think maybe I'll give them some privacy," he said, turning to go. "You coming?"

"Alas, I am . . . chaperone to this congress. By order of my Lady."

"Good luck with that," Merle said as he left.

"I hope we meet again, Merlin of Ambrosius," said the elf.

Merlin didn't look back. "I don't," he said through his teeth.

"This is it," Merle said now, in the truck. "We're right on top of it." They'd passed through the town and emerged at the foot of a tall hill. Taller than Dinas Emrys had been.

Merle, Scott, and Mick got out and stood around the poppadum truck in the dark, in the quiet little town of Glastonbury, in Somerset, in the west of England.

"Well," said Mick. "*This* doesn't look right."

CHAPTER 14

It was only when John looked in on him hours later that Erno realized the night had passed and he had quite possibly fallen asleep with his eyes open, half focused on the bleak and bleary poem. The unicat was curled in his lap.

"Up already?" asked John. "Polly's still conked out. Your sister, too."

Erno rubbed his eyes. "Good. Good, she needs the sleep."

The small square window was an ocean-bottom blue. It was very early. John was wearing a three-piece gray gabardine suit with a pink tie and handkerchief.

"Don't know when this so-called car is coming for me," he explained. "Must be ready."

Erno stood, upsetting the cat, and followed John downstairs.

Biggs was standing in one corner of the front room, asleep. Prince Fi paced back and forth like a sentry in front of the goblins, who seemed to be engaged in talk of good ol' Pretannica with Harvey.

"Jutht thurprized we didn't know each other already," Harvey told Pigg and Poke. "Uth havin' the thame uncle and all."

"We're nearly brothers, when it comes down to it," said Pigg.

"A pooka's more goblin than elf, so they say," added Poke.

Harvey nodded. "Thatth true."

Just then a tinny rendition of "For Those About to Rock (We Salute You)" started playing from somewhere. Everyone but the goblins looked around.

"Is that a phone?" asked Erno.

"Not one of mine," said John.

"It is, actually," said Pigg, tilting his head toward the folds of Reggie skin hanging down around him.

"It's the mobile we stole off you at the Goodco factory last year," Poke added, smiling apologetically.

"You changed the ringtone," John said, aghast. As if this was the final straw, the ultimate indignity. Not the identity theft and character assassination so much as the ringtone. He set about the distasteful task of rifling through the pockets of a full-length Halloween costume of himself and found the phone.

"Hello?"

"That's it today?" said the voice on the other end. "Just hello? No 'Queenpunchers Anonymous' or 'You have reached Reggie's House of Fruit' or whatever?"

John winced at Erno. "It's early," he said.

"That it is. Car's out back."

"I'm on my way."

The sun was up, and Merle, Mick, and Scott had driven in and around Glastonbury and the surrounding countryside twice; asked for directions three times; breakfasted in the truck; and made mildly personal comments to one another on the subjects of eating habits, driving ability, age, height, and all-around usefulness. Scott made the mistake of mentioning that in books about magic villains and world saving, there was always a main character who died, and they had a spirited discussion about which of them, if any, it would be. Or if any of them even qualified as a main character. Then they didn't say anything for a long time.

Finally, in unspoken agreement, they gave up.

They were sitting now in a pretty garden on the edge of a stone ring around a two-thousand-year-old hole in the ground called the Chalice Well. It was apparently one of Glastonbury's chief attractions, purportedly the last

resting place of the Holy Grail.

"This mission of ours," said Mick. "'Twas always doomed, wasn't it? That's why they sent the likes of us?"

"It was a long shot," Merle admitted. "Assuming this place was the mythical Avalon, we didn't even know where to begin looking for the queen."

Scott could just barely see Glastonbury Tor from here, a sharp hill with a church on it that rose up from the surrounding plains. This hill had been an island back when the area was flooded, but the lady at the Chalice Well admissions gate said it hadn't been *that* flooded for a while.

"So when the Freemen's files said Avalon, do you think they meant somewhere else?" asked Scott. "When I saw the queen with my salmon sight, she was hard to focus on."

"Is that definitely what we're callin' it?" said Mick. "Your 'salmon sight'? I vote for somethin' else."

They'd driven all night for nothing and were all a little grumpy. Scott read aloud from the visitor's brochure again, just because he knew it annoyed Mick.

"'The interlocking circles on the well cover represent the inner and outer worlds, a symbol known as the Vesica Piscis. A sword bisects these two circles, possibly referring to the legendary Excalibur, sword of King Arthur, who is believed by some to be buried nearby.'"

"Please shut it," said Mick.

Scott put the brochure away. Merle appeared to have nodded off.

"Maybe I should check in at home," Scott said, dialing one of the new disposable cell phones they all had now.

"Hi," said Polly on the second ring.

"Glastonbury's a bust, maybe," Scott told her. "It doesn't look like Avalon. What's going on there?"

"Dad left awhile ago. Erno and Biggs are working on the puzzle poem with Archie the owl. Erno wants to thank Merle again for leaving Archie."

"What about Emily?"

"She's sleeping in. Hold on, Erno wants to know how you're doing." Scott listened to Polly explain to Erno that they hadn't found the queen, that Avalon didn't even look like Avalon. Then there was a pause. "Um, Scott?"

"What?"

"The goblins overheard me talking," said Polly, "and one of them, I think Pigg . . . no, maybe that's Poke. Which one's the ugly one?"

Scott didn't know how to answer that question. "Does it matter?"

"I guess not. One of them just said, '*Course* they didn't find Her Majesty. She's in the *other* Avalon.'"

Scott felt suddenly more tired than he could have thought possible. "You're kidding."

"I'm not, but maybe they are?"

"No, it makes sense, actually—I bet they're telling the truth." Scott sighed. "I think they kind of like telling the truth if they know it isn't gonna make your life any easier. The queen is in Pretannica," he said, and Mick groaned. "How are we going to get to Pretannica?!"

"I dunno," said Polly. "Maybe Mr. Wilson's poem is a clue?"

"That'd be nice. Can you put Erno on?"

"Just a sec."

Erno took the phone. "Hey."

"Hey. What have you worked out so far?"

"Well," said Erno, and Scott could hear papers rustling. "Practically all the lines are about time or temperature. It has the words year, week, frozen, hours, day, degrees, minutes, sec—"

There was silence on the line for a bit. "Seconds?" finished Scott.

"Yeah, hold on," said Erno. "Saying those words out loud got me thinking. Degrees, minutes, and seconds. What does that sound like to you?"

Scott thought. "I dunno. Two words about time and one about temperature?"

"No. No. I think I just figured something out. I was always kind of into military history, and maps and stuff."

"Okay."

"So coordinates of latitude and longitude are written out in degrees, minutes, and seconds. Like a specific point on the globe might be written as minus fifty-three degrees, ten minutes, eighteen seconds latitude; twelve degrees, twenty-three minutes, five seconds longitude."

"So do you think the poem tells you a point on a map?" asked Scott.

" . . . Maybe. I wonder—" There was a faint noise on the line, like a shout from far away. "What was that? Hold on."

Scott hummed to himself until Erno returned.

"Man," said Erno. "Emily is, like, shouting in her sleep. It's hilarious. She must be having a dream."

"What's she saying?"

"I couldn't make out any words. You coming back?"

"I guess so, when Merle wakes up."

"Hope your dad's doing better than you guys."

"He'd almost have to be."

CHAPTER 15

That was not strictly true.

He was an actor, John told himself as he exited through the back door of his house; a good actor, and today he was not John Doe. He wasn't even Reggie Dwight—he was two awful little monsters in a suit, ready to take tea with a pantomime queen.

The car that waited for John outside his home in St. John's Wood was an ordinary black London cab, but it had an extraordinary driver. He was a black-suited, hard-headed man with stubbly black hair you could strike a match on, and so large and powerfully built that it seemed the car must have been manufactured around him. *Soon he'd have to leave the shell of it behind for another, larger one,* thought John, *like a hermit crab.*

"Lads," greeted the driver as John got in the back.

"So what was decided?" asked John. "British Museum?"

The driver frowned. Not that John could see his face, but he'd swear you could hear this man frown. "You weren't supposed to know that yet."

Oh, thought John. "Well, I have my ways."

"I?"

Shoot shoot shoot. "Yes, I. Mister Pigg, speaking. Mister Poke hasn't got my ways, you understand. He's got his own ways."

"That I do, Mister Pigg," John added.

"Right," said the driver with another frown, and the sound that made. Sort of a meat-tenderizing sound. Anyway, the moment had passed. John was supposed to get the driver to confirm the location of the meet, then make a quick sign through the rear windshield to Erno, who was watching from a window. But he'd gotten flustered and forgotten, and now they were blocks away.

It was early, and traffic was light. When they were near the museum, John asked, "So where are we setting up? Reading Room?"

"Look," said the driver, craning his neck. "You didn't tell anyone, did you?"

"Only our grocer. And the lady who does our hair. And this nice bloke from the *Daily Telegraph*, what was his name?"

"Funny. You're funny. Never have I known such a funny pair of goblins."

They pulled up Great Russell Street to the museum grounds and were waved through gold-tipped gates that would normally turn away all automobiles. They came to their final stop right in front of the building's columned facade. John's door was opened for him, and he stepped out to be frisked by police officers. They didn't find him to be carrying a weapon, even though he was.

The museum wasn't yet open, so everyone here was attached to the queen in some way. John wondered how many of them were in on the joke—how many of them knew the queen wasn't the queen, that John wasn't John. There was a distinct lack of winks and knowing smiles, so he was inclined to think most of them were legit. Then a prissy and pucker-mouthed little man who looked like he was sucking on boredom itself came alongside him.

"I thought I'd talked you both into the navy-blue check," he whispered.

"Be happy we're wearing pants," said John. Who was this man? Was he a Freeman? Was he even human?

"At least you had the good sense to wear pink," the prissy man conceded. He was wearing pink himself—an ascot and a small carnation. John scanned the crowd— there were maybe only ten others wearing some little blush of color, including one police officer with a breast cancer awareness pin.

The Great Court of the British Museum was vast,

clean, a gleaming blue-white at this time of the morning. A round, bright, modern structure with tall, evenly spaced windows like a zoetrope stood in its center, boxed in by more classical peaks and pillars and sheltered beneath a curvilinear lattice of metal and glass. A wide walkway clasped its staircase arms around the zoetrope, tapering down to rest its cold hands on either side of a door that led into the old Reading Room. This room was currently showing an exhibit of reliquaries, which, if John understood correctly, was a collection of the body parts of famous dead religious people. But they weren't going into the Reading Room.

Between the staircases, a blue backdrop had been erected, and in front of that, a table and tea set. He thought this place had the sort of symbolism the royals liked—a bit of old, a bit of new, a place of learning where he and the queen would supposedly come to a better understanding of each other blah blah blah. He took his place at the table and immediately started working out escape routes.

"Where are Katt and Bagg?" whispered John, hoping he'd gotten the other goblins' names right.

"First you, then the press are called, then the Goblin Queen makes her royal entrance."

"We hate waiting," said John.

The new year has a week to wait till waking, thought Erno with an atlas across his lap. *Could that mean December twenty-fourth, then, or maybe twenty-fifth? Or . . . or, if there's a week until the new year, then that means fifty-one weeks have passed.* He checked the atlas. Assuming that the first number in the poem would be the first number of the coordinates, then fifty-one degrees latitude was far enough north of the equator to possibly be in England. *Or Canada or Germany or about five other countries*, he thought. Still, it was a nice coincidence.

The water's almost frozen in the well. "Archie?" Erno said, and the owl turned. "What temperature does water freeze at?" He read the answer off Merle's watch. Thirty-two degrees Fahrenheit, or zero degrees Celsius. *So if water's almost freezing, it would be thirty-three. Or one.* Again, fifty-one degrees, thirty-three minutes latitude could keep him in England, and Erno started feeling the thrill of discovery.

Within a half-hour, John was told the press had assembled outside the Great Court, waiting to be let in. He checked his phone and found the more traditional news outlets predicting a staged and uneventful reconciliation, while the tabloids speculated wildly about fresh queen punchings and royal retaliations. One newspaper was calling the event the "Tussle on Great Russell."

The table was real wood beneath the tablecloth, some expensive antique. The china teacups looked as delicate as fingernails. There was a small creamer of milk and a bowl filled with perfect sugar cubes. Somewhere, someone was making the tea. The whole tableau glowed under powerful lights. This kind of ridiculous stagecraft, this was his world—Reggie's world, really. He could do this.

Now the press was let into the Great Court and began immediately to snap pictures and pepper John with questions. They were kept at a distance, and he smiled and waved back and pretended not to hear them. A servant (who was *not* wearing pink, John noted) came with a bone china teapot on a silver tray and placed it in the center of the table. John took the lid off the teapot, under the pretense of smelling the tea, and slipped a four-leaf clover and a primrose unnoticed into the brew.

"Please don't touch the service, sir," said the servant.

"Sorry."

Erno rubbed his palms into his eyes and tried to focus on something apart from his sister mumbling in her sleep in the next room.

The hours of the day
pass swiftly by, then drift away . . .

Twenty-four hours in the day, obviously, thought Erno, and he wrote 24 beside 51 and 33.

and yet there's nothing, less than nothing left to tell.

Here he stumbled, until remembering that a coordinate could be positive or negative. Negative latitude meant it was south of the equator. Negative longitude was west of the prime meridian. *So less than nothing is negative one, maybe? Or even negative zero.* The way Mr. Wilson had repeated the word "nothing" made Erno think the latter was more likely.

More muttering from Emily, and then a sustained hiss. Erno would check on her. He'd do it right after he'd finished the poem.

Polly sat downstairs with Biggs and the goblins and Harvey, ripping paper, ripping, specifically, the pages of an '80s magazine she'd assumed was so old it was disposable. She would have panicked if you'd told her it was actually an expensive collector's item, but it wouldn't matter in the long run—everything in the house was going to burn soon anyway.

Conversation had vanished, replaced by one of those clock-ticking kinds of silences, a savagely quiet kind of thickness, and Polly was just rolling her bits of paper into pellets to throw at the goblins when they turned to her and spoke.

"Nothing to do, eh?" said Pigg.

"No secret mission, like the others," said Poke.

"Quiet," said Biggs.

"Eh . . . ," said Harvey. "Why don't you leave thith one alone, boyth. She'th all right."

"All right?" said Pigg.

"All *right*?" said Poke.

"She's our captor."

"Our rightful mark."

"We have our natures to consider."

"It's a big house, you know."

"She *could* sit somewhere else."

"Okay, okay," said Harvey with a shrug and a be-my-guest wave of his arms.

Polly looked squarely at the goblins. "So your question was, why no secret mission for me?"

"That's right."

"I'm only *seven*."

Pigg nodded. "That's what your Prince Fi said. 'Just a little girl,' he told your brother last night, in passing."

Polly gasped. "He said that?"

"Pixies're like humans that way," said Poke. "Don't respect children like the Fay do. Queen Nimue, you know—she wants to build an *army* of children."

"Don't listen," said Biggs.

"The big lug's right," said Pigg. "Don't listen to us."

"Forget we brought it up."

"I mean, even if she *could* win Fi's respect—"

"It's not possible, Mr. Pigg. I hope you aren't suggestin' what I think you're suggestin'—"

"Oh, I agree, Mr. Poke. We could show her, and it'd be *amazing*, but still it wouldn't melt Fi's cold, cold heart."

Polly tightened her fists. "You don't know him. You're wrong about him."

"I'd like to be wrong," said Poke. "I would."

"And stop talking about me like I'm not in the room," said Polly, getting to her feet. "Grown-ups always do that, and I hate it!"

"An' well you should."

"You know what else I hate?"

"Tell us, tell us."

"I hate TV shows where the character *knows* the bad guy's trying to trick her into setting him free, but still all he has to do is say *one kinda true upsetting thing* and she's all like, 'You're wrong! I'm gonna unlock your handcuffs and prove it to you!'"

The room fell silent again, and Biggs smiled at her. She took her seat.

Harvey snorted. "Ah, the girl took you to thchool, ladth," he said. Then Polly allowed herself a little smile, too.

174

The goblins just stared, their chains hanging limply around them.

"Not scared of monsters anymore, you know," Polly added. "Or the dark. I haven't been scared of any of that since I was little."

Poke let his attention drift to the empty fireplace, feigning disinterest. But Pigg continued to watch Polly, and said, "You invented the darkness, you know. You humans. Filled it with stories of bogeymen and bridge trolls and sharp little hands snatching children in the night."

Polly narrowed her eyes. "That's not right. You Fay, you *are* those things. You *do* steal children. Mick told me."

"Yes," said Poke, turning.

"Oh yes," said Pigg.

"But only because we were invited."

"Only because you let us in."

John shifted in his seat and eyed a plate of shortbread on the table. He hadn't eaten any breakfast. Finally the queen herself appeared from behind a blind, wearing a pink dress, pearls, and a diamond brooch. John stood, bowed at the neck, and they sat down together as the cameras flashed.

"They can't hear us if we talk quietlike," said the Goblin Queen in a gruff, sailorly sort of voice. "There ain't no microphones."

John pretended to celebrate this by saying a rude word.

"Thassa spirit. Just lie back an' thinka England, an' it'll all be over soon."

John was fairly certain he was supposed to wait for the queen herself to pour. He was her guest here. He calmed himself by studying the queen's diamond brooch and discovered that what he'd mistaken for an abstract design was actually a giraffe throwing up a smaller giraffe.

"Where'd you get that?"

"Had it made."

Finally the Goblin Queen asked if John took milk, and when he said no she lifted the teapot and filled his cup, then her own. John didn't want any sugar either, so the queen helped herself to two lumps and stirred.

"I suppose you've both grasped the comedy a' this sitiation," said the queen. "It was *you* two what got punched, when you were 'personatin' Her Majesty. An' now it's *you* apologizin' t' us!"

"Misters Katt and Bagg," said John, "always with such a fascinatin' analysis of the facts. Except we're *not* apologizin' to you lot, we're tellin' you to shut your gobs and drink your tea."

"Heh," said the queen with an unladylike leer, and she took up her teacup and pressed it to her lips. Then a man, the same man who'd brought the tea, rushed from the blind and came to a stop by her side. This man gave John

a queer look, then leaned close to the Goblin Queen and whispered something in her ear. She lowered the teacup, the tea untouched. Then she gave John a bit of a queer look herself.

Soon the final days are numbered, then forgotten, read Erno, and he thought, *If there's a week left until new year, then there must be seven days.*

    and the new year's hardly worth the time it's taken.

  So it's the new year now? All right.

    By degrees the hourglass reckons
    all the minutes, all the seconds . . .

He was pretty sure this bit was just there to get him thinking about coordinates.

    and the next year still has weeks to wait to waken.

  So if it's the new year, then the next year has . . . fifty-two weeks to wait?
    He looked at the notes he'd been taking. They read 51, 33, 24, -0, 7, 52.
    He felt iffy about it but asked Archimedes to show him

exactly where fifty-one degrees, thirty-three minutes, twenty-four seconds latitude; minus zero degrees, seven minutes, fifty-two seconds longitude would be on a map. And the owl sent him an answer, and it was a north London house three miles away.

Only three miles. He could hit it with a rock from here. No, he couldn't. But still! This had to be the answer—and he'd found it without any help from Emily, he thought, with a rush of pride. Then, as if rebuking him, Emily shouted in her sleep from the next room.

Polly came up the stairs. "It sounded like Emily yelled real words this time," she said.

"Yeah . . . it did," Erno agreed, and he shifted himself closer to the bedroom door. They were both silent, waiting, and then it came.

"St. John's Wood!" shouted Emily in a mumbly dream speech. "We're in St. John's Wood!"

"Ohhh," said Erno. "That can't be good."

CHAPTER 16

The queen had sent her servant away, and now she stared at John with a little smile. John sipped his own tea, just to show it wasn't poisoned or anything, but the queen went on considering him for another dreadful minute. He thought even the reporters collectively sensed something was amiss. They had the reverent hush of sports fans watching to see if a ball thrown from half-court and backward was going to go in the basket or not.

"There's a wonderful story from the Hebrew Bible," said the queen in a queenly voice. John thought it could only be a bad sign that the goblins were using a queenly voice. "The Gileadites had defeated the Ephraimites in battle, and the surviving Ephraimites were trying to cross the River Jordan back into their homeland. Do you know the story?"

John coughed. "Don't think so," he answered.

"The Gileadites stopped every man crossing the River

Jordan and asked, 'Are you an Ephraimite?' But of course no one answered yes. So the Gileadites told every man, 'Say the word 'shibboleth.'"

There was a pause. John said, "What is—"

"It's a Hebrew word for a part of a plant or something. The meaning isn't important," said the Goblin Queen. "What's important is that the Ephraimites had no *sh* sound in their dialect, while the Gileadites did. You see?"

"So—"

"So any man who said '*si*bboleth' was killed. Say it with me: shibboleth."

John breathed. "Shibboleth," he repeated.

"Say it with both your voices," said the queen.

The Great Court was crushingly silent. Gather enough quiet in one place, in a big enough room, and John thought it could almost kill a man. It almost killed him now.

"Say it," said the queen. "Say shibboleth with both your voices at once, and I'll drink my tea and smile for the cameras and we'll all go home to our plum house-sitting jobs."

John was momentarily stuck for an ad lib.

"Sir Richard!" called the queen. And from behind one of the blinds came Sir Richard Starkey, drummer for the Quarrymen. This had the effect of really warming up the reporters. They shouted and surged against the velvet rope, a seething mass of nonsense.

"I'm sorry, Reggie," said Sir Richard. "I had to tell. You need help, you and your friends."

John rose sharply, and his chair clattered to the floor behind him. "You were always a mediocre drummer, Richard!" he said, pointing.

"Oh, look here, now—"

"You didn't even play on *The Pennyfarthing Policemen Ride Again*! It was a studio drummer!"

Speaking of policemen, several were now advancing on John. He sighed.

"I'm about to do something stupid, lads," he said.

"We sort of figured," said an officer.

"I wasn't," said John, grabbing the teapot, "speaking to you." Then something unexpected happened.

For weeks the world would buzz over the mystery of this unexpected thing, and the things that would follow. Television news cameras these days catch a lot of detail, and those at the British Museum appeared to show Reggie Dwight unfurl his arm with a flourish, and a small bird fly from his sleeve. One of the reporters went, "Oooh." Then the bird started breathing fire, and John punched the queen again.

She tumbled backward onto her royal bum. "THE QUEEN IS AN IMPOSTOR!" John shouted. It appeared to everyone present that he was about to pour hot tea on Her Majesty's face, but a couple of fearless staffers managed to avoid Finchbriton's canopy of fire and grabbed hold of his arms. John struggled, they held him fast, but then each in turn yelped in pain and lost their hold, retreating to nurse fresh cuts on their hands and arms. And the news cameras may or may not have captured the likeness of a four-inch-tall man with a sword, clinging to John's suit coat.

John turned, teapot still in hand, but by now the Goblin Queen had scrambled to safety. "Finchbriton!" he shouted. "Right flanking screen execute!"

They'd worked out some plans in advance. But John wasn't certain how much the bird had understood until now, when it fluttered to the right of the Reading Room and laid down a wide screen of perfectly smoky fire while John ran behind.

"I think today went really well," John said as he ran.

"Is this sarcasm?" asked Fi. "My family didn't believe in sarcasm."

Behind the Reading Room and through the Great Court there was another exhibition space, dimly lit, that was dominated by a large stone moai statue from Easter Island. For a moment John thought this moai moved. But no, it was just the seven-foot-tall figure of his cab driver stepping out from behind it. The brute cracked his knuckles and grinned.

"Good," said John, "our ride's here."

Fi said, "Once again—"

"Sarcasm, yes."

Finchbriton was all too occupied keeping the queen's guard out of the hall. Fi said, "Coin toss! Execute!" and John threw him high in the air. The driver arched his neck to watch Fi's trajectory, and it occurred to John that he was still holding a teapot. So he hit the driver with it. It shattered against the big man's jaw, and hot tea got on everything, including John's hand. He winced from the pain of the strike and the scalding liquid, but the driver howled. By now Fi had landed on the man's shoulder, and he proceeded to stab him in the eardrum before he was shaken off. He hit the floor hard, and John ducked to scoop him up.

"You okay?"

"I am fine. We pixies are a hardy lot."

"Finchbriton!"

The driver, meanwhile, was taking the tea pretty badly. His face was cut up, but now it also seemed to be bubbling, steaming. The big man spat liquid, hunched over, and with a wrenching squelch, transformed suddenly into the Incredible Hulk.

Or something like that. He doubled in size, his black suit opening like a time-lapse blossom and then hanging limply in ragged petals all around him. The ridge of his brow had thickened and his skin had lost all color. He

swung a massive arm and cracked the moai in half.

John goggled. "What?"

"Ogre," said Fi.

"Only grab what you can carry!" shouted Erno, who carried the unicat. "We have to go now!"

Biggs was holding six suitcases, and Emily. She was still asleep. No one seemed to be able to wake her.

"Why?" said Polly as she rushed around, grabbing things, new things, things that didn't make sense. Stuff from John's house that she'd never even seen before yesterday. "Just 'cause Emily shouted in her sleep?"

"She shouted our *location*," said Erno. "She told me she's been dreaming for weeks about her mother or . . . *someone* trying to find her. What if it's Nimue, sneaking into her head?"

"How will Dad and everyone know how to find us?"

"Everyone still has the new cell phones. We'll have to call them, tell them where we're going."

"Where *are* we going?"

"Can't say right now; the goblins might hear."

"WHAT?" Pigg shouted from downstairs.

"Keep trying to wake Emily," Erno told Biggs. "We can't have her talking in her sleep anymore."

They dragged their belongings down the stairs, and Erno dialed Scott.

"How'd you get through?" griped Scott. "I've been trying you, but the network's been overloaded."

"Why?" said Erno. "What's happened?"

"Haven't you been watching the queen's tea?"

"We couldn't figure out how to work your dad's TV. What?"

"We saw it on at a gas station. John's in trouble. We're coming back."

"Well, don't come here. I don't think it's safe anymore. I'm texting everyone a new address."

John's new phone rang, and then chimed to report a text, but he ignored it because he was being chased by an ogre. It chased him down the steps to the street, it chased him northeast toward the parkland of Russell Square. It might have overtaken him already if its broken eardrum hadn't been sending bad signals to its limbs and brain, causing it to stagger at times and jostle tour buses. Londoners screamed and ran from the sight of the monster; cars swerved. The only nice thing about being chased by an ogre was that the sight of it caused the policemen who were *also* supposed to be chasing you to pull back a bit and think about what they wanted out of life.

The ogre found a motorcycle and threw it at John. "Duck!" shouted Fi, who was clinging to John's collar and watching his back. John obeyed without question, and the bike skimmed his head and skipped against the pavement some fifteen feet distant, searing a blackened path toward the square. It broke down a section of iron fence John had been worried about jumping, so that was all right.

"So what do you know about ogres?" asked John.

"Dim-witted when angry," said Fi. "But also less sensitive to pain."

The park was teeming with people, strollers, little dogs off the leash.

"RUN!" John shouted to everyone around him.

"Is that Reggie Dwight?" said someone.

By his watch, the ogre should have crashed into the park already, but a quick glance told him it wasn't behind them anymore. Had it given up the chase? Or was it calming down, starting to think? John heard distant screams.

"Are you Reggie Dwight?" asked a man with a stroller. "My wife just called, said you punched the queen."

"Everyone knows that, mate," said another man.

"No, I mean, he punched her this morning. *Again*."

"Pull the other one."

"No, it's true."

"Finchbriton!" called John. "Where are you? Can you make these people run like I asked?"

The finch swooped down and drew a fiery little swoosh in the air.

"Thank you," said John as the men retreated. "Oh, look

at that! Perfect!" He'd spied a couple of teenagers facing off near the center of the park, wearing glasses and chain-mail armor and wielding longswords.

"Hi!" shouted John, approaching the kids. "Hello. Fancy selling me one of those swords? Say, a hundred pounds?"

"Are you Reggie Dwight?"

Then a moped sailed through the trees, crashing to the ground right where John and the boy would have been standing if John hadn't heaved them both out of the way.

The teens cursed and ran off as fast as their complicated outfits would allow, and John noticed with some satisfaction that the one had dropped his sword when tackled. John stooped to retrieve it, and it was only for this reason that he avoided getting flattened by a second moped.

Now the ogre came plowing through the trees, bellowing and holding a third moped over its head. John's phone rang and went to voice mail. He readied his sword, and Finchbriton set the moped alight so that the beast dropped it on itself. Then the little bird let loose with an inferno that engulfed the ogre itself, transforming the monster into a crackling blue blazing nightmare. And still it advanced, oblivious. Finchbriton sputtered, his flame spent, and barely made it back to John's shoulder.

"Tell your daughter . . . ," said Prince Fi. "Tell her I rode in a pocket."

"Come now," said John. "You know neither one of us is going to see Polly again."

The ogre slammed his fiery fist down, and John rolled to the right, came up with his sleeve smoldering. He struck the ogre's arm with his sword.

"I don't think this thing is even sharpened," he muttered. Then he ducked another swing from the ogre and plunged the sword tip into its belly. Sharpened or no, the blade went in, but then the monster turned and yanked the weapon from John's hand. John's phone rang again.

"Perhaps we should answer?" said Fi.

John took off running and called the number back. The ogre followed, dizzy and half blind from the smoke of his own burning flesh.

"Dad!" said Scott. "I've been calling."

John was shocked into silence for a moment, and so was Scott. He'd said *Dad*. But it didn't seem like the time to discuss it.

"I know," John answered. "Sorry. Been busy."

"Are you still near the museum? We're circling Russell Square right now in the poppadum truck."

"That's terribly good news. Meet me at the northeast corner."

He pushed through a wild hedgerow and emerged at the corner of the square, but the truck hadn't arrived yet.

And now he found he was right against another of those pointy iron fences he hadn't wanted to vault before. He set about gingerly climbing over it.

"Hurry, man!" said Fi. Finchbriton chirruped.

Then there was a great rustle behind him, and he turned to see the ogre break through the bushes. It swayed, lurched, a smelly black cinder. It raised both arms and roared in horrid victory. A frozen moment followed. Then it pitched forward, falling on its face and driving the longsword deep into its gut. And then it was still.

The truck pulled up, and John stumbled over the fence to meet it. The back opened, and Scott put out his hand.

"Punched the queen again, didn't you?"

"To be fair, this was an entirely different queen."

When he thought they were far enough away, when he heard distant sirens, Erno allowed himself a glance back. There was a dark tower of smoke rising up from where he thought John's house should be.

Emily was half awake, squinting foggily over Biggs's shoulder. "No surprise," the big man said. "Like t' burn things." Erno agreed—he remembered what the Freemen had done to Biggs's treehouse—but he was thinking of the goblins. So was Harvey.

"We should have let them go," said the rabbit-man.

CHAPTER 17

The new address, the one Erno had found, was on a sunny little street called St. George, in Islington, in the north of London. It was lined with friendly trees and tall row houses. They'd all made it here, and they'd all converged quite naturally on this particular house without even checking the address—it was like one rotten fang among a set of otherwise fine teeth. A neglectful gray, with scabby wood and pockmarked masonry. A tiny yard that somehow gave the impression of being both dead and overgrown at the same time. A garden where all the troublemaker plants came to smoke.

They'd converged on this house because they all felt, without realizing it consciously, that they belonged in a place like this. They were home. They stood in front of their new home now, exposed and unsure how to proceed. It wasn't even noon.

"Why is there a big sign that says TOILET?" asked Erno.

"Because you can't read," Emily answered. "It says TO LET."

"Oh, right. Why is there a big sign that says TO—"

"It means for rent. The house is for rent."

There was a phone number at the bottom of the sign. On a whim, Erno dialed it. After a moment, he held the phone to Emily. "Listen."

It was a voice-box message from the building's owner. He was on holiday, it said, wasn't showing the property right now, but leave your name and number, etc.

"It's . . . Dad," said Emily. "It's Mr. Wilson."

"Really?" said Scott.

"Then this is definitely th' place," said Mick.

"Whatever place this is," said John.

They continued to stare at it and didn't notice the little girl approaching from behind until Finchbriton twittered.

"'S haunted," the girl said, her tone letting them know that haunted houses bored her personally, but she thought maybe these nice people with their bird and cat might be interested.

"It does look pretty scary, doesn't it?" John turned and said, smiling.

"These squatters?" said the girl. "Were squatting in it. That means they were living there for free. And one

of them? Turned into a stag. So the other squatters ran out screaming, 'HE TURNED INTO A BLOODY GREAT STAG,' and no one's been in since."

Everyone mulled this over.

"Haunted," the girl concluded. "I can't play right now. My mum's making curry. I'd invite you, but I'm not allowed to talk to strangers. What's a ghost's favorite fruit?"

"Is it booberries?" asked John.

"Specterines?" said Merle.

"It depends on the ghost. Okay, bye."

They watched her cross the street.

"That girl was weird," said Polly.

"You were exactly like her not two years ago," Scott replied.

Emily was studying the house. "Are you guys all thinking what I'm thinking?" she said.

"Yes," said Scott, nodding. *There's a fairy in there, turning people into animals.*

"There's a rift in that house that leads to Pretannica, the magical Britain," Emily finished.

Scott looked at the others. "Wait—is that what we were all thinking?"

"I wasn't really thinking anything," said Erno.

"I was thinking of my brothers," said Fi.

"I was thinking about that chip shop we pathed back

by the tube thtation," said Harvey. "Could anyone elthe go for thome chipth right now?"

Emily looked exasperated. "When someone makes the Crossing, they have to trade places with another living thing of similar size on the other side, remember? Some squatter got a trip to Pretannica, and a stag ended up here. C'mon." She strode right up to the house, stepped onto the porch, and pushed through the door.

The building was broken up into single-room flats and zippered up the middle by a staircase so out of plumb it was nearly a ramp.

"Nobody try going upstairs," said Merle.

The ground floor had two flats, a bathroom, a kitchen, and a door to the basement. The ceilings were clouded over with water stains. The electricity was off, but John showed them little coin-slot boxes in each room that could be paid with pound coins to turn it on, as if the whole house was a grim nickelodeon. They got the juice flowing in the kitchen, which flustered an anxious, naked lightbulb in the ceiling and set the refrigerator to jittering back and forth between the cabinets like a bumper car. There was a single sheet of paper stuck to the fridge with a pie-shaped magnet, and the vibrations sent it skating across the surface of the freezer door until Erno unstuck it and gave it a looking over.

Emily, meanwhile, was blithely leading everyone into

the basement. The door opened onto a creaky but serviceable set of stairs and a pull chain that wasn't attached to any actual lightbulb. And now Emily hesitated at the edge of the dense blackness. "Here," said Merle as he lit his flashlight. The cold spill of it fell on an old stone wall, a concrete slab floor, the flinch of a cricket, other bugs, lots of bugs—and then horns, hooves, bones.

"Gah! Skeleton horse!" said Scott before he could stop himself. There was a polite pause.

Emily said, "I think it's the stag—"

"Okay, yeah. I got it."

It was almost entirely skeletonized. The lower jaw had nearly fallen away and gave it a look that was more or less completely terrifying. Its ribs had come loose and were set like kindling on the floor. Something slick and dark twisted in the kindling.

"Ooh, careful there," said John. "That looks like a black adder." The snake coiled itself into a question mark, a formal written request to be left alone.

Further investigation of the basement would reveal a lot more bugs, some food wrappers, and another skeleton (they'd eventually agree on badger), but the real discovery was a large cabinet against the wall opposite the stairs.

It was tall and plain, shabby really, with symmetrical doors. They opened these carefully to find that the back and floor of the cabinet had been removed, and a small octagon was drawn in chalk just behind it on the wall. Emily waved at it.

"Ta-da, the rift. He put a wardrobe in front of it," she added, smirking. "I guess that was his idea of a joke."

"I wonder if the rift's open," said Merle.

"It's open," said Scott.

Most of the rest turned to look at him. Not Polly and John, though. They were still staring at the octagonal rift as well, tilting their heads and squinching up their eyes.

"It's kinda . . . glimmery," said Polly.

"It looks like oil on water," said John.

Emily frowned at the chalk octagon. Because she could still only hear and not see the Fay among them, she said "Mick, Harvey, are you down here? Can you see what they're talking about?"

"Nope," said Harvey.

"No," said Mick. "Maybe it's 'cause they've fairy blood, but they were born here? They're of both worlds."

"The rift's bigger than the octagon Mr. Wilson drew," said Scott. "Like, four times bigger. Mick could walk right through it."

"It's growing," said Emily. "Probably gets bigger and bigger toward May Day." She grinned. "Who wants to go to Pretannica?"

CHAPTER 18

Scott slept through the afternoon in one of the musty ground floor apartments and awoke to find plans crackling all around the house. They'd gotten the lights working in the basement, which didn't really do the basement any favors appearance-wise, and had moved the wardrobe aside. The rift was noticeably larger even than it had been before Scott went to sleep. In the corner now was a stack of metal cages, ropes, stakes, and bags and bags of animal feed.

Scott eyed the cages blearily. "For the . . . snake?" But the snake was still coiled in its little tepee of ribs.

"We seem to have a working arrangement with the snake," said Emily. "Just don't put any part of yourself near his mouth; he's poisonous. No. The cages are for whatever comes through the rift."

Scott thought. "Because . . ."

"Because some of us are going through there, and when we do, it'll only be because something else happens to be on the other side. Hopefully it'll be an animal, and we can capture that animal and keep it here in the basement to swap it back for our team when they're ready to be extracted."

"When our team is ready to be *extracted?*"

Emily shrugged. "Your dad is big on this kind of talk."

"But then . . . ," said Scott. "What if the thing that comes through isn't an animal? What if it's a Pretannican human, or an elf?" *Or an ogre? Or a dragon?*

"At this point our plan is mostly hoping it won't be."

Scott glanced at the snake again. "Do you think that thing is from Pretannica? Maybe it isn't even a regular snake. Maybe it's magic or, like, an enchanted prince."

Polly walked up as he said this. "You should definitely kiss it," she said.

"Ha ha. Shut up. Speaking of enchanted princes—"

Just then Fi surfaced from Polly's jacket pocket. "Well met, Scott," he said.

"Oh. Oh, hey, Fi. I didn't think you liked pockets."

"It's been brought to my attention recently that I should try new things," said the prince.

Mick hopped down the stairs with two walkie-talkies. "Got 'em," he said. "We ready to do this?"

"Ready if you are," said Emily.

"Wait," Scott said to Mick. "Are you going to Pretannica right now? And a walkie-talkie? That's never going to work, is it?"

Emily took one of the walkie-talkies from Mick. "We know it will, thanks to your mom's research. Remember? She said so in an email."

"Asking her all those scientific questions was your idea," Scott reminded Emily. "I was mostly skimming to make sure she hadn't been kidnapped by Freemen."

"Well," said Emily. "Her research showed that all wavelengths of the electromagnetic spectrum bounced back from the rift in Antarctica except radio waves."

Mick got in position where the octagon was drawn and said, "This abou' right, kids?"

Scott narrowed his eyes. The shimmering octagon was transposed over and around and through Mick—he couldn't believe the elf couldn't feel it. "Step just a hair to your left. That's good."

"So now what?" said Polly. "We just wait for something Mick's size to wander by on the other side?"

"That's right."

Polly fidgeted. "That sounds like it'll take forever. I'm gonna get a snack."

"No, Polly, please stay," said Emily. "We may need help with whatever comes across."

Mick looked anxious but excited. "Goin' home,"

he muttered. "Never thought I'd see it. Scott? If . . . if somethin' bad happens an' I can't get back, don't yeh cry. Livin' ou' my days in a doomed world won't be so bad if it's home."

"You . . . you don't mean that."

"I'm Irish. We all think we're doomed anyway."

It would have been a good exit line, but the truth was they had to wait another fifteen minutes before anything happened. But then it happened. Polly gasped, so Scott knew she saw it, too. He didn't think Mick and Emily realized anything was going on. Mick's shape grew dark, flat, and then it joined with another shape, something sharp eared and bushy tailed and quadrupedal. Behind Scott, the adder hissed. Then Mick was gone, and a fox was in the basement instead.

It crouched low and darted off to a corner as Polly made a grab for it. Scott took a cage from the stack and tried to help her, but the little fox was everywhere, its claws ticking on the hard floor—up and down the stairs, nearly bitten by the adder, U-turning around Emily, who so far hadn't even gotten up from where she was sitting.

"Come in, Mick," she said into the walkie-talkie. "Are you there? Over."

The radio crackled. "It's IRELAND!" said Mick. "I'd know it wi' my eyes closed. An' the *glamour*! Sweet Danu, the glamour. I'm gettin' fluthered on it. Um, over."

"Hmm," said Emily to the others as they scrambled around her. "If it leads to Ireland, then the snake can't be from the rift. There are no snakes in Ireland, you know." The fox turned, an orange firecracker, and the Doe kids turned too, their sneakers scuffing, Scott accidentally whanging Polly with the metal cage. "I bet a lot of little Pretannican rodents and things trade places with all the bugs down here, and the adder just realized this basement made for easy hunting." Emily spoke into the radio. "Mick, it's going to be a minute before we extract you, we have a rogue fox situation in the basement. Over."

"No rush. Over."

"Now that I think about it," Emily told Scott and Polly and Fi, who had just managed to maybe corner the thrumming little fox with the cage and a jacket, "we should have started out with Mick already in the cage. Then the fox would have just popped up in there. I'm sorry, I've been so distracted."

Finally they coaxed the animal into the hutch, and everyone seemed relieved, fox included. They put it back in position over the rift.

"Mick, fox is in the henhouse. Over."

"Is that a code yeh just made up to mean it's back on the rift? Over."

"Yes. Over."

Maybe thirty seconds passed, and then the fox's form

went dark, and was conjoined with Mick's, and then it was just the leprechaun in the cage, looking sort of magnificent.

"Get me out of this thing," he said, smiling.

"Mick!" said Emily, jumping to her feet. "I can see you! Is that really what you look like?"

"More wrinkled than I recall," said Fi.

Scott opened the cage door, so Mick tossed him a tip—a gold coin, almost worn smooth, the faintest portrait of a bearded king on its obverse side, a dragon on the other.

"Where'd you get this?" asked Scott.

"Found it," said Mick. He was grinning from ear to ear. "An' for the lady," he added, and handed Emily something small and green.

A four-leaf clover.

CHAPTER 19

Scott had slept in the afternoon, and so wasn't tired at night. And that was good—someone had to watch Emily. Erno was certain that she'd somehow told Nimue and Goodco their location in her dreams, and she couldn't really assure them that this wasn't the case. Scott was to watch her and try to wake her at the first sign of any disturbance in her sleep.

"But it's not Nimue I keep dreaming of, it's my mom," she told Scott as she crawled into bed. She had tired eyes. Old eyes. "Why isn't he just here? Dad. Mr. Wilson, I mean. He could just be here, waiting for us. He could just tell us things, instead of leaving us stupid games. You know Erno thinks the thing that was on the refrigerator is another clue? I'm too angry to look at it."

"He's helping us, at least, in his own way," said Scott, taking a chair.

"I wonder if he's still taking it. The Milk. I mean, I know it was messing me up, but Scott! I'm getting dumber!"

Scott winced. "I'm not sure you are—"

"I think I am. I don't know. I can't say anything for sure without doing some tests. But I think one thing's clear: I'm not going to get any smarter."

Scott smiled. "I wouldn't worry—you're smart enough already."

But Emily looked at him squarely, soberly. "No. Think about what I'm saying." She blinked her red eyes. "You don't realize it maybe, but you're always discovering new doors and stepping into bigger worlds. Bigger and better worlds, with more doors to open. As long as you keep learning, your world gets bigger. Mine's just shrinking, now."

Scott hesitated until he was sure of his answer. "You got a bigger world than I'm ever going to, though. You got that."

"And I got to visit, and now I have to come back to the basement."

Scott looked at his hands.

"Help me fall asleep," said Emily. "Tell me a story."

"I don't know any stories."

"Please."

"You know who has good stories? Merle. I mean, he was the *wizard of King Arthur's court*. Merle!"

Merle poked his head in. "What's up?"

"Tell me a story," said Emily. "About the sword in the stone."

"Yeah, no kidding," said Scott. "Was that real?"

"Sure," said Merle. "Sort of."

"So . . . nobody but Arthur could pull the sword out? Was it a Fay spell? Or was it really a sign from God that Arthur was rightful king of England or . . ."

Merle was smirking. "It was magnets."

They stared.

"Maybe I should begin a little earlier," said Merle. "I told you about Vortigern, Scott, and the whole tower-and-dragons debacle. That gave me a bit of a reputation as a wise guy. So maybe you know that King Uther Pendragon was Arthur's father."

Scott made a sour face. He didn't like this story. King Uther squabbles with the Duke of Tintagel, and invites the duke to his castle. During the visit, Uther falls madly in love with the duke's wife, Igraine. The duke and Igraine flee, so later Uther gets Merlin to disguise him as the duke while his forces are fighting the real duke on the battlefield. Igraine thinks Uther is her husband, and they spend a night together, the same night her actual husband is killed in battle. After Igraine learns her husband has been killed, she wonders who that fake duke was, but she keeps the whole thing to herself, and when Uther proposes marriage, she says yes. Months later she gives birth to Arthur and tells her husband that the son belongs to a mystery man who looked like the duke, and Uther says, "Surprise! It was me," and everyone's happy. Then they give up Arthur to Merlin, because that was the deal. It was an all-around gross story.

"Calm down," said Merle. "I know you've read the books, but it didn't turn out like that. Of course, I had read the books too, so when Uther's man Sir Ulfius comes to me wanting help with his king's love life, I'll admit I didn't know what to do. I think, *If I don't help Uther, then Arthur is never born*, and that's a tragedy. But this is a terrible thing to do to Igraine. So I tell Uther I can help, not knowing what I'm going to do right up until the night itself. And that night King Uther is drinking a lot of wine 'cause he's nervous, and Sir Ulfius is drinking a lot of wine, and I'm trying to come up with a way to disguise us all and make this work, maybe something with fake mustaches, and finally I panic and put everybody to sleep."

Scott frowned. "Then what?"

"Then nothing. I rode them back to the castle, and when they woke up the next morning I told them the plan had gone off perfectly."

"What?"

"I saw the look of doubt on Uther's face, right, but I explained that people shape-shifted by the spell I used might experience a little memory loss. After that he looked happy, and if Uther was happy, there was no way Ulfius was going to argue. But in the back of my mind I feel a little weird, because I didn't do my duty. Arthur would never be born. Then nine months later Arthur was born."

"How?"

"Arthur was the duke's son. He was *always* the duke's son. But Uther says to Igraine, 'I know how your son was really conceived—on the night your late husband was killed, a man with his likeness came to you.' And Igraine was like, 'Uh, no, that never happened,' but Uther insisted and said, 'Fear not! For I was that man, ensorcelled to resemble the duke! Ha ha!'

"So Igraine's probably like, 'He thinks this is his son? Okay, great! Awesome. He's an idiot, but whatever.' Because Igraine was probably expecting Uther would just have the baby killed. Son of your enemy, and you don't want to look weak, right?"

"And they gave baby Arthur to you?" said Emily softly.

"Yeah. That was the deal the books said I made, so that was the deal I made, and like I said, I think Igraine was just thrilled not to have any of her family members murdered. She married her daughters Elaine and Morgause off to rich guys, and put her youngest, Morgan, in a nunnery, all at Uther's request."

"Morgan—that's Morgan le Fay, the sorceress, right?" asked Scott.

"Yeah. I realize now she must have been a changeling. I mean, not a changeling like you and Polly and your dad, who're mostly human with a little drop of fairy in you. I mean an Old World fairy, swapped in the cradle, who doesn't realize she's not really human—that kind of changeling. Anyway, you wanted to know about the sword in the stone."

"Yeah."

"Yeah."

"So I take baby Arthur away to this really nice knight I know, Sir Ector, who's recently had a son of his own. And Sir Ector and his wife raise Arthur, and I sort of help teach the boy things I think he needs to know. And I really grow to love this boy. He's a great kid. In another age he'd have made a great scientist.

"But during this time King Uther gets sick and dies, and England kind of falls apart a little. Everyone's vying to be the guy who takes over and rules as the new king, because Uther didn't leave any heirs. So I do what I'm supposed to, and I tell the Archbishop of Canterbury to demand that all the lords and gentlemen come to London at Christmastime, upon pain of cursing—"

"Upon pain of cursing?" said Scott.

"You like that? I thought that was a nice touch. I have him demand they all come upon pain of cursing and promise that God will show by some miracle who should be rightful king of the realm."

"But . . . ," said Emily.

"You see the hitch, right?" Merle smiled.

"Arthur *wasn't* the rightful king of England," Emily mumbled. "He was the duke's son."

"So I knew I couldn't depend on any miracles, and I had to make my own," said Merle. "I had a big hunk of marble carved, and an anvil stuck in it, and a deep groove cut in the anvil. Took forever. And I had a sword made by an illiterate swordsmith, with words written in gold that said WHOSO PULLETH OUT THIS SWORD OF THIS STONE AND ANVIL, IS RIGHTWISE KING BORN OF ALL ENGLAND. Cost me every penny I had.

"But the genius part," said Merle, really puffing himself up, "was the magnets made out of fairy gold. I suppose you both know that you can make a magnet with a coil of electric current around a nail or whatever."

"Yeah, we did that in science class," said Scott. He felt suddenly weary, wondering if he'd ever get back to doing anything so simple as electrocuting a nail.

"So I managed to scrape together a little bit of fairy gold," said Merle, "and with that I could make a battery to hide inside the stone and anvil. I had to hide my watch in there too, but then I could use Archie to transmit a signal and turn the battery's current on and off. Stick the sword in the stone, run the current through the anvil, and suddenly the strongest man in England couldn't pull it back out. Cut the power, and my tante could do it."

Emily smiled.

"Maybe you kids know the rest. No one could pull out the sword, so they put together a big jousting tournament so everyone can stick around and keep trying. And Arthur's foster brother, Kay, forgets his sword back at the inn, so Arthur, being his squire, runs back for it. But the inn is locked, empty, everyone is at the tournament. So Arthur takes the sword out of the stone, easy as anything, and brings it to Kay. 'How did you come by this?' everyone wants to know. And he tells them, and they're all, OMG!"

"Don't say OMG," said Scott.

"Hey! I can say slang. I haven't even been born yet— technically I'm younger than you."

"Sorry."

"Anyway, he tells them and they kneel down to him

and he's crowned King of England. That's the really short version, anyway."

Scott huffed. "You could have made *anyone* King of England. You could have made yourself."

"Yeah, but I don't like hats."

Scott looked over to see what Emily thought of all this, only to find she'd fallen asleep. He watched her anxiously, but her breathing was gentle and easy, her face finally untroubled.

Now seemed as good a time as any to ask Merle something that had been bothering him. He felt like everyone had been dancing around it. He leaned close and lowered his voice and said, "Mick told me that the Gloria that separated the worlds . . . he said it happened right after Arthur and his son battled each other, when they supposedly died. And that's when you and Arthur traveled to the future, right? So—"

"No."

"I didn't even say it yet—"

"You were gonna say that maybe it was us and our time machines that cracked reality in half? Separated the worlds? That maybe I'm responsible?"

Scott squirmed a bit.

"Well, honestly . . . ," said Merle. "I started wondering about that too, ever since getting mixed up with you bunch. But I've checked and rechecked the math. Emily's checked it, too. There was *nothing in my designs that could have caused this to happen.* I swear. It's some kind of crazy coincidence. I'm sure we'll learn the truth soon enough."

"Yeah. I'm sure we'll learn the truth soon enough."

CHAPTER 20

"I think everybody should have a copy of this," Emily said to all the others, seated on folding chairs in the dank basement. She passed them a stack of pages she'd made up at a local copy shop. They each unrolled their papers to find maps of Great Britain. "They're maps of Pretannica, courtesy of the Freemen and their big filing cabinet," Emily added. "Maps with rifts. That circle around the British Isles is the current edge of the universe, according to the Freemen. Everything beyond that doesn't exist. Those of you going through the rift should try not to get too close to the edge, or it's my understanding that you'll stop existing, too."

"What's this world map for down here?" asked Scott.

"That shows the locations of stable or semi-stable rifts in our world that Goodco knows about. Notice all the little dots around New Jersey."

Scotland
North Sea
Eidynburh
Glasgow
Ireland
Wales
England
Cardiff
London

"Why so many around New Jersey?" said Polly.

"So," said Emily. "A little primer: rifts open up on Earth all the time. Most of them are unstable, only open for a moment, and nothing goes through them, so nobody notices. They're attracted to magic, so mostly they pop up in places where there's a little bit of magical buildup, which pretty much means any city where Goodco's built a factory. Magic is everywhere in Pretannica, so the openings on the Pretannica side are totally random. Point is that at any time a rift could open up in Pretannica so large that you could lead all the armies of the Fay through it at once, but you could never plan your day around it."

"But some rifts aren't unstable," said Merle.

"Right. They stay open for a few weeks, getting bigger, then smaller again around May Day and November Day. Some are even open all the time. Goodco knows about a lot of these, and as you can see on your maps, they're exactly where you'd expect—Goodborough, Slough, towns where there's a Goodco cereal factory. Though there's still a certain amount of randomness. For example, the great big rift in Antarctica that Scott's mom characterized, or that one in Iran."

"There's a rift in . . . Chad?" said Erno. "Is that a country? I thought it was just the name of that eighth grader with the missing earlobe."

"Anyway," said Emily, "all the stable rifts Goodco

knows about are really small, too small for even Mick to get through. Or else they're big but at the bottom of the ocean."

Fi was looking at his map. "I was sent through a rift and found myself in the Atlantic Ocean, near this rift you've marked here. Yet I was near the surface, not at the bottom."

"Yeah, it must have been a different one. You've said this pixie witch of yours had four stable rifts? Nimue would kill for those. She could start the invasion tomorrow. Well. I think John has a report."

John stood up and Emily sat down. "As you know, after the British Museum incident, I sent out a press release through Archimedes to all the news outlets, explaining our position. Of course most of the chatter on the internet is that I'm, er . . . crazy."

"Crazy talented," said Polly.

"No, just the regular kind. But serious journalists are devoting a lot of time to analyzing that footage from the museum and trying to prove that there weren't a fire-breathing finch and a tiny man there, and they can't. So that's all to the good. And people are asking questions, and Goodco has had to release an official statement, so I'm going to send out another missive and try to keep the ball rolling."

"Good," said Emily. "Well—"

"I have something," said Erno.

Emily's shoulders fell. "Is this about the thing from the refrigerator? It's not a clue."

"It definitely belonged to Mr. Wilson—"

"I'm not saying it didn't, but he didn't write it—it's just some page from an old handbook."

It was, specifically, a page torn from the 1921 Young Freeman's Handbook, and it began midsentence.

YOUNG FREEMAN'S HANDBOOK 1921

all know that the Sickle and the Spoon was developed from the vesica piscis, an ancient Christian symbol shown in some medieval traditions to be bisected by the sword Caliburn, or Excalibur.

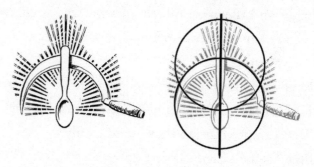

The enterprising young Freeman can draft his own Sickle and Spoon with everyday objects he'll find around the home or temple. Dr. Octopodes Bray (K. o. t. R.) has invented an ingenious method that requires no compass but may be accomplished with a straight edge and by tracing the circumference of any cup, plate, or pie tin.

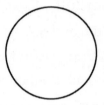

Once the circle has been traced, the first and most important step is to determine its center.

That was all it said. The opposite side was just an etching of Dr. Octopodes Bray, Knight of the Round, probably an otherwise nice man who was born twenty years too early to know how bad he was going to look in a Hitler mustache.

"I know he didn't write it," said Erno, "but he must have left it for a reason. We should at least think about it."

"That can be your job then," said Emily.

"Fine," sighed Erno, sitting down.

"Anyone else?"

Scott stood up. "I want to go to Pretannica."

John turned. "You do? I don't know how I feel about that—"

"Oh, come on. You can't really be pulling the fatherly 'It's too dangerous' thing on me at this point, can you?"

"I'll be happy to have 'im," said Mick. "He's good in a scrape. We may need all the help we can get, savin' the queen."

"Except I don't want to go after the queen," Scott said. "I want to visit the fairies."

"What?" said Emily.

"*What?*" said John. Out of the corner of Scott's eye, he saw Harvey prick up his ears and start frantically scrawling on the back of his map.

"Like a . . . diplomatic mission," said Scott. "If they're all going to invade, it's because Nimue's been feeding them lies all these years. Lies like that the humans are responsible for their world dying. I'll go visit the High Queen . . . Titania, right? And plead our case. Maybe I can just prevent the whole invasion and get everybody talking instead."

"No," said John. "No way. It's too dangerous." And when Scott gave him a look, he added, "Yes, I *am* pulling that. I am pulling exactly that."

"Hold on now," said Mick. "This could actually work. Scott's part fairy, so he has ev'ry right to request an audience wi' the queen. An' if I go with 'im, an' demand his safety as a member o' the queen's court? Then none can harm 'im. Them's the rules."

"I'll go too," said Polly. "Please? I wanna go."

John sighed. "I can't imagine how I'll explain this to your mother next year if something goes wrong."

"Yeah." Merle coughed. "*This* is the part you'll be at a loss to explain."

"Okay," said Emily. "Scott and Polly and Mick and Finchbriton go to the court of Titania. John and Merle rescue the Queen of England. My current projections show this rift is never going to get big enough for Biggs, so he stays here and takes care of whatever animals come through. I keep studying the rift, Erno studies . . . that piece of paper. You all get walkie-talkies souped up by Merle with fairy batteries, thanks to that gold coin Mick found. Fi?"

"I will protect Polly."

"Ooh, better not, mate," said Mick. "You know I like yeh, but a pixie in the court of the Fay? That's an insult, that is."

Fi sighed. "I will go with the men, then."

"Happy to have you," said John.

Emily called to the rabbit-man, who was still writing. "And what are you going to do, Harvey?"

"Nuthin'."

"Right. I guess that's it, then. Let's all make ready."

There was the scuffle and squeak of chairs as class was dismissed.

"Maybe this is a stupid idea," Scott said to Mick. He had half expected everyone to talk him out of it, and now he felt like he was sitting on the edge of a cliff while all his friends said, *Go on, then, jump the motorcycle.*

"Prob'ly. But it speaks well of yeh that you're the first to think of tryin' it."

Harvey made a beeline for Scott and unfolded his map to show a scribble of handwritten notes. "I've made a litht of thingth you do that offend me."

"Oh good."

"One: you turn your clotheth inthide out."

"What?" said Scott. "When have I done that?"

"When you took off your thocks that one time."

"Yeh should listen to this," said Mick. "Harv an' I have been in your world awhile, so these kinds of things don't bother us so much anymore. But the fairies o' Pretannica will have certain hang-ups. The same fairies you're meant to impress."

"Fine," said Scott. "What else?"

"Two," said Harvey. "No ringing bellth."

"Bells? Why would I ring a bell?"

"Tho don't, then."

"Three," interrupted Mick. "Try not to give or receive any gifts. Or food or drink."

"Got it. If they try to give me anything, I won't take it."

"Oh, you'll *have* to take it," said Mick. "Only thing worse than gettin' a gift from the Good Folk is not acceptin' one when it's offered. Yeh want to end up belching flowers the rest o' your life? Just try not to get offered anything."

"How am I supposed to do that?" Scott squeaked. This list was making him nervous.

"If it seems like any fairy's abou' to give yeh somethin', change the subject. Create a diversion."

"Like what?"

"*Don't ring any bellth!*"

"Try singin' somethin'," Mick suggested. "They'll like that. Just don't be surprised if yeh start up a whole big musical number, like in a Disney movie. That can happen."

"It's contagiouth."

"Like a yawn."

"Remember . . . ," said Harvey. "Remember when Jack Muthtard thtarted up with that thong and danthe about thinging and danthing?"

"Do I." Mick groaned. "Hard to know how to end something like that. Eventually everyone's singin' abou' how we can't stop singin', an' we'd be doin' it still if the Milesians hadn't invaded."

"I'm going to lie down," said Scott.

COMMERCIAL BREAK

CHIP
Ah, this is the life!

SPARKLE
The sun, the sand…

PIP
And the frootycrisp
flavor of Puftees!™

CHIP
Blueberry blue!

SPARKLE
Raspberry red!

PIP
And new crispity
Purplegrape!™ Now with
Intellijuice™, the magic
juice that makes you
smarter!

KID ONE
Look, there they are!

KID TWO
Real pixies!

SPARKLE
Oh no! Giants!

KID THREE
Grab the pixies!

CHIP
Why grab pixies?
Why not grab the
delicious taste of
crispy froot?

PIP
Part of this
complete breakfast!

KID ONE
Mmmm! Puftees!™
With new Purplegrape!™

SPARKLE
We'll always outsmart
those kids as long as
we have Puftees!™

KID TWO
You can't fool us
anymore, pixies!

KID THREE
New Intellijuice™
has made us smarter!

CHIP
Aw, blueberries! Outsmarted
by our own pixie magic!

ANNOUNCER
Only YOU can help the pixie
brothers escape from the
jars of giants! Find out
how inside every box of
new, improved Puftees!™

CHAPTER 21

Then the big day came. Everyone was in a tizzy. Polly sat in the kitchen and tried to breathe calmly as the ship tipped around her. A cartoon was playing quietly on the tablet computer, a cartoon in which ordinary kids defeated the forces of darkness in extraordinary ways. Fi sat cross-legged on the table.

"So that's the plan," Polly whispered.

"An ignoble plan," said Fi. "Surely we can do better. We've made promises—"

Just then the cartoon broke for a commercial. Three blue-skinned cartoon pixies were relaxing on a beach.

Polly and Fi watched in silence. Fi's tiny eyes reflected the flickering screen dimly, like distant stars.

John appeared in the doorway. "Did that just say there's Intellijuice in the Puftees now? That's bad news."

Neither Polly nor Fi answered.

"There are already reports of smarter kids, better test scores," John added. "Have you heard? The news is reporting it like it's all a joke, but a mob bought every last Goodco box from a grocer's in Chelsea."

The cartoon children crunched spoonfuls of cereal while the pixies tiptoed away.

John clucked his tongue. "Does anyone really *want* a grape-flavored cereal? You know what kind of fruit people never put on their corn flakes? Grapes."

The commercial ended with a final image of the pixie brothers under glass. "Only *YOU* can help the pixie brothers escape from the jars of giants," it said.

"Oh," John added then, and cleared his throat. "Um. I'll bet that makes you think about your . . . I'm sorry, Fi, I forgot."

Fi stood and turned to Polly. "All right," he said quietly. Then he slid down a chair leg and went off toward the basement.

Polly clicked off the cartoon. John looked adrift until Scott squeezed past him through the door.

"Hey! Did anyone tell you the latest?" John asked Scott as they both tried to move and eat their way through the kitchen. "The Goblin Queen got some questions about the British Museum event this morning and got so flustered she hissed at the minister of health!"

Scott smiled. "Nice to think about *them* being on the

defensive for a change," he said. "Maybe if they think their plan is falling apart, the Fay will be willing to talk to me."

"Yes. Yes, break a leg with that. Really."

"Yeah, you . . . you too," Scott answered. Then they stared at each other a moment, having lost all momentum. Finally Scott turned and retreated down the basement steps. Polly followed him.

Mick and Finchbriton were already in Pretannica. So now they had a Pretannican mouse, who was burrowing in the wood chips of a little plastic hutch inside the wardrobe. And another fox (or maybe the same fox) was crouching in the corner of one of their wire cages, with Biggs unsuccessfully trying to feed it. Polly made kissy noises at it. Merle was down here too, apparently in conversation with Prince Fi. Emily was in radio contact with the leprechaun.

"I bought some sheep from a certain Robert Shepherd nearby," said Mick through the radio. "Over."

"With what money? Over."

"Found some more fairy gold. Over."

"That's unethical," Emily groused. "Fairy money is an illusion. Over."

"Isn't all money technic'ly an illusion? Over."

"Oh, whatever. Just get them back here. Emily out. Biggs? We're going to have sheep."

"Yuh," said Biggs, and he commenced to pounding

metal stakes into the mortar of the walls and floor. The adder swayed along with the hammer blows.

Polly lost interest in the fox and crossed to the stairs.

"Don't go far," said Emily. "You leave soon."

"I know." She climbed and met Erno in the kitchen. "Where are you headed?" she asked him. He shrugged.

"Emily wants my help with animal wrangling or something. I dunno."

"Do you wish you were going to Pretannica?"

"Does it matter?" asked Erno, looking out the kitchen window, which only faced an alley. "John and Merle and Fi don't want kids along on their mission, you can tell. And I don't have any fairy blood, so I'm not allowed in Queen Titania's clubhouse."

"Emily's got Biggs for the animals, though," Polly said. "Why aren't you working on that clue? That's important."

Erno scoffed. "You're the only one who thinks so."

"Yeah, but it *has* to be, right? That Mr. Wilson left *so little* in this house. Just a couple chairs and a wardrobe and a jar of Nutella and *that piece of paper.*"

"*I know!*" said Erno. "Thank you! Finally!"

They stared at each other a moment.

"You know what? I *am* going to work on the clue," said Erno. "Tell Emily I'm in the back bedroom if she really needs me."

"Okay." Polly followed him out into the stairwell,

watched him shut himself up inside the back bedroom, then arched her neck to look up at the gap in the ceiling. A little aspect of the second floor could be seen at the top of the ruinous stairs. It wasn't going to be the easiest throw, but she was the athletic one in the family. She took Harvey's cell phone from her pocket, squared her shot, and threw—a perfect sky hook, something the WNBA was going to be interested in if she ever got her growth spurt. Then she sauntered back to the basement.

Everyone was accounted for except Erno—and Harvey, who wasn't really expected to show anyway.

"So how are we doing this?" said John as he got into place near the octagon. "Everyone at once?"

"Should work," said Emily. "The rift's wide enough. It's held at the same diameter for three days now. I calculate you have as much as two months in Pretannica before it gets too small for the tallest of you to return, but let's not test that unless we have to, okay? Get home quickly."

"Guys?" said Merle. "Fi has something to say." He held up the little prince on his palm. Fi cleared his throat.

"I am sorry, my compatriots," he said, "but I have decided not to go to Pretannica. I believe I am honor bound instead to make inquiries into the fortunes of my brothers."

The basement was silent.

"Oh," said Scott. "Right. Sorry, Fi, we've been so

234

wrapped up in saving the queen—"

"There shall be no need for apologies among brothers-in-arms," said Fi. "Truly the welfare of your English queen is paramount. She can knight a thousand soldiers to slay the Great Dragon. But I think I can no longer serve you well when my heart is cut in twain. Merlin, please set me down."

Merle put Fi on the floor, and the pixie strode proudly, if slowly, across the basement floor.

"Good speech, right?" Polly whispered to Emily, next to her. Fi got to the stairs and paused.

"Merlin, please help me up the stairs."

Merle helped him up the stairs.

"Can't beat a prince for a good speech," Polly agreed with herself.

With Fi gone, Scott, Polly, John, and Merle arranged themselves in the rift and waited. Merle handed Archimedes off to Emily.

"Take care of him," he said.

They were dressed warmly, with backpacks, radios, Swiss Army knives, canteens, water purification tablets, and plastic flare guns. John had his sword. Emily got back on the radio.

"Mick, how far out are you? Over."

"'Bout ten minutes. Over."

"This is it," said John. After a moment no one had

confirmed or denied this, so he said it again.

"You mentioned something on the cruise ship," Scott murmured to John. "About how actors want to be loved and are afraid of rejection. That's why you never visited, all those years. Isn't it. You were afraid we'd reject you."

John pulled his lips back into a thin smile, a sad smile, and he raised his head as if to nod. But then his head just sagged.

"No."

Scott frowned. "No?"

"Not at first, no. That wasn't it." John stared at his shoes. "I want to be honest with you kids, and . . . honesty isn't always easy."

Scott and Polly watched him as he gathered his thoughts.

"Your mom and I weren't really happy anymore, but I wanted to stay together for your sakes. Then I went off on a film shoot and came home to find your mom had left, and had taken you with her.

"I called your grandparents. I called all our friends. And no one could tell me where you'd gone. But then I had to leave on a press junket, and on another trip after that, and . . . I stopped looking. I figured your mom would get in touch eventually, when she was ready, and so I went off and played movie star for a while. It was kind of a relief, really: knowing I could have fun, be famous, and that it wasn't my fault. *She* was the one who'd left."

"Didn't you ever think of us?" asked Polly, in a voice that made you want to lift her up, carry *her* around in your pocket.

"All the time. But maybe I'd be leaving on a world tour so I'd think, *Well, obviously I shouldn't call just now.* Then there'd be another film shoot looming, and I'd say, 'Well, of course *now* isn't the right time for a visit.' And somehow seven years slipped away."

Scott discovered he was making fists. It was startling. He abruptly unclenched and shook out his fingers, no less alarmed than if his hands had changed to werewolves.

"And now by this time," said John, "by this time I really *was* afraid. Afraid I couldn't blame everything on anyone but myself anymore, afraid you wouldn't want to see me. I'm trying to be better, I *want* to be better. I want to be here. Not . . . not necessarily in this basement especially, but . . . you know. Here. With you. But even if it's harder, even if it doesn't make you feel any friendlier toward me, I still think you both deserve honesty."

"Honesty," Polly repeated flatly. Scott thought maybe she felt the way he did, like this honesty was something they hadn't asked for, like it was an unwanted gift they had to pretend to appreciate while the Christmas music was still playing.

"Anyway," said John. "So. Pretannica. This is it."

"This is it," said Merle. "Good luck, everybody."

"Saying good luck is unlucky," said John.

Meanwhile, Polly fiddled with something in her pocket. She knew she could count on Biggs to hear it first. After Harvey, he had the best ears.

"Phone," said Biggs.

"Phone?" said Emily. "I don't hear it." They were all silent and still, and then they could all hear it, a phone ringing faintly, somewhere in the house. "That's one of our special rings. But everyone's here, except for Harvey."

"And except for Erno," said Scott.

"Erno," said Emily. "Where's Erno? Oh, geez, Biggs, could you get that phone?"

Biggs left the basement, followed the noise out into the stairwell, and determined without question that the ringing was coming from the second floor. To say that he grimaced at the ramshackle staircase would be an overappraisal of his talents for expression, but he frowned on the inside. Then he took his first, hesitant step.

"I should tell Mick to wait," said Emily. "I don't want to try to corral four sheep by myself."

Then the pounding started. Someone was knocking, knocking hard, on the front door of the house. Emily flinched, looked forward and back. She spoke into the radio. "Mick? Don't get the sheep in position till I give the word. Copy."

"Ten-four."

"Hold on," said Emily, and she ran up the stairs as the pounding came harder and faster.

Polly turned to her father. "I don't want to go to Pretannica anymore," she said.

"You don't? Why not?"

"I'm . . . I'm scared. I didn't want to admit it, but—"

"No, no, that's okay, Polly," said John, smiling. "Really, I'm relieved. I mean, I know you're a very capable seven-year-old, but—"

"I'll go help Biggs and Emily," Polly said, and she rushed up the stairs, spooked the unicat, and took out her walkie-talkie, the one she would have taken with her to Pretannica. She switched it to Mick's channel.

"Mick, we're back on," she said in her best Emily voice. "Sheep in place. Over."

"Copy that."

Then Polly climbed up onto the kitchen counter, opened the window, dropped down into the alley, and shut the window behind her.

Inside the house, Emily was at her wits' end. The moment she'd get to the door, the knocking would stop. She'd peer out through the narrow windows beside it and see nothing, no one. Then she'd turn, and the knocking would start again. Meanwhile, Biggs had managed to answer the upstairs phone (hang-up, blocked) and was trying to get down again without collapsing the staircase. Erno stormed out from the back bedroom.

"Do you all mind? Some of us are *trying* to decipher a *clue!*"

Sometime later the three of them descended back into the basement to find the black adder being menaced by three of the thickest sheep in two worlds.

"Woah," said Emily. "Mick must have gotten the sheep too close. And there's only three? Mick?" she said into the radio.

"I'm here. Over."

"Did everyone make it? Over."

"Everyone made it. Your knocking stop? Over."

Emily listened. It *had* stopped. "Yeah."

"Maybe that little lass was right an' the house *is* haunted. Over."

Emily went to press the radio button, then stopped. "I'm not going to dignify that with a response."

Outside, Polly met up with Prince Fi and Harvey.

"You were right," Polly said to Harvey. "That was easy."

"People like uth can alwayth manipulate otherth," said Harvey. "We can get them to do what we want."

"So is that what you're doing?" said Polly. "To all of us?"

"Naw, not me."

Polly studied him. "Why not?"

"Haven't figured out what I want, yet."

Fi was watching the both of them and signaled to be lifted into Polly's pocket. "There is nothing about this I like," he said. "The deceit. The danger for Polly. I am without honor."

"I'll be a big help to you. I'm even a bit stronger than you."

"It's not strength of body that's required. It's strength of mind, and of character. Which, I must admit," Fi conceded, "you have showed in great measure if I ignore today's escapades."

They walked off toward the tube station.

"What I did today," said Polly. "Was it bad?"

"It was not good," said Fi.

"It wath fine," said Harvey. "Ath long ath you had good reathonth. And didn't enjoy it. You have to try not to enjoy it."

After another block he added, "Not that I didn't enjoy knocking on Emily's cage a bit. Little prith."

CHAPTER 22

Pretannica.

"What . . . what color is everything?" Scott asked Mick.

"'S green."

"Are you sure?" This was the green of camera ads and television commercials for other televisions.

Pretannica.

The trees were brawny, titanic hosts for ivy and velvety moss, shade for fern and flower and fungus. *Oh, man, the fungus,* thought Scott. All prehistoric shapes and back-of-the-refrigerator colors. He thought maybe one mushroom in particular had called him a name when he passed.

But more than any particular sight was the smell, the air, the everything of the place. The *otherworldliness* of it. The magic, the glamour. *Pretannica!* He could see his father was caught up in it too, so could it be the fairyness

of them both that was tuned to this trill, this connection?

"I feel like," he said, struggling to put it into words, "like my fingers have to sneeze. I feel like . . ."

"Running through the hills and twirling like a nun in a movie," finished John.

"That isn't what I was going to say."

Merle was watching them. "I have no idea what you guys are on about. I'm okay with that."

They'd emerged from the rift in a tangled glen, tearing through shrubbery and scattering field mice in every direction. There was no way to get your bearings in a land with no sun, no moon, no stars, but Mick assured them they were in Ireland, in the forests near Killarney. Close to his old mound, in fact. The sky was a Prussian blue above, warming to pumpkin orange at the horizons. Everything seemed brighter than it should have. As if the whole world might be faintly luminous, like a dying glow stick.

"All right, enough gawkin'," said Mick. He addressed Merle and John. "Unless yis have plans to the contrary, England is that way, an' may the road rise to meet yeh. If Scott has no objections, I'd like to stop off at my old mound an' see if anyone's been waterin' my plants. Finchbriton?"

The little bird chirruped.

"I love yeh like the ugly son I never had, but I wan' yeh

245

to consider goin' with John an' Merle here. They have the more dangerous mission an' could use a real powerhouse like you. Of course Scott an' I'd be delighted to have your company—all your little stories, your thoughts on love an' life an' so forth."

Finchbriton seemed to consider the options, then he tweeted his decision and flew to John's shoulder.

"Oh, thank goodness," said Merle. "You know my Slumbro doesn't even work on the Fay."

John was lingering, like he wanted to be knighted just for refusing to lie. Honesty wasn't all *that* hard.

"So, bye," Scott said finally.

John nodded, taking his medicine.

They all said their good-byes and parted. Scott and Mick pressed through the woods—Mick easily, gracefully, Scott as if he were being pranked constantly by a spiteful slapstick universe. He tripped on roots, stumbled over logs, was poked by thickets, had his face raked by brambles.

"It's just up ahead," said Mick. "The ol' mound. An' when I say mound, I'm not bein' modest—'s a mound. But inside it was as cozy as your mother's handbag. Here we are."

They arrived at a small clearing and a mound of earth ringed by small mushrooms. Atop the mound was a weathered and whitewashed wooden cross. Mick stared quizzically at the cross.

"Well, that's new. I hope you won't be offended when I tell yeh it has no place on a leprechaun's domicile."

"There's something tied to it," said Scott, and he climbed up, wondering too late if it was bad manners to just hike up another man's house like this. At the base of the cross was a pair of very old, shriveled baby shoes. They'd probably been calfskin or something similar, but now they were hard and dry as raisins.

"Well, Monday Tuesday an' Wednesday—it's you, Finchfather. Isn't it," said a voice, and they turned to see a man in the nearby trees. He wasn't a tall man, but he nonetheless appeared to be a sprightly, smartly dressed human.

Mick squinted. "Lusmore? By my baby teeth, it *is* you. Older, sure, but still alive, after all these years."

"It's thanks to all that fairy food an' drink I ate, plus all the gifts the Good Folk gave me," said Lusmore.

Scott gave Mick what he hoped was an appropriately what-the-heck? look.

"Exception that proves the rule," said Mick.

"How have you been, Finchfather?" asked Lusmore. "*Where* have you been? Is it true there's another Ireland out there, beyond the veil?"

"I'm going by Mick these days. This here's Scott, a changeling friend o' mine." Lusmore bowed. "An' there *is* another Ireland, an we're hopin' to speak with Her Majesty the High Queen abou' that. Yeh know where she can be found presently?"

Lusmore smiled. "Just so happens I do. It'll be nice to do yeh a favor, after all your people did for me."

"Oh, come now—we only paid yeh in kind for improvin' on that song we all had stuck in our heads. What's the story here?" Mick asked, hitching his thumb toward the cross atop his mound.

Lusmore gave the cross a sad smile. "The day you disappeared, she arrived. Just a wee babby, no aul' wan to care for her. The Good Folk tried to take her in, make a changeling of her, but yeh know how it is. Sometimes they don't thrive. They gave her a Christian burial, as they thought proper for one such as she."

"Baby Ann," whispered Mick. "Poor lass."

"Aye."

They took a moment. But then old Lusmore stepped up the mound.

"If yeh want to catch up to your queen, we'll have to move fast," he said. "Now Mick, yeh're lookin' as glamourous as the Lord's haircut, so I'll bet if yeh rummage through your things yeh'll happen to find two oilskin sacks just big enough for you an' your friend. 'Cause that's what yeh're going to need."

CHAPTER 23

It turned out Mick did have two such sacks in his mound, not to mention a fresh red tracksuit, which didn't even make any sense. They took the sacks and followed Lusmore through the wilderness.

"Hustle now," he said. "Not much time."

Their movement stirred all manner of creatures—unseen, but they rustled the underbrush. High above, the trees groaned and clicked, clicked, clicked, as if speaking to one another in their own language,

"Have ta admit," said Mick, "things have changed in the last hunnerd an' fifty years. The forests seem more built up, wilder."

"A lot has changed, an that's the truth," said Lusmore, and Scott thought he heard a grim note in the man's voice. "Now, while we walk we'll be lookin' for a particular plant. Weedy-lookin' thing, with little white flowers and fleshy leaves. Try not to touch any others."

"Any other whats?" asked Scott.

"Plants. Here's a helpful little song: Leaves o' one, turn an' run. Leaves o' two, not for you. Leaves o' three, leave it be. Leaves o' four, instant death. We used to have a better rhyme for that, but too many little ones were dying for the sake o' poetry. Leaves o' five—"

"And why are we looking for this plant?" asked Scott, trying to hold his arms as close as he could to his body.

"Right. So abou' sixty years ago Titania grew tired of moving her whole entourage from one castle to another all the time, season after season, so she asked the sorceress Queen Morgan le Fay to enchant the Tower o' London. She moved herself an' her whole retinue inside, an' now it just disappears from one place and pops up in the next, quick as yeh like."

"The whole thing?"

"Every last brick. Well, the whole White Tower, anyway. Ah! Here we are!"

Lusmore took a small knife from his belt and carefully cut a cluster of weeds free of the earth. Each had a spray of tiny white flowers. He handed them to Mick and Scott.

"Don't let the young one put these in his mouth."

Mick gave Scott a stern look, and Scott rolled his eyes. "So," he said, "the Tower of London is nearby?"

"*Was* nearby. She was just off the peninsula this

mornin', inspectin' the boundaries of the Gloria Wall.
Now she's up in Dub Linn."

"All respect, Lusmore," said Mick, "but this helps us
how? Dublin is two hundred miles away."

"Follow me into this meadow, an' all will be revealed."

Scott was noticing the first signs of a path, and a tall,
rough stone, standing upright, with symbols carved into
its face. An octagon and a moon. After another twenty
feet, there was another on the opposite side of the path,
with a moon and two stars. Then they broke through a
hedge and into a meadow, and there stood three ravens
the size of cement trucks.

"Woah," said Scott, taking a step back.

"Gentlemen," said Lusmore, "the famous ravens of the
Tower of London!"

The meadow narrowed to a wide stone wall, the ruins
of some old fortress. Here and there were more standing
stones, like jagged fingers reaching out of the earth. They
also bore carvings of spirals, moons, octagons, stars, a
crude dragon with outstretched wings. One prominent
stone showed two overlapping circles, bisected by a sharp
line. Mincing among these stones were the three blue-
black birds, their nightmare feet pulling up tufts of grass
and soil. Their beaks were clacking like gunshots. One
of them watched Scott and Mick and Lusmore with its

glassy black eye, followed them with brisk movements of its head.

"The famous what of what?" Scott whispered.

"The Tower o' London has always been famous for its ravens," said Mick. "For its *perfectly ordinary-sized ravens*," he added, glancing at Lusmore. "What's the story?"

"You know how spellcastin' can be," said Lusmore. "Unintended consequences. The ravens got caught in the edge o' Morgan's spell, became a part of it. Now yeh can't separate 'em. The ravens don't disappear along with the tower, but as soon as it's gone they pick up an' follow it. It's uncanny, but they always know where to find it."

Scott watched a fourth raven, just beyond the ruins of the stone wall, amble into view.

"Poor things have gotten fat an' stupid on all the magic they've been soakin' up over the years, though. They can only fly a short bit before they're knackered."

"So we capture one and ride it to Queen Titania's court," said Scott.

That wasn't the plan, but Lusmore made sure to let them know that he thought it was adorable.

Lusmore explained the actual plan, explained that people did it all the time, which was how Scott and Mick came to be hopping into the middle of a meadow, covered head to toe in oilskin sacks, while the Irishman shouted

to them from the trees that they needed to wiggle their bums more.

"I can't see," said Scott.

"That's probably for the best, don't yeh think?" asked Mick.

"You two are the most unappetizin' grubs I ever did see!" Lusmore called to them, distantly. "Wiggle it! Wiggle it!"

"Maybe this isn't any kind of plan at all," said Scott. "Maybe this is just a joke he plays on out-of-towners."

Then it happened. Scott couldn't see anything, but he was certain he was swallowed whole by a giant raven. He felt the lacquered black coffin of a beak snap around him with a thunderclap. He tipped up and slid back, and felt himself being forced in fits and starts down the creature's esophagus, then dropped down with a little splash into what science class had told him must be the stomach. A few seconds later he heard another splash beside him.

"Mick?"

"Yep."

Scott sighed and tried to breathe through his mouth.

"I'm glad we ended up inside the same bird."

"Aye."

It wasn't long before the flock took flight, and Scott sloshed around, trying to touch the oilskin sack as little as possible, doing his best to stay dry. He knew the sack was supposed to be waterproof, but he'd owned enough supposedly waterproof raincoats to know that the rain always won in the end. He tried to think about what he was going to say to Titania. Public speaking wasn't really his thing. He'd always hated oral reports in school.

Twice the ravens landed and rested, and took to the air again. Lusmore had instructed them that they wouldn't be at the tower until all the ravens cawed at once.

"Mick?"

"Yeah, lad?"

"I'm in a bird."

"I as well, boyo."

He listened to the raven's heartbeat for a while.

"Mick?"

"Still here."

"I'm supposed to be in the sixth grade."

"I know yeh are, son."

"I thought maybe everyone'd forgotten."

Finally they landed for the last time, and heard their raven crow, and the muffled croaks of six or seven other ravens join in chorus. That was the signal. Scott opened his Swiss Army knife and cut the tiniest slit he could in his sack, then pushed the plant with the little white flowers through the slit, into the raven's stomach. It took a second, but the stomach convulsed like a waterbed.

Here we go, thought Scott.

The raven pitched its neck out, *huck huck huck*, and then Mick and Scott spilled to the lawn in front of the Tower of London. Scott finished cutting open his sack and stepped out, hoping for a James-Bond-emerging-from-his-scuba-suit-in-full-tuxedo kind of impression, even though he had to admit it probably didn't look like that at all. Mick did the same. The raven left the scene out of general embarrassment.

They ran, just to get away from the birds, hugging the wall of the castle. It was gleaming even in the twilight of Pretannica, dripping whitewash. It wasn't a huge castle by any means, and Scott and Mick had quickly turned a corner and then another before pausing to calm their nerves.

Scott looked up at the White Tower. "We made it," he said with a swell of pride.

A strange voice said, "Aye, you did, recreants; now who are you?"

CHAPTER 24

Biggs finished sewing Emily a little lab coat covered with pockets, and he made her model it for him while he tried to whistle (couldn't) and clapped arrhythmically. She filled these pockets with all kinds of scientific equipment and devices—an oscilloscope, a laser pointer, concave and convex mirrors, spider-web bolometers for the measurement of the cosmic microwave background radiation; that sort of thing. One pocket alone held something fanciful and unscientific—the shamrock Mick had found in Pretannica—and this was to remind her that there might be limits to what she could learn through science. Even though she didn't really believe this. Even though she currently suspected that "magic" was just another kind of science, with rules she didn't understand yet.

The sheep minced about on their tethers. The adder

slithered around, possibly reasserting the borders of its narrowing territory. They'd all really disrupted the good thing the snake had going in this basement, and Emily wondered if it had eaten even once since their crew moved in. She felt sorry for it, but interested, too—the adder had hissed right before anyone or anything passed through the rift. As if it could see what Scott had seen—the shapes of both travelers merging, darkly, into one shape before they traded places. Emily never saw anything of the sort. To her, Mick would just be standing there one moment, and then the next, a fox. Or four humans, and then, the next moment, three sheep.

Not that she'd actually been in the room for that one. She hadn't actually *seen* it.

She'd been so certain that four humans would require four sheep. She thought as she sat down in front of the rift with Archimedes. *Maybe because Scott and Polly were smaller . . . ?*

"Oh, good," said Erno as he came down the stairs. "Biggs made you a mad scientist costume."

Emily stiffened. *"I'm not mad."*

Erno shuffled his feet. "I know. It was just—"

"You mean because of Mr. Wilson? Because he's crazy, and we were both taking the Milk? Is that what you were thinking?"

"Hey," said Erno, with his hands up. "You know I don't usually start thinking until I'm done talking."

Emily watched him tensely for a moment, then she sagged. "Sorry," she said, barely.

"What's up with you?" said Erno. "You've been chewing on my head for days."

"I'm not mad at you. I'm mad at Dad. Mr. Wilson."

"Well, I'm mad at him too," said Erno.

"Yeah, but you've been mad at him for years. You're better at it. Plus I'm mad that he's a coward, that he's hiding... I mean, yes, it's great he was obviously gathering all this secret information all these years and keeping it from Goodco, great that he's feeding it to us, but now he's letting a bunch of kids do all the dangerous stuff for him while he . . . nibbles chocolates in Switzerland or whatever."

"Why Switzerland?"

"That's where *I'd* go. And then I could tour the Large Hadron Collider near Geneva—"

"Is this why you hate me working on his new clue so much?" asked Erno.

Emily sighed. "Probably. I just don't even want to hear about it. I'm angry at a piece of paper. Proof I'm getting stupider."

One of the sheep made a sheep noise, which was just

the sound effect for a statement like that. Emily frowned at the sheep.

"Stupider or not, I swear I can still count," she said. "Four people needed four sheep. Someone didn't go through the rift."

Polly, Fi, and Harvey got to the Goodco factory in Slough easily enough after Harvey stole a taxicab.

"Itth not thtealing," the pooka explained. "They're public automobileth. Don't you thee them everywhere, those boxy black thingth? You take a free one, you leave it when you're finished for the next perthon. It'th a British thing."

Polly didn't feel like she was in a position to argue. After she'd learned they drove on the wrong side of the road here, she was prepared to believe anything.

Now they lay on their stomachs on a knoll at the edge of the Goodco parking lot, watching the entrance. Polly wished they had binoculars. And costumes.

"Okay," said Polly. "We sneak in, we find the pixies, we sneak out. Easy."

Nobody made any motion to do anything in particular.

"Might not even be in there anymore," Harvey offered. "Rumor wath alwayth that Goodco put pixthie in the Pufteeth."

"*Harvey!*"

"Jutht a little bit of pixthie, mind you, ground up. Pixthie dutht."

"You are a vulgar and hateful beast," Fi murmured.

The little hill was silent and chilly for a minute.

"The Goodco factory back home had groups of schoolkids going in and out a million times a day," Polly grumbled. "If only there was something like that, I could sneak in at the back."

Fi said, "I expect one of my size could enter quite easily alone."

"But then?" said Polly. "And please please please don't take this the wrong way? But you might have to climb some stairs. Or see what's on the top of a counter."

"Forsooth."

"And I'm worried about Harvey, too," said Polly. "I know he's invisible mostly, but they probably have some kind of fairy detection system."

"Oh, there wath never any chanth I wath going in there," Harvey answered.

Polly thought.

"All right. We're going for broke," she decided, not because there wasn't time to plan but more because she was seven years old and impatient. "Forget sneakiness. They're gonna take us right inside themselves."

● ○ ★

And that was how Polly came to walk right past the man at the front desk in the lobby of the U.K. headquarters of Goodco, trying to summon real tears to her eyes. She thought of Grandma Peggy. And when that didn't work, she remembered the giraffe at the zoo that died because a volunteer accidentally fed it oleander. At this she sniffed and felt her eyes well up. *Sorry, Grandma Peggy*, she thought.

The front-desk man got up to follow her, as she expected him to. He bent at the waist and rested his hands on his knees, his face immediately coloring from the effort. "Um, hello? Little girl? I'm sorry, can I help you? Are you looking for someone?" He was an older man, a grandfatherly type, just the sort Polly thought she could handle. He looked like he didn't get a lot of unaccompanied children through here, which was fine.

She turned, and the sweet, earnest look on his face was the perfect thing to really get her tears flowing. "It was supposed to be a secret," she bawled.

"What was, love?" said the guard, glancing over his shoulder, trying to watch his desk and be a hero at the same time.

"My dad couldn't find anyone to babysit me, so my dad's new girlfriend brought me into work here and said don't touch anything and don't go anywhere, but I just wanted to look around and now? I got lost and I can't find my way back." She sucked a snotty breath. She hoped nobody was taping this.

The man relaxed his shoulders and smiled. "That's fine. Just tell me your . . . da's girlfriend's name, then, and I'll have her come get you—"

"NO! No, she said if anyone saw me I couldn't say who brought me or she'd get in trouble, she works in some secret part."

"Well, I think you'd better tell me now—"

"I won't. She'll get mad. Don't make me."

The guard straightened, steadied himself, gathered his features together to regroup.

"I don't know the name of her department," Polly offered, because things weren't moving along as quickly as she would have liked, "but she says it's the one 'with all the bloody pixies.'"

"Bloody pixies . . . ," the man repeated foggily. This obviously wasn't ringing any bells, but at least it suggested a course of action. "You just come back to my desk here, while I call Ms. Aleister. She'll know where to take you." He made the call.

"Ms. Aleister, this is Henry at the front. Yes, ma'am, I do think it's important. I have a little girl here who came in with one of the employees, and now she's lost. No ma'am, she won't say which one. No ma'am, she won't say which department, but she says it's the one with the 'bloody pixies'? Does that mean anything to you?"

Henry the guard flinched and turned off his earpiece. "She said she'd be right down. So." He offered Polly a little brown lump of something from a bag. "Would you like one of my candy lozenges? They taste like horehound."

CHAPTER 25

"Wow, look at it," said John. "Just look at it!"

"Stop telling me to look at it," said Merle. He paused to push some nettles away from his face. "I get it. Pretannica is very pretty. I imagine your slight elfishness is making it all extra sparkly for you."

"How do you know where we're going, by the way? Emily said compasses won't work here, and there aren't any stars or sun to navigate by."

"I'm mostly just heading toward that gap in the trees. Finchbriton, can you fly up high, tell me if there's a lake in that direction? Lough Leane ought to be near here."

"Lough Leane?"

"Really big lake."

Finchbriton scouted up above the trees and returned a minute later, alighting on a low branch before the men.

He twittered back his report, and John and Merle stared at him.

"I've just realized I have no idea what that means," said Merle.

"Mick always seems to kind of understand him," said John.

"Mick has known him for a thousand years."

Finchbriton lowed kind of an annoyed whistle and flew to another branch farther along the same path.

"I think that means we're doing all right," said Merle. "Follow the bird."

A light rain began to fall. Just as John was about to remark that this seemed unusual, as there were nothing but the thinnest whispers of clouds in the sky, he noticed that it did not appear to be raining at all a hundred feet ahead of them, nor a hundred feet behind.

"Hard not to take that personally," he muttered, and pulled his hood up. The trail, if indeed they were even on a trail, dipped into a deeply ferny patch surrounded by young trees. "So . . . we're hiking to this big lake . . . why? I think England is technically in the opposite direction."

"I'm hoping for a shortcut," said Merle, hunching up his shoulders against the rain. "Something the Lady of the Lake told me once, back when we were friendly, or pretending to be friendly. She said, 'All lakes are one lake in my kingdom.' She could sink beneath the waves of one lake and break the surface of another, a hundred miles away. In no time at all."

John waited politely for Merle to explain why this was relevant, but the old man started whistling, so he found it necessary to reopen the conversation.

"Okay, what?"

"We're gonna try to travel from one lake directly to another, in Avalon," said Merle. "Use Nimue's magic against her. Nice, huh?"

Finchbriton chirped something that sounded ruffled and complicated.

"I think I agree with that, even if I couldn't understand the words," said John. "None of us are spellcasters like Nimue. It can't be as easy as just dunking your head underwater and saying, 'Avalon, please,' like a taxi. Can it?"

The bird whistled his agreement.

"Look—I have some small idea of what we might find at Lough Leane," said Merle. "But if I'm wrong, it's only a few miles out of our way. A few extra miles never killed anybody."

"The miles won't," whispered a voice from the underbrush, "but the Hairy Men might, yeh thick idjits! Hide!"

John ducked slightly to look for the source of this new voice and felt a smooth stone whiz past his ear. It shattered against a nearby boulder and resounded like a firecracker. This was followed by a screech, a monkey-house kind of sound.

John pulled his backpack up over his head. "Under the boulders! Quickly!"

He and Merle and Finchbriton dove for cover as the air filled with stones and shrieks, an angry rain, and little hairy men made themselves visible on the high limbs of trees. They were all lean and wild maned, bearded and bigmouthed, maybe eighteen inches tall and wearing only the poor memories of outfits. They chattered to one another in their own language and hurled stone after stone from little leather slings. All around were thuds and cracks.

John slid under one particular boulder, only to find it occupied.

"Oi!" said a small (but nonetheless obviously human) man. "Get your own!"

"Oh, excellent," said a nearby voice, a woman's. "They have gotten the Hairy Men to resume slinging their stones. I was just wondering to meself, *Have they any more stones?* And now, happily, I have my answer."

"Merle!" said John. "Finchbriton! You all right?"

"Not dead," said Merle from beneath a nearby boulder. Finchbriton whistled.

"Your mate there's under a rock," the small man told

John. "Why don't yeh go share wi' him?"

Stones ricocheted off the ground and struck John's side—not terribly hard, but he expected he'd bruise. "There's room for us both," he said, just as the forest grew quiet. "They've stopped. Is that good or bad?"

"Probably just pausin' to gather more stones," said the woman. "They can keep this up long as yeh like."

"Where are you?" called John.

"In the shrubbery, under a shield."

"You have a shield . . . ," John said to himself.

The rain was letting up already, but still it was trickling down into the crevices beneath the boulders where they hid and pooling in uncomfortable places.

Merle was peering out from his hiding spot. "Are those . . . maybe this is a stupid question, but are those *brownies?*"

"Course they're brownies! Hairy Men!" said the woman. "What've I been sayin'?"

One of the stone-collecting brownies, on the ground, approached John's boulder and slung a little spear down off its back. It bared its thick teeth and leaned forward, gave John and his roommate a good look at its fierce face, its flea-peppered mane of yellow dreads.

"EEEEEEEEEK," it said. "Wuh-WEEEEEEEEEK!" Then it commenced to trying to poke some part of John that John wasn't covering with his backpack. Other brownies gathered to watch and holler encouragement.

John anticipated one of the brownie's lunges and grabbed the spear himself, wrenching it from the hairy little man's grip. "HA!" he said. Then he spun it around and started poking back.

"REEEEEEEEEEEK!" the brownie answered, and retreated to a safe distance with its fellows. Then they started hurling rocks again.

"Oh!" said the small man. "Ow! Beautiful!" John wriggled between the man and the barrage, tried to block as much of it as he could. Then there was a whistling, and a burst of blue flame surged past them, sending the brownies hooting and scrambling for the trees. Before long the rain of stones began again, but from above.

"Thank you, Finchbriton!" called John. "You stay under cover, though! I know you're a small target, but just one hit and you're done for! Merle! I don't suppose your wand—"

"Works on this bunch? Nope, like I said—only humans."

"Right. I'm going to try something. Madam? Hello?"

"Are yeh talking to me?" asked the woman in the bushes.

"I was," said John. He paused. "Is there anyone *else* hiding nearby?"

"Just me an' my husband an' my babby."

"Your baby is here? Where is it?"

"Oh, toddlin' 'round about someplace SHE'S RIGHT HERE WI' ME, WHERE DO YEH THINK SHE IS?"

"All right, all right," said John. "Um. Well. That makes this next part harder to ask, but . . . can I borrow your shield?"

"So it wasn't so hard when yeh thought yeh were just askin' for the only means o' protection from a helpless woman, is that right?"

"I will get you to shelter with your husband. But I'll need your shield to fight the Hairy Men."

"Let 'im have it," said the husband. "The Hairy Men won't be satisfied till they've killed a human. Maybe after this one's dead they'll bugger off."

"That's some beautiful gratitude, right there," said Merle from his rock. "If I had a pen I'd write that down."

"Finchbriton!" called John. "A little cover?"

So another plume of especially smoky fire issued forth, and when the brownies paused in their barrage to watch, John ran just behind it and into the bushes. There he found a slight young woman curled up under a battered metal shield painted with a weathered and fading image of a chickadee. She clutched what was perhaps a six-month-old baby to her chest. The baby, apparently used to this sort of thing, was fast asleep.

John huddled down beside them both.

"Hullo," he said. "I'm John."

"Clara Tanner. Oo, yeh're a nice-lookin' one."

"Soon to be dead, though!" her husband reminded her from his rock. "Terrible shame."

"Ready?" asked John, and Clara nodded. "Finchbriton?"

The finch sent out another screen of fire and smoke. But the brownies, despite their mook behavior and monkey chatter, weren't entirely stupid. When they saw the flames again, they rained missiles down even harder, and John did his best to protect what the shield could not as he brought mother and baby back underneath the far side of the boulder. They were nearly home when a stone creased his temple.

"AAH! SSSSS!" he hissed, and pushed all three of them to safety. They curled close in the mud and moss. Clara examined the cut.

"Oo, it's a bleeder—head wounds always are—but yeh'll be all right. Here." She touched at it tenderly, then removed her scarf and tied it around John's forehead.

"Do I look like a pirate?"

"I don't know what that is."

"Enough pillow talk!" said the husband. "Why, I'd almost think yeh're stallin'! Do yeh want to go die or don't yeh?"

"You sure about this?" called Merle.

273

"Never ask me if I'm sure about anything! Finchbriton! Want to come along?"

John launched into the fray, sword drawn, with Finchbriton clinging to his jacket front behind the chickadee shield. Stones clanged noisily off it.

The brownies were concentrated in two trees—a lean-trunked one rather close to John and a taller, stouter one farther away. He aimed his shield at the far tree and hugged close to the leaner one, even using it for cover and frustrating the Hairy Men up above. With John standing almost directly below them, the tree's own thick head of branches got in the way of many of their stones, and the brownies in the lowest branches were now in danger from wayward shots flying across the gully.

There was a lot of angry chatter. A couple brownies threatened to drop down on top of them until Finchbriton sent hot little balloons up at each, and they retreated, singed and barking.

John wasn't sure he could even swing his sword at a brownie—they looked too human, despite everything. But he did start hacking at the trunk of the tree, intending to topple the whole business. The brownies gibbered and yelped. The tree quivered. The tree quivered more than it should have, maybe.

The tree, possibly tired of being hacked at and pelted with stones and filled with tiny hairy people, sprang to life. John leaped away, and Finchbriton flew free. The tree snapped a root from the earth like a tentacle and gave John an uppercut that he only partially managed to absorb with the chickadee shield. He landed hard on his back and looked up to see a spindly fist of branches swinging down at him. He rolled and turned, just as he had done on the set of *Galileo's Revenge*, and carved a few twig-fingers from the fist. Then Finchbriton fluttered in and set the rest ablaze.

The tree pulled back, creaking and groaning, and shook itself like a dog, joggling the some twenty Hairy Men still camped in its branches. Then it plucked one of these Hairy Men free like an apple and chucked it at John.

"WAAAAH!" The brownie whanged off John's shield and landed in a wad a few feet away, then crawled off. After a moment the tree found another brownie and did it again.

"WAAAAH!" (*whang*)

"Stop that!" said John.

"WAAAAAAH!" (*whang*)

The tree hadn't forgotten that the other brownies in the far tree had been pelting it with stones, so it started flinging Hairy Men at them, too. Soon all the brownies were decamping quickly, some of them simply falling straight into the underbrush, and scattering in all directions.

The tree had a few more roots up now and was trying to get ambulatory. Finchbriton set another woody arm alight, which the tree tried to smother in the ferns.

At this John leaped forward and finished the job he'd started—he chopped the trunk from its root system, then went about pruning whatever moved until the tree finally collapsed in the ditch and was still.

John's arms fell limply to his sides. He was dripping sweat.

"Well," he breathed as Finchbriton perched close to his ear. "That was just the *worst*."

Another tree across the gully, seeing what had happened to the first one, uprooted itself and ran off into the bushes.

"Yeh've saved us!" said Clara, and she ran to John, still holding the baby. "This is Mab. My worthless husband is Alfie Skinner."

John pulled his hood back, shook hands with Alfie.

"We were takin' furs in our donkey cart to Agora," said Alfie. "They killed our donkey, chased us down here."

Merle had emerged and stepped over to a brownie that was lying on its back among the ferns. He poked it with his boot.

"Wuuuuuh," moaned the brownie, and it took a halfhearted swipe at Merle with its hand. "Wuh."

"Yeh can keep the shield," said Clara, bouncing the

baby, which had now, just *now*, awakened and started to cry. "I know it isn't much, but it was my da's. I painted that chickadee on it when I was a girl."

"Thank you. It's a good shield."

"I don't believe it," said Merle now as he joined them. "Brownies! They used to be the gentlest of the Fay. Clean-cut, hardworking. They lived in human homes! Did chores for the humans at night when no one was looking."

Clara pulled baby Mab away from Merle a bit and made a face. "Mister, maybe yeh're older than yeh look, but my *granddad* told me stories abou' the Hairy Men." She spat on the ground. "Only help they offer roun' the house is givin' folks fewer mouths to feed."

Merle raised his hands. "Hey, I didn't mean anything by it. Things are just . . . different here than I expected. I'm from very far away."

Clara squinted. "Mister, there's no such place."

John thought it best to interject. "It's probably unsafe to hang about, isn't it? Perhaps we can walk together as far as Lough Leane?"

At the sound of his voice Clara beamed again, and John thought he saw Alfie roll his eyes. "We'll tell everyone what yeh did for us here," she said. "Oo, an' I'll be so proud to tell them yeh're carryin' my da's shield. Folks might even start callin' yeh the Chickadee!"

"It would be all right if they didn't call me that."

CHAPTER 26

Scott and Mick turned to see a dark-skinned, black-haired teen, holding a bow and arrow at the ready. A company of four other beautiful youths were behind him, each with a stylish and richly appointed outfit, each with his own favored weapon. They were the boy band of assassins.

Mick stepped forward. "Well met, young blood. Your reputation precedes you—I believe yeh are Dhanu, most favored changeling of our High Queen—"

"And charged as captain of her Changeling Guard."
(said Dhanu.)
"Alas, I asked you two for your own names,
Sirrah, Sir Runt. I'm freshly vers'd in mine."

Mick looked snookered. "Right. Sorry. I go by Mick,

an' . . . um, I am a full an' trusty member of the Seelie Court, leprechaun in good standing, Crest of Ór. As such, I request safe conduct for myself an' my compatriot here, Scott, a changeling from parts distant."

At this Dhanu took renewed interest in Scott.

"An' Scott an' I both crave audience with our High Queen, as is the right of all with Fay blood, at least once in our happy lives. I'll be obliged, of course, to furnish my True Name whensoever—"

Dhanu, his bow relaxed, raised a hand and stepped uncomfortably close to Scott.

"You cannot be but human. What fairy
Nursery tended this, such fusty fruit?"

"Come now," said Mick, "He—"

"Speaks, yes? If not to me, how to a queen?"

"I was born to humans," said Scott. "I was raised by humans. But my dad and I have fairy blood."

Dhanu looked Scott up and down at this and curled his lip.

"You have but drops of fairy blood in you,
And smell as like the inside of a crow."

As insults go, this was so close to accurate that Scott thought it would be petty to tell him it had been a raven.

"I'm . . . pretty ordinary," he agreed. He looked at these changelings, carrying themselves with red-carpet grace. He thought he was right in assuming they were all human, but a lifetime of fostering in the fairy court had given them a kind of ageless glamour. Still, they were human, and he was not—not entirely. "You need us in a way, don't you," he added, realizing something. "Us ordinary ones. Without us, someone else would have to be ordinary."

Dhanu glowered at him a moment. Then his eyes changed. They didn't soften, exactly, but they looked like a pair of eyes Scott might be able to work with. Like he and one of the popular kids had been grouped together on a science fair project and it would all be over soon. Dhanu turned without a word and motioned for Mick and Scott to follow.

"He's kind of hard to talk to," whispered Scott.

"Man, it's this courtly speech," said Mick. "I don't think I can pull it off anymore. It's been too long, an' I was never very good at it anyway." He pointed at Scott. "Don't yeh even try it. Jes' be polite, an' don't put on any airs."

They walked along the castle wall. Scott liked the

Tower of London. This was the castle a child would design: a white stone box, buttoned with arched windows, topped by a toothy parapet, braced at each corner by a tall tower. It lacked only a drawbridge and a moat. They passed an ogre diligently whitewashing one side with brush and bucket.

Then they turned a final corner, and Scott saw where the Fay had concentrated their improvements. The front facade of the Tower was whitewashed like the rest, but the gaps between every stone sprouted mushrooms, wild rose, clover and foxglove and bluebells and ivy. And here and there the fungi and flowers themselves had been trained to form signs and symbols: the now-familiar stars and moons and octagons that Scott could not help but see rendered in marshmallow and floating in milk. Cracks in the masonry had begun to form—nature was having its way. Eventually the elves would tear down their own castle for beauty.

There was still no drawbridge, no moat, but the main castle doors here were twenty feet off the ground. And emblazoned on these doors was another symbol, of two overlapping circles or spheres, split in two by a line.

"I've been seeing that a lot lately," said Scott.

"*It came to fair Titania in dreams,*" answered Dhanu.

Towering giants stood to either side of these doors,

stripped tree trunks in the grips of their long bare limbs, their belts hung with the tackle of their villainous, storybook lives—skulls, knives, the spine and rib cage of something or other, a lot of iron horseshoes that had been twisted together on chains. Scott thought the Fay weren't supposed to like iron; but then he thought it might be like a tongue piercing—something unpleasant the big kids did to show what they were capable of.

He caught his breath. He supposed the only way up to that door was to have one of these bald-headed, snaggletoothed giants lift you up to it, and he suddenly felt a depth of sympathy for Fi that never would have occurred to him otherwise. But instead Dhanu whistled, and stout vines grew down from the castle door, weaving and intertwining so that when they'd reached the ground they'd formed a grand staircase. Roses bloomed as they climbed.

"'S that you, Cuhullin?" Mick asked the giant on the left when they were at the level of his waist. "How's the wife?"

The giant didn't answer.

"Ah, sometimes I think the Old Mother should have given giants a set o' ears on their ankles," Mick said. "I asked—"

"Not supposed to speak to you, Finchfather," said Cuhullin.

Mick frowned. "Not supposed to speak on the job, or not supposed to speak to me person'ly?"

Still the giant didn't answer.

The doors were open. Dhanu said,

> "So now the stage is set, and it is seen
> How churl and chaff assay to sway a queen."

CHAPTER 27

Near the lake John and Merle parted company with Clara and Alfie and Mab.

"Fare thee well, Chickadee," said Clara with a girlish smile.

John couldn't help twitching a little. "We're definitely calling me that, then?" he asked.

"Chickadee is another name for Titmouse," said Merle. "We could call you Titmouse."

"Chickadee's fine," said John.

They watched the little family disappear, then proceeded down to the water's edge. When Merle saw movement, they paused and concealed themselves behind a copse of trees. Finchbriton hopped nervously back and forth on John's shoulder.

Mermaids.

"Ah," whispered Merle. "If only I were fifty years younger."

"Seriously?" murmured John. He squinted to see better, but he didn't think it helped.

Lough Leane was vast and electric blue, reflecting the dwindling light of the sky above. Down past the rushes the lake met the land, and there were a handful of low, wide stones lapped smooth by water. Lounging on these stones were the mermaids.

John supposed they might be pretty. But like so many things that are meant to be seen in the water, they looked stringy and colorless when out of it. Like seaweed drying on a beach. Their top halves were pasty and bare apart from whatever their lanky hair covered. Their bottom halves looked like low tide. There was a distinct pet-store sort of smell wafting up from the lake.

One thing that really surprised him: nearly all of them were wearing hats. Red silk pointed caps. Those that weren't had red silk capes. A few had both.

"Merrows," said Merle. "A sort of Irish mermaid. With so much of the seas disappeared here, I was hoping they might be hanging out in the lakes. The females are all honeys but the males are all hideously ugly, so they tend to be partial to human men. I'd been thinking we'd have to steal a couple of their caps, but the way that Clara was going goo-goo for you reminded me that I'm traveling with *People* magazine's Sexiest Man Alive for 2010."

"I'm embarrassed for you that you know that. And what about these caps?"

"Don't ask me why, but without one of those caps or capes they can't dive beneath the water. But if we get a couple of them, we can go *SHOOM!* down to the bottom of the lake like rockets. Once we're at the bottom I'm pretty sure we'll find a door, a door that'll take us to any lake we want. So how about sweet-talking those gals out of a coupla hats?"

John sighed and prepared. He couldn't merely be a man who wanted some hats. He needed to be a man who loved fish women. He had to believe this. If he loved them, they would love him. They would *want* to give him their hats. He massaged his temples and searched his past for any and all fish affection he could think of. He'd had a goldfish as a boy, that was something, wasn't it? He'd always enjoyed films about people helping whales be free. As a teenager he'd practically *lived* on fish and chips.

"What are you doing?" asked Merle.

"I'm getting into character!" John answered through gritted teeth. "Okay, fine. Fine. Okay. Here I go."

He breathed and stepped down the mucky bank.

The merrow women flinched, and one moved as if to dive into the water. But John walked with his arms wide, hands open, his face a beatific Get Well Soon card to the universe.

"What treasures!" he said, and beamed them a smile that could be seen from space. "What treasures have washed ashore! And here I thought one had to dive to find pearls."

The merrows exchanged glances. None of them said anything in return, but neither did they swim away, even as John drew slowly closer. One smiled, shyly. A second even giggled. All of them began to fuss in some way with their hair, pushing it back behind their webbed ears or combing it with their clamshell fingernails.

"Ladies." John went down on one knee in the mud and bowed his head. Then he raised it slightly, looked up at each of them with lifted brow, did that thing where his jaw muscles clenched just a little like he had to bite down to keep from crying for joy to the heavens and so forth. All the stuff he'd perfected the year he'd done the Australian soap opera. Now the merrows were all grinning, and one of them made sort of a dolphin noise.

"What . . . what is your name, landsman?" asked one of the merrows.

"I am John. I travel with my elderly and mute and also unfortunately simpleminded father, who rests not far off. And you are of course right to call me a landsman, though I long to explore the beauty of the deep waters

of the lakes of the world."

"*Aw,*" said another merrow.

He wasn't using contractions all of a sudden, thought John. Why wasn't he using contractions? "Is it beautiful, beneath the waves? Tell me, please, so that I may describe it to my brainless and often gassy father."

"Hey!" came a faint shout from the trees. The merrows craned their necks to look until John did sort of a puckery thing with his lips and got them to refocus. So they told him about the inky blue beauty of their home, the easy rhythms of the water weeds and grasses, the corals and sponges that had tumbled in centuries ago, afire with magic they'd absorbed from the Gloria Wall. They told him of the sea monster in Scotland that never left its cave because it didn't believe in itself. They described the silver schools of fish that moved like one body and arranged themselves, just twice a year, into arcane symbols that none could decipher. They told him which fish they thought were stuck up and which ones could be really popular if they weren't always camouflaging themselves all the time.

John listened patiently, nodding, hoping one of the merrows would get around to suggesting what he wanted, all on her own. And indeed, eventually one said, "You know, I have a spare cap in my grotto. I could make a gift of it to you—then you could see these splendors with your own eyes!" She gasped as if she'd surprised herself.

John pretended to really perk up at this. Could he really? One of the merrows with both cap and cape pointed out that *she* really only needed one or the other, so she could give John the hat right off her head. A small squabble erupted over who would give him what. In the midst of this, he sighed heavily and turned all their heads.

"What is it?" said a merrow. "What ails you?"

"Oh . . . just . . . any experience beneath the waves would be a hollow one if I could not share it with my halfwit father, who is not long for this world."

So it was quickly decided that John would be given not one but *two* caps, and also an enchanted comb made from a conch shell. When pressed, the merrow who'd given the comb admitted that it wasn't so much *magic* as it was merely the only thing she'd had on her person at the moment, but John thanked her extravagantly anyway. Then he brought Merle out ("Oh, he's just as you described," said one merrow), and they took up places by the water.

"Where's Finchbriton?" whispered John.

"Zippered up inside my bag."

"Are these bags waterproof?"

"'Bout to find out. But he's in the ziplock with the flare gun."

"We'd better hurry, then."

John blew kisses to the merrows, which they made a great show of pretending to catch in their webbed hands and then devour, noisily. It was disturbing.

The men put on their caps. "So what do we do, exactly?" asked John.

"Okay, I think . . . I think this door, if there is a door, will be right in the middle of the lake," said Merle. "So I think we have to, like, dive in, and if we *think* about the middle of the bottom of the lake, then I think the caps will take us there. And then we find the door, and I think we have to *think* about where we want it to take us, and then we open it and *bam!* We're there."

"Do you know what word I noticed a lot of in that plan?"

"Relax. What do people say in your movies? 'It'll work. It *has* to.' Plans always work after the character says that."

"Do we have to hold our breath with the caps on?"

"Better hold it just to be safe."

"On three?"

One, two, three, and then they breathed, and dove.

CHAPTER 28

John's head surfaced first, then Merle's. Each gasped for air, then Merle scrambled up this new shore as quickly as his old joints would allow and unzipped his bag, then the ziplock. Finchbriton fluttered out, drowsily. He landed a few feet away and fluffed himself.

They looked at the marsh around them, the shroud of mist, the bandy-rooted and bare-limbed trees like the taut-skinned mummies of things that had tried to struggle free from the mire. Frogs chirped and croaked. The air smelled like rotten apples.

"Avalon," said John. "Mick said this place was supposed to be nice."

The plan with the caps had worked better than it had any right to. As soon as they'd hit water their bodies had been whisked downward, spiraling through a flurry of bubbles, to the bottom of the lake. The whole trip took all of two seconds, and that was fine—had it been slower, or had there been fewer bubbles, John and Merle might have been aware of all the colossal eels, or the one merrow who was as large as a submarine, or the fish with the pincushion teeth, or even the moment when their trajectory actually took them *through* the coils of a sea serpent and past its jagged jaws.

But they'd had no idea. They reached bottom, squinted about through the murk for an exit while entirely failing to notice the octoclops barreling down on them, swam over to a pearly door set into a tall stone amidst the weeds, and stepped through, thinking, *Avalon.*

"Well," said Merle, looking at Avalon now. "I haven't been *here* in a long time. Not properly."

They scuttled up to a felled tree and crouched in among the roots. John couldn't help looking at most trees a little suspiciously ever since one had tried to kill him, so a dead specimen like this was sort of a comfort.

He wondered if it was the gloom of this place or merely the fact that the two of them were dripping swamp water that made Merle shiver just then.

"First time I came to Avalon was also the first time I met Nimue, actually," the old man said as he twisted around to survey the island, the sweep of the hill dotted here and there by stones and caves. Dreary as it was, at least he could get his bearings. The place he'd visited in

Somerset back on earth had barely looked anything like this. "It was one of Arthur's early misadventures. He'd gotten himself wounded and his sword broken fighting this enormous knight named Pellinore."

"This was before Arthur was king?"

"Nah, he was king already."

"Why was he fighting Pellinore, then?" asked John.

"Oh, the usual. I don't remember the specifics. A squire or a damsel rushes into the great hall of the king to tattle on some bad knight who's knocking down other knights and taking their lunch money. So the king . . . does what? Tries him in court? 'Course not. One guy goes out to beat him up. Maybe kill him. No talking, no trying to reason with anyone. Just the juvenile belief that the guy who gets beaten somehow lost the argument. Whoever wins the fight is right, and whoever's right wins the fight. I tried to point out that whoever wins the fight might just be lucky or do more push-ups than the other guy, but I never got a lot of traction with that.

"Anyway, the first guy Arthur sends to fight Pellinore doesn't do so hot, so Arthur sneaks off to fight Pellinore himself. And does pretty well, but eventually he's going to die if I don't rush in and put Pellinore to sleep."

"And no one ever thinks to send, like, a posse out?" asks John. "A proper police arrest?"

"Please. It was like high school with swords. All the

cool kids, the rich kids, sitting at the big round cool kids'
table. Acting like the serfs don't exist. Racing around,
playing chicken with spears. Every one of them with some
tragic, heroic opinion of himself. It was the adolescence
of man."

"Was it really as bad as all that?" said John. "Didn't
Arthur bring law and order to England or something?"

"Oh, sure, mostly. It was *much* worse before Arthur
came along. Arthur practically invented chivalry. Honor,
and protection of the weak. Each noble knight must be
willing to lay down his life in service to those less fortunate
than himself. Funny how they still managed to almost
completely ignore all the farmers and poor people, though."

On all the island there was only one footpath that
looked well worn, and it led up to a vault of granite that
protected a shaft into the hillside. Merle and John and
Finchbriton scrambled closer and staked it out over the
edge of a shelf of stones.

"So what does Pellinore and all this have to do with
Nimue and Avalon?" whispered John.

"Well, I take Arthur away to heal up at an abbey, and
remember, his sword is broken. So I know this is the time
in the story where I take him to a particular lake and a
particular lady offers him a new one."

"Oh, right."

● ○ ★

They traveled, Arthur and Merlin, like pilgrims to the lake of Avalon. It looked much sweeter then, but no less mysterious. Mists still hung low and thick as carded wool, but these were often spun by sunlight into brightly colored tissue that robed the island like a fine mantle.

And in the water they saw a milk-white arm, around which was wrapped the band of a scabbard, and the hand of which held the finest sword ever forged by man or fairy.

Arthur inhaled sharply. "I would give my kingdom for such a sword," he said.

"Jeez," said Merle. "Keep your voice down. Somebody might hold you to that."

"The sword Excalibur," spoke someone new, and they found they'd been joined on the shore by a stunning young woman with hair like a moonless sky. It seemed to

please her that this hair be still, but that her pallid gown sailed and slipped on a breeze that touched no other nearby thing. "Do you like it?"

"I like it very well," Arthur answered, "and I would bring much worship to the Isle of Avalon, were I allowed to wield it in your name."

"Hmm," said Nimue, and she poked out her lip. "But if I give you my sword, I'm left just a lake with an empty arm in it. You see my predicament."

"I vow I shall return it to this lake before I die, lady."

"See that you do," said the Lady of the Lake, and just then a small boat drifted to shore through the mists.

While it took Arthur to the arm and Excalibur, Merle stayed with the lady and looked her over. Unless he'd misread the stories, this was the woman who would one day pretend to be his girlfriend and trap him in a cave under the earth. Well, she was a looker, so he could think of worse things.

"Your name's Nimue, right?"

"And you are Merlin," said Nimue. "I've been following your career for some time."

"I'm flattered. So what's your game here? Giving Arthur a free sword? And I know you've been raising Lancelot, and that you're gonna send him to be one of Arthur's knights. His *greatest* knight, a good man, and yet more than anything, it's Lance that's going to end up tearing the kingdom apart."

"Ah, yes," Nimue purred. "This fantastic gift you have for foresight. We Fay get the odd flash now and then, you know—but nothing like this talent of yours. You really must tell me one day how you accomplish it. You *must*."

Arthur was just now returning with sword and scabbard, trying to look solemn and dignified when you could tell what he really wanted to do was swing his new toy around and stab trees. And it was best that they get out of there before Merle said something stupid. He never had learned how to talk to girls. They bowed and said their good-byes, and turned toward Camelot.

"So, uh . . . which do you like better?" Merle asked Arthur later. "The sword or its scabbard?"

The young king examined them both. The scabbard was golden, inlaid with silver and stones. Very nice. But the sword was magnificent. "The sword," said Arthur.

"You should like the scabbard, actually. 'Cause anyone who wears it will never bleed, no matter how badly he's cut."

Arthur was impressed. "The sword cleaves, the scabbard protects."

"Yeah. Really—don't lose the scabbard," Merle told him, knowing he would, knowing that story was already written.

John and Merle and Finchbriton dashed to the vaulted entrance of the mine. They couldn't hear anything, couldn't see any signs of life, so there was nothing for it but to plunge downward. The shaft was dimly lit, though there were no visible sources of light. The tunnel was wide enough for four men to walk abreast, and only about seven feet tall, which was itself a kind of relief—the low ceiling really cut down on the variety of Fay that could be coming and going through here.

At the end the tunnel forked, and they heard a sharp voice approaching from the right, so they ducked into the tunnel on the left. They watched as a scarlet-cloaked and hooded woman emerged, flanked by tiny figures in robes, and continued up the main corridor to the cave entrance.

". . . *you* try to tell the largest dragon in all the isles what she can and can't eat. I say, 'Saxbriton, do you want to stay *cooped up* in this mountain till *YOU DIE,* or do you want to slim down to whale weight and go conquer the universe?' Stupid!"

"MAH," said one of the little robed people.

"Right. Whatever. Anyway, she's an angel for two or three weeks and then she gets depressed and eats a whole orphanage."

When these Fay were out of earshot, John and Merle and Finchbriton stole into the tunnel from which they'd come and followed it into a small chamber made up like a proper bedroom. Oil lamps, chairs with poufy cushions, a lion tapestry on one wall. And asleep on a bed in the center of the room, the Queen of England.

"Huh," said Merle.

"Huh," John agreed. "So. Did you think she was going to look like *that?*"

CHAPTER 29

Scott could see the elves trying to size him up as he passed through the wide hall—who was this stranger with the leprechaun, in the company of Titania's most favorite? Was he changeling or human? They'd appraise his clothes, his glamour (or lack of it), and have a flustered little moment of panic. Had they miscalculated? Was boring the new interesting? Were they all to look like smelly highwaymen now? No, they dismissed their fear finally with a wave. The boy was just some charity case.

"Is that the Finchfather?" said one, a tall elf whose hairline grew birch-wood saplings. He and his compatriot kept pace with the party as it walked.

> *"Methinks it is.*
> *Must this one then beside him be the finch?"*

"Does yonder one resemble selfsame finch?"

"Well, sure I am 'tis not impossible.
Perhaps in time a finch becomes a boy.
Forsooth a finch was not a finch at first—
But does the bird resemble then the egg?
Do crops bear semblance to the excrement
From which they bloom? What majesty might grow
up from the filth that presently walks past!"

The elves enjoyed their joke and shared it with whomever would listen.

"Jester tryouts today?" Mick grumbled.

Scott leaned over to Mick. "Did the tall one just call me poop?"

He wondered if it was magic or just nerves that made this hallway seem longer on the inside than it looked on the outside. They passed winged sprites that flitted about like hummingbirds; dwarfs and gnomes; Scandinavian trolls like bent tubers, massive and shaggy with roots; a rail-thin Hindu who kept his head in a birdcage and fed it apple; a woman made entirely of flowers and leaves that reminded Scott of something awful Emily had done to a Freeman a few months ago; a fairy who was like a well-dressed man with the head of a goat; another Scott would have liked to have called a well-dressed goat with

the head of a man, though in fairness it was really more of a fawn; a column of smoke that Scott assumed was a column of smoke until Dhanu paused to bow to it before passing. Each of these persons and others gave the impression of having had nothing to talk about for the last thousand years, so they seemed glad to see Mick and Scott happen by.

Then Scott and Mick and their changeling escorts reached a pair of intricately carved doors that opened on their own, bleeding light, and they stepped inside the throne room of the High Queen of the Fay.

It was like a chapel, a cathedral, with a dark colonnade to the right and left that shined at the edges, outlining every column and arch. A runner of white marble divided the room up the middle like a spill of cream, and a throng of fairy courtiers stood to either side of it, against the walls, like at certain middle-school dances Scott had been to. It parted ways with a typical middle-school dance crowd due to the sheer number of swords and axes everyone seemed to be carrying.

It reminded him, actually, of every throne room scene of every movie he'd ever watched, where you wondered just what everybody had been doing *before* the strangers came in. Talking quietly? Waiting in line to sit on the queen's lap? Whatever it was, they'd all stopped it in favor of staring silently at Scott and Mick, judging them so scathingly that Scott thought it might set his hair on fire.

But honestly, the first thing Scott saw upon entering, before the axes even, was Titania.

Her throne was a crescent of columns at the end of that spill of cream, framed by rich tapestries and embellished with a carving of a dragon biting a lion on the neck. Atop the crescent was an alabaster dish, and she sat lightly on that dish like a pearl on an oyster.

There was nothing about Titania that was not unnerving.

Her skin was nearly as white as the marble, with a blush of pink at the cheeks, the eyes, the lips, the knees. Her limbs were a touch too long, slightly too slender, and arranged just so out of the confectionery folds of her prom dress. The whole of her body was just too large to be human, but that struck Scott as a whim—she might awake tomorrow with the proportions of a doll, or eat something for supper that disagreed with her and swell up like Alice.

She lowered her head, gave Scott full view of her high-browed face with its strange mix of vixen and child.

Dhanu bowed low. Mick did, too, so Scott followed suit. Then the changeling said to everyone assembled,

> *"Behold her grace, my gift and godmother:*
> *Our kingdom dies for love of this, its queen."*

He turned to Titania.

> "*The fickle stars have quit for jealousy;*
> *The hidden moon retires to gaze at you.*"

Titania smiled faintly and fanned her fingers at him, an "Oh, *you*," sort of gesture. Dhanu continued.

> "*I bring today two children of the Fay—*
> *Two wan'dring sons I've sworn will see no harm*
> *By compact with the changelings of the guard.*"

Dhanu stepped aside, and suddenly it seemed like Scott and Mick's turn to speak. Scott thought he understood how to handle this Titania: talk fancy and kiss her butt. He just needed to *want* her attention. He just had to want to be the golden boy (that's how Mick had put it once), and whatever natural glamour he possessed would rise up to the surface. He had more glamour than Dhanu. His *dad* was a *movie star*. He could do this.

"Your Majesty, High Queen Titania," he said. "I would speak with thee about a great—"

Mick elbowed him in the shin. The peanut gallery tittered. Titania herself inclined her head a matter of degrees, a minuscule gesture that made Scott want to crawl into his own pocket. What had he done?

"I *said* no puttin' on airs," whispered Mick.

Titania spoke, with a voice that sounded like something musical turning inside your head.

> *"They laugh at phantoms; ghosts; a word misheard.*
> *They thought you called us 'thee,' but that's absurd.*
> *Or are you now our lord? We had not known—*
> *How thrilling! Let us help you to your throne."*

Scott could have *sworn* words like "thee" and "thou" were fancy talk. He'd have to ask Mick about it later. And was Titania seriously rhyming? He glanced around, but it didn't seem to be bothering anybody else.

Then a little elf maid approached and tried to offer Scott a glass of cordial, and he was forced to sing "Froggie Went a-Courtin'" until she went away again.

The hall felt chilly. Scott sighed and bowed once more at Titania.

"I'm not your lord. It . . . looks like I'm your jester," he told her, remembering what Mick said earlier. "I'm sorry. I come from a very different place, and I don't think that's the last mistake I'm going to make. But I mean no offense, High Queen."

Mick gave him a smile and a nod before Titania answered.

> *"Well said—our changeling cousin knows his place.*
> *Return you to your thoughts, and plead your case."*

This rhyming—it was like talking to someone who has food on her chin. Scott could barely concentrate on what she was saying.

"Um. I want to . . . I want . . ." Scott breathed. "I've heard rumors of a fairy invasion of Earth. I think you've been told maybe that humans split our world off from all the magic and the Fay on purpose, so I've come here to tell you it isn't true. I know people say Merle . . . Merlin is responsible for the split, for the Gloria, but we don't think that's true either."

The Fay murmured at this. Scoffed.

"He was really worried it was all his fault, honestly," Scott insisted. "But . . . well, I know him, actually, and we've investigated it and this whole thing's a big misunderstanding."

> *"Of course! The fault is ours for being blind.*
> *When man in ancient times behav'd unkind*
> *And stole from us the lands we'd held above*
> *How could we doubt he played but games of love?"*

"Um—"

"And absence made your hearts grow ever ripe!
You slandered us with fables, tales, and tripe—
How mystical we were! How fierce and fine!
Yet tame to hide our flame and keep in line."

Scott shifted from foot to foot. "With . . . with respect, I think humans have changed a lot since then."

"How true—once fate deprived you of the elves,
You humans turned your swords upon yourselves.
How swiftly did you newly fantasize
Of tribes to conquer, then romanticize.
Our Nimue has told me of the wars
O'er Africans, red Indians, and Moors?
You cast us each like actors in the parts
Of all the best and worst in thine own hearts."

Scott thought this might be kind of an oversimplification, but he didn't want to debate history with a woman who had lived through most of it. And *she* got to say thine! How come *he* didn't get to say things like thine? Whatever.

"You're definitely not wrong," he said. "Humans are bad at dealing with things they don't understand. So we tell stories. That's what humans do, is tell stories. I think it's what we do instead of magic."

More murmuring around the hall, but a good kind of murmuring. Thoughtful.

"But I also think . . . in the centuries since we've lost real magic, and the Fay . . . I think we've gone a little crazy. I mean, glamour used to only mean a kind of fairy magic, I guess, but now humans look for glamour wherever they can get it. We look for magic in movies and clothes and stuff, and in believing that certain people can have a kind of glamour. My dad's one of these kinds of people. We treat them like they're more than human, but they're not, so they always let us down."

The room was quiet, really quiet. He thought Titania was ever so slowly leaning forward.

"If the Fay come to Earth," Scott told her, "they won't have to invade. We'll worship you anyway. I'm sure of it. There are already a dozen magazines in every supermarket checkout lane waiting to do it, a hundred cable shows, a thousand websites. Maybe . . . maybe you don't know what those things are, but . . . won't it be better if you don't have to rule us? Won't it be better if we just give you our love?"

> *"And does my new young friend not understand?*
> *We cannot simply stride from land to land.*
> *For ev'ry elf that parts this shrinking sphere,*
> *Some wretched soul must cross from there to here."*

"You could trade places with animals!" Scott suggested. "Cows or sheep or something that would be happy to live out its life grazing in a place as beautiful as this."

But here he'd hit a nerve. The elves began to grumble, to make remarks behind their hands. Apparently they found this idea distasteful.

"Or people!" Scott added quickly. "There are seven billion humans on Earth. How many elves and humans here, a few hundred thousand?" He glanced at Mick, and the leprechaun bobbed his head back and forth, then nodded. "They could totally find enough on Earth who would be willing to trade places. You know, just for the adventure of it. Humans do stupid things all the time for adventure; you have no idea. They have this thing called bungee jumping?"

Mick nudged him. "Stay focused," he whispered.

"Well, anyway, humans are short-lived. They'd die naturally anyway before this world disappeared forever."

Scott took a half step forward. What did they call this on lawyer shows? Closing arguments? He thought Titania might even be smiling a little.

"I know about the Fay's famous sense of honor. I don't believe they want to push a whole species down because of the mistakes of the past. You're right that we tell stories about you. Over the years those stories have only gotten . . . kinder, and sweeter. They all have happy endings now. Let's . . . let's write a happy ending together."

That last bit made him want to throw up a little, but he thought it was probably what was called for. Mick gave him a sock in the leg, and when Scott looked down the little man was smiling up at him.

Titania was smiling, too. She was unquestionably smiling.

> *"I must commend you, boy—you've had your say*
> *And honored both your people and the Fay.*
> *And now will I confess I've played a trick:*
> *I know of all your treasons, Scott and Mick."*

"Uh." Scott felt his heartbeat in his stomach. The throne room was suddenly small. Was everyone closer than they'd been a second ago?

"Okay," whispered Mick. "We're banished. We get out quick, get as far away as we can."

Titania glared at Scott now.

> *"You're but a stranger here, so I'll concede*
> *Your plots have not the bite to make me bleed.*
> *But* Mick—"

Here Scott thought he could hear Mick rasping beside him. The little man's eyes might have been damp.

"—the fabled father of the finch.
If fairy folk have hearts, mine feels thy pinch.
And so we'd quite agreed before you came
To strike you from our court and curse your name.
'Twas foolish to surrender to my power—
You had no claim to safety in this tower."

Dhanu gasped and surged forward.

"And why was I not told? I must protest!
Upon my honor was their safety pledged."

Titania clasped her hands together, all girlish smiles
again.

"A necessary falsehood, pet of mine.
I longed to hear this plaything mewl and whine.
Such fun in one so young! Such grace and poise!"

Her fingers tightened.

"A crime, in time I always break my toys."

And the Fay, and those swords, and those axes,
advanced from all sides.

CHAPTER 30

Ms. Aleister walked Polly down halls, elevators, through complicated-looking systems that analyzed retinal patterns and fingerprints and spit for some reason. She waltzed her past all the best security money could buy, and only because she was under the impression that Polly had already been wherever she was being taken.

Ms. Aleister looked like a pretty velociraptor. Her heels sounded against the tile like a raptor's hind claw, *click click*. Ms. Aleister was explaining that little girls sometimes let their imaginations run away with them, that their eyes can play tricks, that what Polly no doubt *thought* she'd seen in Sensitive Research Area Alpha was not what it looked like.

Polly gave Ms. Aleister a dopey smile. "I know that already—daddy's new girlfriend told me it was all special effects, like in the movies."

"Exactly! Daddy's new girlfriend. What did you say her name was?"

"I'll point her out when we get there."

"See that you do. 'Special effects.' Your father's a lucky man—what a smart lady! Too bad she's soon to be unemployed."

"My dad has enough money for all of us."

"And what does he do?"

"Rocket-car test pilot."

"Uh-*huh*."

They reached Sensitive Research Area Alpha, which was in a wing labeled MICROFICHE ARCHIVE 1940–1959 and plastered with notices that it was shortly to be fumigated for earwigs. To pass through this door, Ms. Aleister had to press her hand against a little mirror on the wall. A green light flashed above the door, then a red.

"C'mon," said the woman, "you too. Fairy detector. You must have done it this morning."

Polly edged forward. Was she enough of a changeling to set this off? "Didn't realize I had to do it every time."

"That's why it's a security system, and not a hand stamp. This isn't the county fun fair."

Polly put her fingers, then her palm against the cold glass. She felt a buzz. All was silent for a moment.

"Got a slight blip off you," said Ms. Aleister. "Very faint. That's odd."

"Daddy's girlfriend said it's been doing that all week."

Polly concentrated and tried to push the fairyness down inside her. She imagined she was Scott—staying home on Halloween; doing sudoku puzzles; eating lunch alone in the library.

The lights above the door flashed green, and the door clicked open.

Inside was a wide and vaulted octagonal room lit up with a branching system of radial florescent tubes like a neon snowflake. There was a small team of researchers (three women, two men) who paused and looked up at the unexpected visitors. There were cases and refrigerators holding vials and samples of chemicals, work stations and computers and miles and miles of cables. And against one wall, cages holding a royal-looking elf and a manticore.

The former was easy to recognize: tall and lean and stately, even as it sat forlornly on the concrete floor in a hospital gown. A foxlike face with large and tapered ears and ginger hair. The latter was something Polly would have to ask about later—she didn't know what a manticore was. But the caged thing had a scorpion's tail on a wasted lion's body, with a nearly human face, and a disconcertingly wide mouth so packed with teeth they were growing in sideways.

Next to the manticore's cage there was a massive, windowless reinforced steel vault painted to say DANGER:

RONOPOLISK. Something huge kept whanging against the door from the inside.

In one corner was a small tank filled with a thick pink liquid. Milk-7. Interesting.

But most interesting was the table near the center of the room, the table with the yellow plastic hamster cage and the Habitrail, because inside this were three pixies.

One prince paced a rut through the wood chips. Another was shirtless, his tunic drying over a tunnel entrance. There were plastic tunnels to three separate sleeping quarters, and dishes of food and water. There was even a hamster wheel, and the last of the princes was running it. Which seemed kind of demeaning to Polly, but she supposed they had to keep fit somehow. It came to her suddenly that they had to go to the bathroom somewhere too, and she looked away quickly before she found it.

"All right," said Ms. Aleister, arms akimbo. "Who's responsible for this kid?"

Of course nobody volunteered anything. They glanced at one another, trying to decipher the situation. Maybe this was a surprise team-building exercise.

"Come on, come on. The longer you string this out, the worse it'll be for you."

Polly moved closer to these people in lab coats, under the pretext of giving them a closer look at her. But what she was really doing was getting closer to that hamster cage.

"I don't understand, ma'am," said one of the scientists as he watched Polly. "Is she a test subject?"

"Oh, for heaven's sake, shut *up*," said Ms. Aleister. And while she had everyone's attention like that for a moment, Polly stretched out her sleeve and released Prince Fi onto the table with his brothers. Then she walked swiftly away. "Girl!" Ms. Aleister continued. "Anni . . . Ann . . . What was your name again?"

"Anastasia de la Taco."

"Just point to your daddy's girlfriend so we can fire her and leave."

"What's this?" Polly asked, picking up the first thing she could get ahold of. Which turned out to be a beaker, and Ms. Aleister told her so. "I can make it stay over my mouth," Polly said, and she held it there with suction.

"Little girl—"

"How many things can I stick to my face?" Polly tested her question by circling the lab, snatching objects at random and affixing them, or trying to affix them, to her cheeks and forehead. A metal washer. Litmus paper. A cell phone, a test tube, a public-radio coffee mug. Some clattered to the floor, or even broke. "My mom says I have 'combination skin.'"

The manticore seemed to chuckle, gruffly.

"Seize the girl," said Ms. Aleister, and you could sort of tell it wasn't the first time she'd said it.

Polly had maneuvered her way to the Milk-7 tank, however, and as the scientists moved on her, she spun the spigot. The goopy pink stuff spilled out onto the floor.

"Pretty!" she squealed. "Strawberry! Food fight!" Then she kicked a spray of the Milk at the advancing researchers. They recoiled as if vampires before holy water. Then Polly moved to an adjacent refrigerator and grabbed a test tube of something yellow. "Ooh, what's this?"

"It's an antidote for children who've grown extra fingers and toes," said a scientist. "Please put it down."

Polly poured the liquid into the pink milk. "What do yellow and pink make?" she asked, then frowned. The answer, apparently, was lightning.

Now the adults were really panicking. A jet of steam rose from where Polly had mixed the chemicals, and some kind of detector started beeping. Ceiling sprinklers activated, and the lights in the room turned red. Everyone rushed for the door as a serious-looking barricade began to slide down in front of it.

"Girl!" shouted Ms. Aleister. "Hurry!"

But Polly made no attempt to escape the room. The emergency door slid into place with a thump and a hiss, and now there was two inches of steel between her and the adults, apart from a little window bricked up with

Plexiglas. They stared at her through the little window, the scientists and Ms. Aleister, shouting silently. Polly found some tape and covered it over with a piece of notebook paper.

Before long Polly found a set of keys, and when the elf was free he kissed Polly's hand while struggling to keep his gown closed in the back. He thanked her graciously while Fi heaved open a hatch on the hamster cage and lowered a string of rubber bands down to his brothers.

The elf appeared to be about to say something as Polly tried key after key in the lock of the manticore's cage, but he checked himself. He nonetheless urged her not to release the ronopolisk.

"I would sooner face a cockatrice, a basilisk, and a catoblepas all at once than fight one ronopolisk," he insisted.

"You're making up words," Polly told him. The door of the manticore's cage clicked open, and the devil beast rubbed against Polly's shoulder as it passed.

"Human girl," it purred. "Though I am hungry, I shan't eat you." He said it like it was a pretty big compliment.

"Thanks."

The sprinklers were cleansing the room and sending the toxic mess down a drain in the middle. The manticore hunched and looked as miserable as any wet cat. Fi introduced Polly to his brothers.

"Denzil, Fo, and Fee, this is the Lady Polly Esther Doe." The princes bowed deeply.

"This was a gallant rescue, brother, Lady Polly," said Denzil, the oldest. "But I fear while we pixies might clinch our escape, those larger than we are doomed."

"I will be proud to die fighting," said the elf, "and will relish destroying as much of this infernal apothecary as I can."

But Fi was watching Polly, and Polly was peering at the refrigerator where she had found the yellow test tube.

"You are thinking," said Fi. "You are hatching plans. I know this because my stomach hurts."

"Goodco did all kinds of weird experiments on kids, I hear," said Polly. "That's what made Biggs big and hairy— some chemical they invented. But he said something once, when we were on the cruise—he said the chemical didn't make everyone big and hairy, just the boys."

"So it did not work on the girls," said Fi.

"No," said Polly, "it made them *smaller*."

"That does not follow. Just because—"

"That's why I'm going to drink some of the same chemical Biggs drank, and I'll get to be the size of a pixie!"

The sprinklers had stopped. The red light had extinguished. Polly crossed back to the fridge.

"You cannot do this!" Fi insisted. "I believe it to be

dangerous." But Fi was trapped on a counter, far from Polly. "Brothers," he said, "help me."

Polly heaved the fridge open again and began pushing around little racks of test tubes. "Emily is always going on about how Goodco doesn't know about any big rifts," she said. "Right? Except that one in Antarctica, but nothing ever goes in or out of it. They don't know where it connects to in Pretannica. That's why the rift in Mr. Wilson's house is so special—regular-sized people can go through it. But if Goodco can't usually send regular-sized people through rifts, then how'd they get the Queen of England through?"

"Nimue forced *her* way through," Fi reminded her. "With witchcraft."

"Yeah, and it nearly killed her, it was so hard. So of *course* they shrank the queen down to tiny size to get her through one of the small rifts. Duh." Polly uncorked a vial of something clear and fizzy.

"Please remember, if you drink the potion that grows finger and toes, that you've already flushed the antidote," says Fi.

Polly swallowed a bit of the liquid. Just a bit. It didn't have a flavor, per se. It tasted a little like the smell of a new raincoat? Or like anger? It was hard to explain. Anyway, she otherwise tried to report that nothing had happened, but nothing happened. She'd entirely lost her voice.

"A most heartrending tragedy," said Fee.

Polly scrambled for an antidote and swallowed something blue, and her voice returned—albeit hoarse and squeaky like she'd been sucking helium and screaming.

The emergency gate was starting to come up. *I need more time!* Polly squealed.

Fi sighed and asked elf and manticore to take him and his brothers to the gate. The manticore and elf braced their hands and paws on metal handles and strained to keep it closed, while Fi jabbed with his sword at any hands that appeared under the gate from the other side.

"An elf and pixies and a manticore fighting as brothers," said the elf. "What a rare death."

"A good death," growled the manticore. "I am old. I had cubs I will never again see. I am ready to die with blood in my teeth."

Polly twisted every sample around in its container, trying to make sense of their labels. "Just another minute!" she squawked.

The elf smirked down at Fi. "Who gives the orders here, pigsie? She is but a human girl."

"Yet see what she has done today," Fi answered. "Is she not something?"

"Fi!" Polly shouted. "I drank another one and

326

something went pop! Can you look?" She hiked up her shirt in the back.

"You have tiny wings."

"I HAVE TINY WINGS? I wonder if I can flap them! Are they moving now? What about now? I don't know which muscles to push."

"We'll find you the antidote," says Fi.

"No we won't. Oh, listen! My voice is going back down."

"Polly, hurry!"

"She is *something*," said the elf.

"The pixies have a story," Fi continued. "You would not know it. But we say that the Spirit, the Spirit that made all things, and who separated good from evil, is reborn from time to time into a mortal person. And that this person cannot help but be remarkable. Remarkable, but not necessarily good."

"An old story," Denzil agreed as heavy-heeled footsteps thundered up to the gate. "The mortal Spirit must decide, as each of us does in turn, what is right and what is wrong. And in this way good and evil is redefined, and the world remade. But the story says the Spirit is born into a pixie, brother."

Fo said, "You don't think this girl is—"

Fi shook his head, and laughed, and speared a scientist's hand. "I think it's a story. You know I do not hold with such things, brothers. If anything, I think we might all be born with a little Spirit in us, pixie and human and elf alike, and we are each the bumbling makers of our own folly. But still and all, the girl—she might be remarkable, might she not?"

"Everyone?" said Polly. They turned to see a two-foot-tall girl, blanketed by her own clothes. "I found it, didn't I? Just a little bit more."

Fi and his brothers rushed to her as she sipped a little bit more of the liquid she'd found. When they'd traipsed through folds of pants and jacket, they found a pixie-sized seven-year-old, pulling a vastly oversized shirt around her. Fi passed her his topcoat, and she ducked down under the shirt collar with it. When she came up again, they saw that it made a fine little dress.

The elf and manticore were tiring. The gate was coming up by inches.

"I wish we could help you more," Polly told them.

"You've done more than you know," said the elf. "You're a changeling, aren't you, girl? A little agent of sacred chaos. I am your servant."

"Then you might lift us to that air vent," said Fi. "We are ready to leave."

"We're all going to leave this place," growled the manticore. "We are all of us going to leave this place, one way or another."

CHAPTER 31

Merle and John stood in the velvety bedroom chamber, over the tiny canopy bed in which slept the tiny Queen of England. She wore a tiny nightgown. They'd fashioned her a tiny pair of slippers.

"No wonder they made the queen on the Clobbers box look like Mick," said Merle. "They're the same height."

"She looks good otherwise though, right?" asked John. "Well rested."

"I bet they've had her asleep ever since she came here. An enchanted sleep."

John massaged his jaw. "Do you think we have to kiss her?"

"I don't think there's any 'we' about it. Knight of the Realm, seems like your duty."

"I'm . . . going to try the forehead first and work my way inward," said John. He leaned in.

"Now if you feel yourself about to punch her," said Merle, "just step back and count to ten."

"Shh."

John kissed her little forehead and straightened again. Nothing happened immediately, so he was just thinking, *All right, cheek then,* when she woke and trained her eyes on his.

"You're that pop star we knighted," she said creakily. Her throat was probably pretty dry. "I thought you were too young, but my advisers thought it would be good for public relations. You appear rather larger than I remember."

"We have a lot to explain to you, Your Majesty," said John. "And not a lot of time. But first and foremost, it is fundamentally important that you get inside this backpack."

Scott and Mick sat on the cold floor of a little bell-shaped cell high above the ground. There was nothing for light but a single cross-slit hole in the wall and a tiny torchlit window in the door. Just enough to see the occasional dim shape that you'd mistaken for a stone suddenly lift itself up from its torpor, shuffle a few inches, and die.

"Prison sucks," said Scott. "They make it look like fun on TV, but it secretly sucks."

"Try to at least have a sense o' pride abou' it," said

Mick. "Yeh're a prisoner o' the *Tower o' London*. There's none more famous jail."

"Alcatraz."

"No sense o' history," Mick grumbled.

In a way, Scott did not so much mind the dim light—it concealed his red eyes. In the darkness Scott wished to be comforted. He wanted, not to put too fine a point on it, his mommy. He would never admit as much to Mick, however, so instead he said, "Eleven months until Mom comes back."

"So 'tis."

"No matter . . . no matter what happened, whether we won or lost, I thought at least I'd be there when she reappeared. But now maybe—"

"We'll be there, lad. Somehow. I always escape my cages, 'ventually."

"You know," said Scott, "in Arthurian stories they got thrown in cells like this all the time. Arthur and Lancelot and the rest."

"How'd *they* get out?"

"Pretty girls would let them out in exchange for favors, mostly."

They watched the window of the cell door as if that might be some damsel's cue, but none was forthcoming.

"You ever hear Merle tell about how he got out of his prison under the earth?" asked Scott. "The one all the stories say Nimue put him in?'"

"Don't think so."

"He knew she was gonna do it, and he knew he couldn't really stop her from doing whatever she wanted. So he found a cave on Avalon with a tunnel he could dig out that led far away, and had a back door. And one day, when he and Nimue were still acting all smoochy, they went by this cave, and he told her, 'Oh no! I'm getting a vision that I'm doomed to die in that cave! But how could anything bad happen to me on Avalon?'"

"Heh." Mick chuckled. "Smart man. Nimue wouldn't want to spoil the story."

"Right. So she 'trapped' him right where he wanted, and he could work on his second time machine, the one for Arthur, in peace."

They fell silent. After a few minutes of this, Scott decided there may be nothing quieter than two people not talking to each other in a dark room in a tower they can't leave. If they weren't careful, they might just forget how to speak altogether, and the decades would pass without notice, and Scott would be dead ten years before Mick mentioned, *"Yeh've been awful quiet."*

"He gets a weird look on his face sometimes when he talks about the old days," said Scott. "Merle, I mean."

"I'll bet he does do."

"He almost even talks like he and Nimue cared for each

333

other a little bit. But how could he like her? She's awful."

Mick said, "Ah, love she's a python/she'll pull yeh in snug/an' yeh'll die with a sigh/'cause yeh think it's a hug."

"Did you just make that up?"

"Aye."

"I'm gonna let my mom give me the boy-girl talk, if that's okay with you."

"Aye."

"Thing is, maybe Nimue actually cared for Merle a little too? 'Cause he asked her for a final favor before she sealed him in, and she actually did it. It starts out as one of those Arthur-in-prison stories, actually."

"Any useful tips?"

"Mmm . . . no."

"Well, tell it anyway."

"Okay, you know Morgan le Fay hated her half-brother Arthur, right?"

"Hoo, yeah. Pretty li'l changeling, but she was always barking."

"Well, she manages to snare Arthur in this enchantment while he's out hunting. He wakes up, doesn't understand what's happened, but he's in the dungeon of this real nasty knight named Damas.

"Damas is feuding with his brother, Ontzlake, and needs a champion to do his fighting for him because he's a coward. So a pretty girl comes to the prison—"

"Natcherly."

"—and tells Arthur that Damas will let him go if he fights Ontzlake's champion. So Arthur agrees, and Morgan le Fay, pretending to be the good sister, sends him his sword Excalibur and its scabbard. But they're both fakes. She sends the real ones to Ontzlake's champion, Sir Accolon.

"The day comes, and everybody's gathered to watch. Arthur and Accolon both fight bravely, and both score a lot of hits. But Accolon can't bleed because he has the magic scabbard, and meanwhile his sword is the best in the world. Arthur's sword actually *breaks*. But still he won't fall, though he knows there's been some trick. And now Nimue comes and stands at the edge of the crowd, watching."

● ○ ★

If there is one thing on which the old stories agree, it's that Nimue did not act right away. She waited and watched as Accolon and Arthur landed still more blows. But only Arthur's wounds bled, and the lawn was dark with his blood. Near to Nimue, a seated woman remarked that it was a wonder the swordless knight could still stand. No one knew who either man was— they wore helmets.

"Fools, both," Nimue muttered, though whether she meant Merlin and Arthur, or Arthur and Accolon, or Merlin and *Nimue*, was a secret she was keeping even from herself.

She didn't kill Merlin. She would never kill, not like that mad Morgan. Now *there's* a girl she should have left at the nunnery—still barely more than a spoiled child, and getting ever harder to control. But no—she didn't kill Merlin. She left his fate to the gods. And to story! The stories that clung to that man, like the stink of every mess he'd ever stepped in. Such a man would have another chapter, surely.

She'd trapped him to protect her interests. The interests of her people.

But oh, his last request, that she rush here and save Arthur. Naturally. And humans say the *Fay* are overdramatic.

Nimue sighed. *"Fine,"* she said, and waved her hand just as Accolon was about to shamefully slay the weaponless king. The fact that her timing made for the best possible story was not lost on her. By her magic arts, the sword Excalibur fell from Accolon's grasp and landed near Arthur. The young king seized it, and attacked. Nimue didn't stick around for the ending.

After he'd gotten his sword, Arthur snatched back the scabbard. He ceased to bleed, and now Accolon was suddenly bleeding profusely. The contest was over soon, though both men were sorely wounded. Accolon died shortly thereafter.

Arthur was taken to an abbey to heal, where he slept with Excalibur in his arms. But he was careless with the scabbard.

Morgan le Fay stole into the abbey while Arthur slept. Not daring to touch the sword, she snapped up the scabbard and rushed back to her horse. Arthur woke and pursued her with his men, but she ran her horse dead from exhaustion, then alit on the tip of a sawtoothed cliff over the sea. She held the scabbard aloft, and for a moment it was edged with fire against the setting sun. "So sorry, *brother,*" she hissed through clenched teeth as her hair blew ragged around her. "Brother. Brother brother *brother.*" She could hear horses approaching as she threw the scabbard off the cliff into the sea. Then she turned herself to stone.

"He lost the scabbard," repeated Scott. "If he'd kept it, maybe things would . . . I don't know . . . would have turned out different."

"Yeah," said Mick. "Like maybe he never would have gotten in Merle's time machine in the first place, an' the worlds wouldna' have split."

Scott shook his head. "Merle says the time machines didn't cause the split."

"I know what he says. An' I know he needs to believe it. But I don't believe it."

"I wouldn't believe a bit of this," said the Queen of England to Merle and John, "if it weren't for the fire-breathing finch. Nothing better to convince you that you're trapped in a Harry Potter novel than a fire-breathing finch."

"We're not out of the woods yet, Your Majesty," said Merle. "Better keep our voices down."

She shifted in the backpack, unused to keeping her balance while being borne along by a man three times her size. "I shan't argue. But if my continued imprisonment is so important to the . . . fairies' plans, one might expect them to have me a shade better guarded."

"I don't think they believed it possible that anyone from Earth would make it to this world, much less to this cave," said John. Still, he was pretty pleased himself with how well things were going. Then they reached the mouth of the cavern and heard an intake of breath behind them.

They turned. The woman in the scarlet cloak had appeared at the bottom of the passage, and she pulled down her hood to reveal a frizzy mushroom of red curly locks. She was a ginger, a wild-haired, half-feral woman-child.

"Oh, shoot," Merle muttered. "That's Morgan le Fay."

"MEN!" she screamed. "MEN OF ADAM! TAKING THE PRIZE!"

Her scream raked down the corridor like nails on chalkboard, rattling shale loose from the walls and ceiling.

John and Merle stumbled, ears ringing, down the hills of Avalon. Morgan shrieked once more behind them, a keening, birdlike noise. And now the Hairy Men were pouring like roaches from every cave, every hole in the ground, scurrying in clusters, long lines, converging on the interlopers. And all of them appeared to have slings and stones.

"Their caps!" screeched Morgan. "Merrow caps! Don't let them get to the water!" She chanted behind them and swung her arm like she was throwing an imaginary fastball. And where that invisible pitch would have landed, the earth heaved with a seismic belch, flinging John and Merle to the ground in a shower of sod and tossing brownies everywhere.

"She's not one of those killing-is-dishonorable Fay, is she?" John groaned.

In a moment they were completely surrounded. Which was, ironically, the only thing keeping them alive, since the brownies were reluctant to sling stones when they were all facing one another.

"I always suspected I'd die like this," said the queen.

Merle started. "Really?"

"No. Not really. That was something we in Britain call 'humour.'"

"What do you think, Finchbriton?" said John.

The bird winged his way forward and burned them a path through the crowd. The brownies eeked and howled.

"Forget what I've told you!" screamed Morgan. "KILL

THEM ALL! KILL EVEN THE *QUEEN* RATHER THAN LET HER ESCAPE!"

Stones came down, thudding, clanging, cracking against larger stones. John did his best to cover them with the chickadee shield as he brought up the rear. Merle was shouting something about knowing where he was going.

"Oh," Merle said now. "Whoops."

"Whoops *what?*"

"This is . . . my old cave," said Merle, pointing to a pile of boulders. "The one I was, you know, trapped in. I thought we could hide in it, use the old back door. But of course it's collapsed."

They ducked behind a cairn of stones. The brownies' bullets chipped away at the edges of it. The water's brink was maybe a hundred yards away. John tried to remember his better track-and-field times from school.

"Think we can make it?" he asked.

"No, I do not," came the queen's muffled voice in answer. "Don't let's be reckless."

"Well, they're afraid to get too close because of Finchbriton, but there's nothing to keep them from circling around and firing on us from all sides."

In fact, that seemed to occur to the brownies as well. They were starting to skirt a wide perimeter around the stone bunker. Merle dug into his sack and produced his flare gun. He shot a couple flares to either side, and they landed near the advancing brownies, who backed immediately away. The flares didn't burn long on their own, but while they did, they made an odd green light that the Hairy Men could plainly see wasn't natural.

"Well done," said John. "They think we have some kind of magic. Magic ammo. But how long is that going to last?"

Sometime after the flares burned out, the brownies resumed their hesitant advance, so Merle gave them another couple of flares to look at. After that they seemed content to hunker down and sling stones.

Every now and then, some patch of earth exploded. As if Morgan was blindly casting about, not caring who or what she killed.

Another stone landed near them, which was nothing special in and of itself, except that this one was on fire. So was the next. They made the grass smolder and give off a dark smoke.

"Fantastic," said John. "*They* have magic ammo now. Fire ammo."

More flaming stones fell all around. One bounced off the boulders and into Merle's lap, and he hooted, pitched it off quickly, and then sucked on his fingers.

"Is that what magic smells like?" asked the queen. "Smells of paraffin."

Merle peeked over the boulders. "She's right," he said.

"It's not magic—they've got a big vat of kerosene. They're dipping the bullets in it and lighting 'em on fire. Heh. Bet they'd rather not get a flare in it. Get ready to run."

John heard the Hairy Men chattering and a petulant voice joining them from afar.

"Well, I'm here *now*. Morgan le Fay doesn't run for you or anyone."

"Better zip into the sack, Your Majesty," said John. "You too, Finchbriton. When I say so, hold your breath."

"CHILDREN OF ADAM!" Morgan screeched, closer now. "I'M COMING TO RECLAIM THE PRIZE!"

John stole a look and instantly regretted it. Now he'd have the picture of furious Morgan—face like a gash, tramping across the pockmarked and smoldering island while a petrified rain thumped around her—to take to his grave with him.

"Hold on," said Merle. He shot a flare. "Missed."

Morgan sneered at the flare but didn't break stride.

"Missed again," Merle said a second later.

"Give me your flare gun," he told John after firing a third time. "I'm out."

John handed Merle his gun, but as he shifted around, a sling bullet grazed his shoulder.

"YEEEEAAH!"

"Missed again. Are you okay?"

"Erg. *Fine*. Do you want me to do that for you?"

Just then Merle fired a final flare, and it landed in the vat. The kerosene ignited, sending up a bright FOOSH of flame. The Hairy Men scattered, wailing and covering their eyes, and Merle and John raced to the bank and dove beneath the water.

CHAPTER 32

Emily couldn't sleep. She sat up, listened to the old mattress springs bray and creak. Erno was supposed to be watching her, making certain her sleep wasn't disturbed, but there he was, snoring in the chair by the bed. She reached out to where Archie perched on the headboard, and he stepped down onto her arm. Then she tiptoed out of the room and shut the door behind her. She might as well get some work done.

Scott couldn't sleep. He wondered how many hours straight he'd been awake now, in this prison cell. Twenty-four? Thirty?

"How long do you think we've been in here?" he asked Mick.

"Six hours, maybe."

"Six—that's all? Are you sure?"

"No, I amn't sure. I didn't bring my Rolex. Is it important?"

"Well, I was thinking of scratching marks into the wall, to count the days, but . . . never mind," said Scott. "It's not like we'll ever be able to count them anyway without a sun or moon. What makes this world work, anyway? Where's the light coming from? What makes the plants grow? What keeps it going?"

A voice said,

> *"What keeps our kingdom going, glowing on?*
> *Suspense—suspense and stubborn expectation.*
> *A wish to witness how the story ends."*

Scott squinted at the silhouetted face in the door's window. "Beautiful damsel?"

"Nah," said Mick, "it's just Dhanu."

> *"What fools you were to come and court the courtly,"*

the changeling said through the door.

> *"More fool was I to lend you my good name.*
> *What covenant could you have hoped to gain?*
> *The mission of the Fay is right and just.*
> *It must be just—for if their cause were not?*
> *For lack of glamour's blush they'd wilt and waste."*

347

"Thassa crock," Mick said cheerily. "We've gotten it all turned around, we Fay. I think we used to tell ourselves we needed to be good, to be honorable, an' that the glamour was our reward. Now 's our barometer. If we still have our glamour, then we're sure we *must* be good, no matter how heinous we've become. I think yeh know what I mean."

Dhanu watched them for a moment.

> *"It was* my *honor pledged,* mine *on the line*
> *When conduct safe I promised in the court."*

"I know," said Scott. "I'm sorry."
Dhanu smirked.

> *"And now apology, from you to me.*
> *From jailed to jailer; that is passing strange.*
> *For all your folly, still I'm fain to think*
> *You spoke with honest valor in the court."*

Scott and Mick were silent.

> *"If I arrange your swift release, will first*
> *You swear what you foretold will come to pass?*
> *The Fay, all Fay, led safely to your world?*
> *Admired and living free among your kind?"*

"Sure," said Mick. "That's what he thinks. That's what we both think."

> *"He made predictions all his own in court,*
> *So now I'll have his answer for myself."*

Scott opened his mouth to reassure Dhanu as well, and it would have been easy, so easy to lie. Instead he grimaced as he realized he was about to be honest. It really wasn't all that simple after all. What do you know.

"No."

Mick turned his head. "Lad?"

". . . No," Scott told Dhanu. "I won't promise that. It wouldn't be right. I think that's what will happen . . . mostly . . . but I can't make any guarantees. I'm just a kid—I don't have any power in my world."

"*Scott*," said Mick.

You couldn't read Dhanu's dim face there, in that small frame in the door, but when he spoke again it seemed to be with greater urgency.

> *"I trust you grasp the pact I'm offering?*
> *An oath, mere words, and then I'll set you free."*

"Sorry, Mick," Scott breathed. He turned to Dhanu. "Yeah, I understood you the first time. Thanks, but . . . I guess I'll have to stay in here."

Dhanu studied him, then turned and motioned to someone who must have been standing with him there, in the hall. There was a jangling, and the bolt slid free of the lock. The door opened, and Scott and Mick scrambled to their feet.

Dhanu was accompanied by another changeling Scott recognized from before. This second teen had Scott's backpack. Now Scott could just see Dhanu's face in the blue light of the cross-shaped window, and he was smiling. Sort of a rueful smile.

> *"Our horses wait in secret down below.*
> *Now softly, and attend to what I say.*
> *And if your drop of fairy blood bestows*
> *A drop of fairy grace, do use it now."*

Scott was stunned. "Thank you."

"I think you'll be a king among your kind," said Dhanu.

"Nah," said Scott, shrugging uncomfortably. "I'm thinking maybe a lawyer."

CHAPTER 33

"If you were truly Merlin," said the queen, "then I think you have much to answer for. All that I-know-the-terrible-future-but-I'm-going-to-let-it-happen-anyway business."

"Oh." Merle laughed. "*That.*"

Merle and John were still dripping wet, though Her Majesty and Finchbriton had remained relatively dry inside the backpack. They walked back through the southwest of Ireland, toward the rift, on their guard but otherwise enjoying a rare moment of triumph.

"Putting aside the tragedy of Lancelot and Guinevere," said the queen, "you must have known that Arthur would have a bastard son who would grow up to oppose him."

"Mordred," Merle agreed, nodding. "So why didn't I stop it? I actually tried. I did. Just like I got Arthur born by doing everything wrong, I got Mordred born by doing everything right. All the old accounts agreed that Mordred's mom was Morgause, so I never left her and Arthur alone together for even a second. Sure, some newer versions of the legends said Mordred's mom was Morgan le *Fay*, but I knew that was just because modern writers think Morgan's a fun villain and they wanted to make the stories simpler by getting rid of characters. Right? So I'm watching Morgause like a hawk, and meanwhile Arthur and Morgan le Fay are sneaking out the back together."

The queen pursed her lips but said nothing. John said it for her. "Arthur and that . . . wild child?"

"She had a more alluring glamour back then, I swear. And actually ran a comb through her hair every now and then. So Mordred was born after all, but I was there to meet Arthur on the battlefield of Camlann. Arthur killed his son, but Mordred got Arthur pretty bad, too. The books all say that four queens took him off to Avalon to rest and heal, but I guess that's just 'cause no one was around to know the truth. It was actually me."

Merle drove his skittish horse and cart through the field of the dead, a hundred thousand men, looking for movement that was not some crow or snake in the grass. Quiet as an anvil. Only the dry curses of scavengers creaking under a leaden sky.

When his horse quailed and wouldn't go any farther, Merle got down and walked, slipping occasionally on things he didn't care to identify, looking for that extraordinary sword and the Pendragon device on a shield, looking for his friend.

He found Arthur breathing shallowly on the ground next to the body of his son. He pressed on the king's wound until the bleeding stopped, mostly, and dressed it with fresh linen.

"Merlin," said Arthur, fluttering his papery eyelids. He looked so much older than Merle remembered, so much older than his years. "So I've died, then. Is this heaven or hell?"

"What a thing to say. I've missed you too."

"What are you doing now?"

"I am trying," Merle grunted, "to drag you back . . . to

353

my cart. The books said Lucan . . . and Bedivere would be hanging around to help?" (*Cough.*) "But I guess they just made that up?"

After the better part of a sweat-soaked hour, Merle had Arthur in the wagon, and they were away. Merle had to keep nudging Arthur to keep him awake.

"Whither we travel?" asked the king after one of these proddings.

"Avalon."

"Good. I shall return the sword Excalibur to the lake and fulfill my vow."

"Mmm . . . yeeeah. Why don't you hold on to that, actually," said Merle. "You're gonna need it where we're going, and I don't intend to let you die."

"Old friend," said Arthur. "My wound is mortal."

"Let's let twenty-first century medicine decide what's mortal and what isn't. You'll be amazed how different the doctors are from the ones you have here. Like, do you know what they'll almost never put on an open wound? Moss. And they're gonna wash their hands and everything. You'll feel like a king. The Once and Future King."

He snuck them both through the back door tunnel to his secret cave, explaining all the while that there was a new kingdom, another world that needed his help more than any other. They were going there. Inside the cave Arthur found Archimedes, and some work benches,

crude tools, copper and tin wire, pipes. The time machine
Merlin had built for him was a hundred times larger than
his own and would have looked to the modern eye more
like plumbing than science. But to the medieval man,
plumbing *was* science, and Arthur was much impressed.
Merlin told the king that he must place himself within
a large octagonal ring, surrounded by batteries of fairy
gold.

"You can sit," said Merle.

"I will stand." Arthur was barely on his feet, but he
raised Excalibur, pointed it before him as if ready to
cleave his way into the next millennium.

Merle and Archie gripped their little octagon. "Okay,
Archie," said Merle. "Sync us up and do the math. Then
jump."

Arthur's machine rattled and hummed. And glowed.
There was a lot more light than Merle expected.
Especially from Arthur's trembling sword. Excalibur was
incandescent.

Then there was a *pop*, and Merle and Archie were in
New Jersey.

Alone.

He'd tumbled to the grass, so now Merle rose near the
edge of a park, squinted at a boulevard of row homes just
visible through the trees. The breeze was in his face, a
summer breeze. He smelled . . . marshmallows.

"Arthur?" asked Merle, looking all around him, but nothing. The legendary king was legendary once more.

Scott clung, stiff fingered, to the galloping pony, Mick in his backpack, with Dhanu and the Changeling Guard riding alongside. The forest was a panic of log-jumping, low-hanging boughs, grasping branches, and the ever-changing kaleidoscope of dappled twilight that pinholed through the trees. This was a truly excellent pony and didn't seem to need steering or even the slightest encouragement from Scott, which was good—after his initial order of "Giddyap," he'd entirely exhausted his horsemanship.

Dhanu caught Scott's eye and nodded. The other changelings looked grim. Their treachery hadn't escaped notice for long, and they had a battalion of the Trooping Fairies of Oberon on their tails.

"'Why don't you go with John and *Merle*, Finchbriton,' says Mick," Scott grumbled. "'We shouldn't have any need for you.'"

"Oh, enough already," said Mick.

Arrows whizzed by. Small ones, like the elves only wanted to murder them a little bit. One lodged itself into a flowering elder, and Mick got a look at it as they passed.

"Ooh, did yeh see the craftsmanship on that arrow? Sure to be poisoned, too, that was. 'S like they're tryin' to kill us with the good silverware."

"Neat."

Dhanu drew his horse near and called out over the thunder of hoofbeats.

"We'll scatter at the border of the shire.
Perhaps my guard will draw off their pursuit."

Scott nodded, grateful. The changelings, all the changelings, would probably never be welcome back in fairy society again. What would happen to them?

"The horse you ride is fairy bred, and bright,"

Dhanu added.

"Just tell her where you'd go, and she'll abide."

Before Scott or Mick could say a proper word of thanks, Dhanu had reined his horse away, and less than a minute later they could neither see nor hear the Changeling Guard anymore. They must have crossed the county line, and now they were on their own.

After a time Scott felt Mick twist around in the backpack and lean into Scott's ear. "Good news an' bad news," said the leprechaun.

"What's the good news?" asked Scott as another arrow whistled by.

"We have us just two pursuers."

"And the bad news?"

"It's the same news."

They were dogged pursuers, these last two, and better riders. They gained ground. Mick ducked into the backpack and popped up, facing backward, with a flare gun. He fired a flare, and it cut a spectral laser trail through the blue wood. The elves forked to avoid it, then came back together again, losing a little ground as they did so. Mick reloaded and played this card again and again until they couldn't see their hunters anymore.

Scott smelled water. The trees were thinning out ahead, too—they were coming up on a river. "We can't keep this up," he said. "Hold on. I'm going to try something."

"Can I maybe have a little more explanation than that?"

Scott arched forward and spoke into the horse's ear. He hoped it understood.

It wasn't an especially wide river—that was good. They careened down the bank and plowed into the water, sending a heavy swell to either side. Then, of course, their mythologically nimble horse became suddenly sluggish as she surged against the water and the current.

"Come on, come on," Scott whispered, terrified the elves would catch up while they were so exposed.

Then, when they were halfway across the river, Scott fell sideways off the pony's back and let the current take him. He and Mick took breaths and went under. They could hear the water being breached as their pony emerged on the far bank and galloped on. They heard the disturbance, underwater, as the elven riders entered the river a few seconds later, and crossed, and then were gone.

Scott and Mick surfaced, gasped, and swam to shore, panting.

"What . . . what did yeh say to the pony?" asked Mick.

"Told it to keep running without us, fast as it could. Wonder how long the elves'll follow before they realize they aren't chasing anyone?"

CHAPTER 34

In the basement, Emily was conducting an experiment with Archimedes, and a lead box with slits in it, and some photosensitive paper, and a spoon. She looked at the spoon. Why did she need a spoon? The answer was she didn't, and she set it aside, quietly, so as not to wake the house.

In the basement, Emily returned to her experiment with Archimedes, and a lead box with slits in it, and some photosensitive paper, and she needed the spoon for ice cream. *That's* why. Her research would lead to a heretofore unimagined flavor of ice cream, with tiny rifts in it. And brownie bits, maybe.

In the basement, Emily was nodding off.

"Don't fall asleep—you know it's dangerous," says a voice.

Emily looks up, dimly. "Oh, it's *you*," she says. She

smiles. "You found me."

Her mother is beautiful. She'd forgotten how beautiful. Tall and raven haired, like a storybook queen. Her mother leans in close, asks what she's working on.

"A rift! A stable rift! A really big one," Emily tells her mother.

Her mother is silent for a long time. "You don't say," she breathes.

"I've learned so much about them," says Emily. She's excited to be talking about it.

"I'm so silly," says her mother. "I don't remember exactly where we are. Is it London?"

"Did you know that each rift is a pair of tiny white holes with a black hole in the center? Is that not crazy? And there's no time displacement. Also I think I've discovered a new elementary subatomic particle I'm calling the Emilyon."

"The house we're in, dear. It's in London?"

"Yes, London." Emily winces. There is a sound, like a ringing in her ears, but it isn't a ringing. The sound goes *shhhhhhhhhhhhhhhhhhhhhhhhhhhh*. "Can you hear that?"

"I hear nothing. What part of London?"

Shhhhhhhhhhhhhhhhhhhhhhhh, goes the sound.

"Is . . . Islington. That snake . . . do you see that snake there? It could see something coming through the rift just before it happened. There's no reason a reptile should

362

be able to do that naturally, but it *has* been eating a lot of mice from Pretannica—I think that has to be the explanation."

"Pretannica?"

"That's . . . what we call the world on the other side." Emily's face is suddenly hot. Her forehead is damp.

Shhhhhhhhhhhhhhhhhhhhhhhhh.

"Is this . . . ," she asks, ". . . is this real life?"

"Of course, silly mouse. Now where in Islington, do you think?"

Don't.

"On a . . . on a street called St. George, which is funny, because *he* slew a dragon, and we have to slay a dragon, too—"

"Very good, Emily," says her mother. "Stop talking. There we are. Now come upstairs."

Don't.

Emily doesn't want to disobey her mother, who looks familiar, like someone she's seen before, doesn't she? Emily can't remember. She's sweating through her nightdress to the white lab coat Biggs made her.

She ascends to the kitchen. The woman with the coal-black hair is already standing in the center of the room like a bent needle.

"Look there on the counter," says the woman.

Emily looks. It's a knife.

363

"It's a knife," the woman agrees, nodding, though Emily hasn't said this aloud. "Why don't you pick it up?"

In Erno's dream, there was a dog that could say Erno's name. In fact, all it seemed to be able to say was "Erno, Emily, Biggs, come in—over." It wasn't much of a vocabulary, but still Erno expected the dog would make him rich, somehow. He was going to name it Walkie-Talkie because dogs like going for walkies and also this dog could talkie. He was just trying to remember why this name seemed so familiar when he woke with a start and realized Merle had been shouting through the radio for five minutes.

"Sorry. Sorry," said Erno. "Was asleep. Um, over."

"Don't worry about it," Merle answered. "But hey! Good news! John and I got the queen, and we're on our way. So ready two sheep and the fox—we'll have to get something else to swap for Mick later. Over."

"We got a rabbit at a pet shop," said Erno groggily. Then, "Hold on. Emily should be here. Shoot, I fell asleep while I was supposed to be watching Emily."

Just then Scott came in on the same channel. "Are you guys there?" he asked. "We need you to get the rift ready soon. Mick and I are coming back."

"How did it go with the elves?" asked John. "Did you make your case?"

Scott thought before answering. "It went pretty bad.

But I told the truth, and I'm glad I told the truth." He hoped he was being understood. "You know what I'm saying?"

After a pause John said, "I know what you're saying."

Scott smiled. "But yeah, otherwise I made our case pretty horribly."

"The Fay are sendin' us some pointed comments," said Mick. "Some sharp retorts. Some barbed replies."

"That's Mick's way of explaining that they were shooting arrows at us," said Scott. "When he gets a lot of glamour in him he's like a bad poet or something."

"Guys, I'll get Biggs up and get the animals ready, but first I have to find Emily," said Erno. "I screwed up." Erno rose and crossed to the door, turned the handle. But it wouldn't budge. "I can't open the door," Erno said into the radio. "Guys, something's going on—I can't leave my room."

Emily is in a different room, and she's looking at Biggs there, sleeping. He sleeps standing up. He says he's done it that way for a long time. Emily can't remember how she got here. She can't remember climbing up onto the desk. She's holding a knife.

"It would be so much better if all your friends were gone," her mother is saying. "Then it could be just you and me. None of these weird characters about. They would hurt me if they could, you know. Do you love me?"

Emily loves her *so* much. She's crying, silently. Her mother was gone, but now she's come back. That makes sense, doesn't it?

No.

"I would never kill another living thing myself," her mother is saying. "It goes against everything I believe in, you must understand that. And I would never ask another person to kill for me. But then I don't know how *you* feel about it, this idea of killing. I don't want to make up your mind for you. You do love me, *don't you.*"

No. No.

But Emily nods, her breath coming loose with each jerk of her head.

"He seems like a sound sleeper, but still," says the beautiful black-haired woman. "Can't have him thrashing about. Is that a ratchet strap I see in your right pocket? You might secure it around his ankles."

Emily reaches a shaking hand to the lower right pocket of her lab coat.

No. Upper pocket. Upper pocket, says the voice in her head. The *other* voice in her head. The one that sounds an awful lot like herself.

"The strap isn't *in* the upper pocket," says Emily.

"What's that, dear?" says the mother woman.

No, it isn't. Is it.

Frowning, Emily reaches, trembling, into the upper

right pocket of her coat and feels something small, delicate, like a tiny flower. She curls her fingers around it, and the sun shines inside her mind.

She pulled it out and looked at it, this tiny delicate thing. The four-leaf clover Mick gave her. Dainty little spell breaker. Emily breathed deeply, powerfully, and stepped from the desk to the bed, to the floor. Past the woman with the pitch-black hair, who suddenly looked altogether more familiar.

"Dear, what are you doing?"

"I want to show you something. It's really cool. I'll kill Biggs later."

She walked back through the kitchen with the knife and stepped down the basement stairs. The sheep shifted at her approach. They never seemed to sleep. She walked right up to the adder, which shimmied back and coiled. Before she could give herself time to really think about what she was doing, she snapped her hand down and seized the snake at its tail, using the blunt edge of her knife to keep it from striking her.

"If you wanted to show me the adder, darling," said Nimue, "I've seen it already."

"You've seen it, I suppose, because you're looking through my eyes? Is that how this works? I know you're not really here. You're in my mind." *Listen,* she thought. *I can speak to you without speaking.*

Nimue didn't say anything for a long time. Meanwhile Emily was holding the struggling snake near the rift.

"I don't need to be there," said Nimue. "My men will be there soon."

Emily put the shamrock in her mouth and swallowed it. That would keep her hands free. Then she removed her radio from another pocket and opened a channel.

"I know your men are coming," she said, and everyone heard it. Erno, Scott, John, Mick, and Merle. "I know I blew it, told you where we are."

"RUN, EMILY!" shouted Erno into his radio, but he was shouting to a locked and empty room. Emily still had the channel engaged.

"I've told you where we are and given you a rift. Let me tell you a little bit about your new rift, then," said Emily. "First of all? You were . . . you were right about something. Magic split from the world when Merle and Arthur left for the future. I'm sorry, Merle, it's true."

In Pretannica, Merle sat heavily on a nearby stone.

"I've been studying the energy from the rift, and I'm a hundred percent certain," said Emily. She looked at Nimue, or rather the illusion of her by the stairs. "He didn't do it on purpose. He didn't want it to be true, and it wasn't entirely his fault. There was some kind of interference. Some big, magical hoo-ha. It confused me, because I was sure that if Merle's time machines were responsible, then the bubble . . . well, never mind about the bubble."

In his room, Erno sat down, stood up again. "That's *it*," he said. "The bubble. Finding the centers of circles."

"Anyway," Emily continued into the radio, "you found the remains of Merle's time machine, and it taught you how to make magic milking machines, is that right? That's how you've been stealing glamour all these years, storing it in batteries so that you can overload yourself and tear the rifts open, start your invasion, even if it kills you? But now . . . *now* you think it's going to be easy. Now I've given you a big stable rift, so you think it won't come to that."

"It seems it won't," said Nimue. She was letting herself sound smug. "You have to learn to admit when you've lost, dear. It's a part of growing up."

"Oh, please," she said to Nimue, and to everyone else on the radio. "I know we've lost. All we've managed to do so far is slow you down a little. Delay the release of a cereal. Waste some of that magic you've been saving. I mean, who ever really thought John was going to slay a dragon? No offense, John, if you're listening."

"None taken," John said weakly into his radio.

"But you know something?" said Emily "Aha! There! Look!"

The snake had suddenly recoiled back upon itself and struck, seemingly at nothing. Its crisp and startling mouth

clenched around something invisible but clearly there.

"See? It's caught something. The adder can see it before we do. Do you know that in the instant before two creatures trade places, they're actually a single mass? One interdimensional being? What do you think happens when that interdimensional being swallows itself in the middle of a rift?" said Emily. "I'm asking because I'd love your opinion—I'm honestly only about ninety-five percent sure."

The snake engulfed the mouse on the other side, and the rift shrank. Emily couldn't see that, but she could see the brick wall contract as if squeezed by an invisible fist.

"NO!" Nimue screamed in Emily's mind. "NO NO NO!"

"Sorry," Emily whispered to the snake, to the mouse. Then she set free the animals they had in cages, and cut the sheep's tethers with her knife, and tried to shoo them all up the basement stairs.

Emily breathed heavily. Now the ceiling seemed to be crumbling. The floor was buckling and moving in toward the collapsing rift like the tide. She ran up the stairs behind the animals. "Wake Biggs!" she told Archimedes.

"Little *witch*!" said Nimue. "Do you know what I'm going to do to you and your friends?"

"Nothing bad, I'm sure," said Emily, turning her back on Nimue, or on the idea of Nimue. "It would go against everything you believe in."

Erno came tumbling out of his room with the unicat, Nimue's influence suddenly broken. He was already packed. "What's going on? Are they really coming?"

"They're really coming. Help me get my things. And these animals out the front door."

"I'm going to win," said Nimue in her mind.

Emily sighed, exasperated. "I *know* you're going to win. Of *course* you're going to win. It's just not going to be *easy*. You're going to have to *die*. Now let me ask you something," said Emily. "Seriously. Was this really your plan? To make someone super-intelligent and then TURN HER AGAINST YOU? How did you think *that* was going to work out?"

There wasn't any answer. But still Emily knew she wasn't alone.

"You," she said. "You paper doll. You nothing. You're not my fairy godmother, you soft-witted figment." Emily breathed. "NOW GET OUT OF MY HEAD!"

She was alone. She could feel it.

Finally Biggs was awake, confused and pajama clad, and they left—not out the front door, but up the rotted staircase to the roof, then in Biggs's arms across the rooftops of London just as the white vans pulled up.

Across the street from the house, a little girl was up late (as she was most nights) filming the haunted house with

372

an old camcorder, just in case something interesting happened. So she captured it when the front door opened and something small like a rabbit hopped out, followed by a fox. Followed by three sheep, which fumbled right and left and smack into one another like a comedy trio before cantering off in separate directions. Then a squad of white vans screeched to a stop in front of the haunted house, and the little girl saw what might have been movement up at the roofline. It was hard to say. Men in black outfits and helmets and guns rushed from the vans toward the building, which sort of flinched, as if they'd startled it. The men stopped short, looked at one another. Then the building crumpled like a soda can, flicking bits of brick and mortar every which way, cracking helmets. The men retreated as the whole haunted house collapsed into a super-dense lump and sank beneath the earth.

The little girl watched this, wide-eyed. It wasn't exactly what she'd been expecting, but still she whispered, "I knew it," because she'd been waiting to whisper that for a long time.

The following evening she tried to show the video to her dad, but her brother had erased it to record himself burping the alphabet. "He already showed me," her dad told her. "As soon as I got home. Say, did you notice your haunted house is gone?"

CHAPTER 35

Tiny Polly and the pixie brothers found Harvey, right where they left him.

"Thomething'th different about you," he said when he saw Polly. "Ith that a new dreth?"

"Harvey," said Polly, "this is Fee, Fo, and Denzil. Your Not-So-Highnesses, this is the pooka Harvey."

They exchanged uncomfortable handshakes.

"We were afraid you'd have run into trouble, since we were gone so long," said Polly.

"No. No trouble. Should we go?"

Harvey was quiet on the way back to the house. He hunched over the steering wheel and paid a lot more attention to the road than usual. But then the brothers were doing most of the talking—sharing the details of their misadventures, their failed attempts to rescue Morenwyn.

"Fi said that Fray said that Morenwyn likes him," Polly announced.

"I . . . do not remember saying that."

"You did."

"Nonsense," said Fo. "Anyone at court would tell you she found me most handsome and Denzil the best conversationalist."

"She would want me," said Fee, "if only I wasn't the youngest."

"Or perhaps she does not want any of us, my brothers," said Denzil. "We have to accept it: fair Morenwyn does not wish to be saved. We cannot make her change."

"That'th exactly it," Harvey said, suddenly animated. "You've put your tiny finger right on it. Can't save everyone. Can't change anybody. Gotta play the cardth you're dealt."

"I don't believe that's what I intended—"

"You know, when I wath a captive of Goodco mythelf . . . I remember the day the guardth brought me the firtht box of Honey Frothted Thnox. Fresh off the line, they told me."

Harvey ran a red light, but Polly didn't say anything.

"They pointed at the Thnox Rabbit in hith shirt and tie, jutht like the clotheth they'd drethed *me* in, and thaid, 'Look. You're trademarked. You belong to *uth*, now.'"

Polly crawled up to the front. "Did something happen

376

while we were inside the factory?" she asked.

"Courth not. What could have happened?"

Nobody spoke again until they pulled up St. George Road.

"Weird," Harvey said, leaning over the wheel. "Could've thworn there wath a building here when we left."

"I can't believe it," said Merle, in Pretannica. "All my fault. I mean . . . I was afraid it was true, but then the kid didn't used to believe it, and she was so scary smart. . . ."

Finchbriton hopped to Merle's shoulder, nipped his ear in what was presumably an affectionate way.

"She said there was something else that caused it," said John. "Some 'magical hoo-ha.'"

"We don't lose ourselves to self-pity," said the queen. "We keep calm and carry on. If this rift has been closed, then how are we to get home?"

"I can't believe it," said Mick. "Emily marooned us. We're doomed."

"No," said Scott. "No, she wouldn't do that," he added, convincing himself. "She did the right thing. She kept the rift from Nimue." Scott fiddled with the walkie-talkie. "I think this thing is dead—whatever happened when the rift collapsed must've fried the batteries. Not only can

I not reach Biggs and the Utzes, I can't reach John and Merle, either."

They had a moment to themselves right now, but Mick was sure the elves would be good trackers. They had to keep moving.

"Don' know what we're gonna do," said Mick. "We might find a rift close to May Day that's big enough for me, but I'm not leavin' without yeh."

Scott smiled at him. Then he thought. "But that's not true, is it? Emily knew we had other options. I'll see my mom again, and Polly. And my dad. We can visit Fi's pixie witch! She has rifts. Big ones. We can talk her into letting us use one."

"Yeah, that's good. She sounded like a real nice lady."

"We just have to get to the Isle of Man," Scott continued. "How hard can that be?"

"Have yeh ever heard of anythin' good comin' of a person sayin', 'How hard can that be?'"

"Sorry."

Polly and the brothers and Harvey sat in the car in utter silence for several minutes, staring at the house-sized hole in the neighborhood.

"I do not understand," Fee said finally. "We are looking at what, exactly?"

"A house that used to be there," whispered Polly.

"A mysterious absence that knells like a bell in our hearts," said Fi.

"Yeah," said Polly. Then she noticed a bit of movement—a dash of white. "Is . . . is that an owl at the end of the street? Harvey, drive to the end of the street."

Harvey complied, and at the end of the street they spotted Archimedes sitting in a willow tree. "Roll down the window!" said Polly. And when Harvey did, the owl glided down from its perch and into the car. Fi's brothers scattered everywhere. Denzil came up hooting.

"He's not a real owl," Polly told him. "Look! He has Merle's watch." Polly struggled with the hugeness of it, and read the face. "Emily says she figured out that I didn't go to Pretannica. Well, course she did. And Erno and Emily and Biggs are okay! They just had to make the building vanish, is all, and now the . . . the rift is gone."

Polly and Fi looked at each other.

"It also says that John and Merle rescued the queen, but they're still in Pretannica and that Scott and Mick are too, and that Scott and Mick are on the run from elves. Oh *no*. Scott's in trouble and he can't get home!"

The car was respectfully quiet.

"There's also . . . there's also this stuff about that thing Erno was working on, but I don't get it. Stuff about finding the centers of circles, and about how the circles

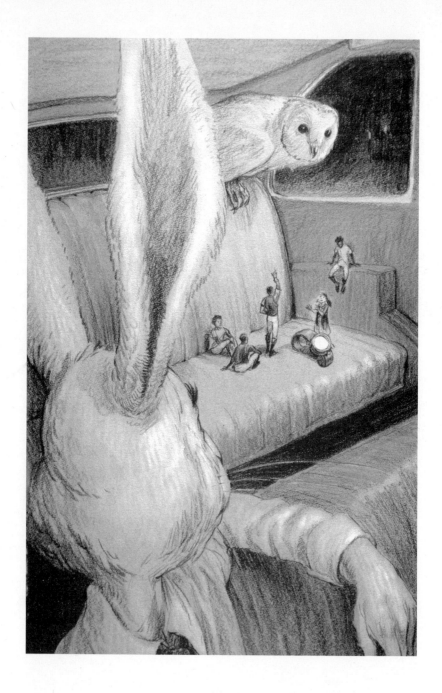

don't match, and . . ." Polly's eyes were welling up.

"Hey now," said Harvey. "People like uth, we don't cry—"

"Well . . . well . . . *sorry!*" Polly seethed, tears streaming. She turned from the others, pressed her hands against her hot face. "I guess . . . I'm not a person like us then! 'Cause I can cry if I FEEL LIKE IT for my brother who's gonna get killed and *I'll never never see him again*—"

"*Impossible!*" Fi roared, and there was such panache to it that Polly was startled out of her misery. "You are *Polly Esther Doe!* Rescuing brothers is what you do! The witch Fray has doors that lead home, and we will help Scott and Mick to use them! Our size is our strength! There are any number of rifts we may use! We go to Pretannica!"

Polly sniffed. "We do?"

"Harvey! Will you take us to one of the small rifts on Emily's map?"

Harvey stared, then shrugged. "Yeahshure."

Fi turned to the other pixies. "Brothers! Will you join us?"

The princes glanced at one another. Then Denzil stepped forward and gave Fi his hand. "I will go, brother. To the isle of Lady Fray and the lovely Morenwyn." Fee and Fo joined their hands as well.

"To Pretannica," said Fo.

"To Morenwyn," said Fee.

Polly wiped her eyes and smirked. "You'll get to see Morenwyn too," she told Fi.

Fi took a knee, and then grasped her hand.

"Ah, dear Polly—little sister—*you* are my love."

Polly blushed.

"Now. Shall we go?"

"Let's go."

They went.